BOOK OF HAN

Records of Emperors

Gu Ban

Wei Fangfang

CONTENTS

INTRODUCTION

The Book of Han, also known as the Former Book of Han, is the first dynastic history in biographical - chronological style in China and one of the Twenty - Four Histories. It is collectively referred to as the "Three Histories" together with the Records of the Grand Historian and the Eastern Han Records, and is also known as the "Four Early Histories" together with the Records of the Grand Historian, the Book of the Later Han, and the Records of the Three Kingdoms. It was compiled by Ban Gu, a historian of the Eastern Han Dynasty, and took more than twenty years to complete during the Jianchu period of the Han Dynasty. The eight tables of the Book of Han were supplemented by Ban Gu's younger sister, Ban Zhao, and the Treatise on Astronomy was completed by Ma Xu, a disciple of Ban Zhao. Yan Shigu of the Tang Dynasty annotated it. It was a regular subject in the imperial examinations of the Tang Dynasty.

The Book of Han mainly records the history of the Western Han Dynasty (including the Wang Mang regime). It chronicles a total of 230 years of history from the first year of Emperor Gaozu of the Han Dynasty (206 BC) to the fourth year of Emperor Huang of the Xin Dynasty under Wang Mang (23 AD). It consists of twelve Records of Emperors, eight tables, ten treatises, and seventy biographies, totaling one hundred chapters.

VOLUME 1 PART 1: RECORDS OF EMPEROR GAOZU, PART 1, NO. 1

Emperor Gaozu was a native of Zhongyangli in Pei Fengyi, surnamed Liu. His mother, while resting by the marsh's edge, dreamed of encountering a deity. At that moment, thunder and lightning filled the sky, and his father, Taigong, went to see what was happening, only to witness dragons intertwining above. Shortly thereafter, she became pregnant and gave birth to Emperor Gaozu.

Emperor Gaozu had a high nose bridge and a dragon-like countenance, with a fine beard and seventy-two black moles on his left thigh. He was generous and benevolent, with a broad and open-minded disposition. He often displayed great magnanimity and did not engage in the mundane tasks of household production. Upon reaching adulthood, he took a position as a local official, serving as the Tingzhang of Si Shang, where he was familiar with and mocked by all the officials in the court. He had a fondness for wine and women. He often borrowed wine from Madam Wang and Wu Fu, and would frequently drink until he was drunk and fell asleep. Both Wu Fu and Madam Wang noticed that there were often strange occurrences around him. Every time Emperor Gaozu stayed to drink, the amount of wine consumed would multiply severalfold. Upon witnessing these strange occurrences, by the end of the year, these two households would often tear up the IOUs and forgive the debts.

Emperor Gaozu often traveled to Xianyang, where he observed the Emperor of Qin from afar. He sighed deeply and said, "Ah, a true man should be like this!"

Shanfu's Lü Gong was on good terms with the magistrate of Pei. Fleeing from enemies, he followed the magistrate as a guest and thus settled there. The local heroes and officials of Pei, hearing that the magistrate had an important guest, all went to offer their congratulations. Xiao He, as the chief official, was in charge of receiving the gifts and instructed the various officials, saying, "Those who present less than a thousand coins shall sit in the lower hall." Emperor Gaozu, being the Tingzhang and usually dismissive of the officials, deceitfully presented a note saying, "Ten thousand coins as a gift," but in reality, he did not bring a single coin. When the note was presented, Lü Gong was greatly astonished, stood up, and went to the gate to welcome him. Lü Gong, who was skilled in physiognomy, upon seeing Emperor Gaozu's appearance, held him in high regard and led him to the seat of honor. Xiao He remarked, "Liu Ji often boasts but rarely accomplishes anything." Emperor Gaozu, accustomed to mocking the guests, took the seat of honor without any hesitation. As the drinking came to an end, Lü Gong signaled to keep Emperor Gaozu behind. After the feast, Lü Gong said, "Since my youth, I have been fond of physiognomy and have seen many faces, but none as remarkable as yours, Ji. I hope you will take good care of yourself." "I have a daughter who is of marriageable age, and I wish to offer her to you as a humble servant." After the wine was finished, Lü's wife angrily said to Lü Gong, "You always wanted to make this daughter of ours special and marry her to a nobleman. The magistrate of Pei is on good terms with you and asked for her hand, but you refused. Why did you recklessly promise her to Liu Ji?" Lü Gong replied, "This is not something for women to understand." In the end, he gave his daughter to Emperor Gaozu. Lü Gong's daughter was Empress Lü, who bore Emperor Hui and Princess Lu Yuan.

Emperor Gaozu once returned home from his duties to the fields.

Empress Lü and their two children were in the fields when an old man passed by and asked for a drink, which Empress Lü provided. The old man, after observing Empress Lü, said, "Madam, you are destined to be a noblewoman of the world." He then asked to see the two children. Upon seeing Emperor Hui, he said, "The reason for your nobility, madam, is this boy." When he saw Princess Lu Yuan, he also predicted that she would be noble. After the old man left, Emperor Gaozu happened to come from a nearby house, and Empress Lü told him in detail about the visitor who had passed by and predicted that both she and her children would be greatly honored. Emperor Gaozu asked, "Has he gone far?" He then caught up with the old man and inquired. The old man said, "Earlier, I saw that the lady and her children all have the bearing of a noble family. Your destiny, sir, is of such high honor that it is beyond words." Emperor Gaozu thanked him, saying, "If it truly is as you say, I shall not forget your kindness." However, by the time Emperor Gaozu rose to prominence, the whereabouts of the old man were no longer known.

When Emperor Gaozu was the Tingzhang, he made a hat from bamboo skin and had it crafted by a thief from Xue, which he wore from time to time. After he rose to prominence, he often wore this hat, which came to be known as the "Liu Clan Hat."

Emperor Gaozu, as the Tingzhang, was escorting convicts to Mount Li for the county, but many of the convicts escaped along the way. He reckoned that by the time they arrived, all would have fled. Upon reaching the pavilion in the marsh west of Feng, he stopped to drink and, at night, released all the convicts he was escorting, saying, "You all go now, and I will disappear from here as well!" Among the convicts, a dozen or so strong men were willing to follow him. Emperor Gaozu, having drunk, walked through the marsh at night and ordered one man to go ahead. The man returned and reported, "There is a large snake blocking the path ahead; we should turn back." Emperor Gaozu, in his drunken state, said, "A strong man walks on; why should he fear?" He then went forward, drew his sword, and cut the snake in two, clearing the path. After walking several miles, he became drunk and weary and lay down to rest. Later, when others came to the place where the snake had been, they found an old woman weeping at night. When asked why she was crying, the old woman said, "Someone has killed my son." The people asked, "Why was your son killed?" The old woman replied, "My son was the son of the White Emperor, who had transformed into a snake and was lying across the road. Now the son of the Red Emperor has slain him, hence I weep." The people then thought the old woman was being deceitful and intended to punish her, but she suddenly disappeared. When others arrived, Emperor Gaozu awoke. They told him what had happened, and he secretly rejoiced in his heart, feeling a sense of pride. His followers increasingly stood in awe of him.

The First Emperor of Qin once said, "There is an aura of an emperor in the southeast," and thus he traveled east to suppress it. Emperor Gaozu hid in the mountains and marshes of Mang and Dang, and Empress Lü, along with others, often found him when they went searching. Emperor Gaozu found this strange and asked her about it. Empress Lü said, "Wherever Ji resides, there is often an aura of clouds and mist, so we always find him when we go looking." Emperor Gaozu was pleased. When the youths of Pei heard of this, many wished to join him.

In the autumn of the first year of the Second Emperor of Qin, in the seventh month, Chen She rose in Qi, reached Chen, and declared himself the King of Chu. He sent Wu Chen, Zhang Er, and Chen Yu to conquer the lands of Zhao. In the eighth month, Wu Chen declared himself the King of Zhao. Many commanderies and counties killed their chief officials to join Chen She's cause. In the ninth month, the magistrate of Pei wanted to have Pei join the rebellion. His subordinates, the chief officials Xiao He and Cao Shen, said, "You are an official of Qin; now you wish to turn against it and lead the youths of Pei, but they may not obey. We suggest you summon those who are hiding outside, and you could gather several hundred people. With them, you can coerce the masses, and they will not dare to disobey." Thus, they ordered Fan Kuai to summon Emperor Gaozu. Emperor Gaozu's followers already numbered several hundred.

Thereupon, Fan Kuai followed Emperor Gaozu to Pei. The magistrate of Pei regretted his decision and, fearing a revolt, closed the city gates to defend it and intended to execute Xiao He and Cao Shen. Xiao He and Cao Shen, in fear, climbed over the city walls to seek protection from Emperor Gaozu. Emperor Gaozu then wrote a message on silk, shot it over the city walls, and addressed the elders of Pei, saying, "The world has long suffered under Qin. Now, although you elders are defending for the magistrate of Pei, the feudal lords have risen together, and they will soon massacre Pei. Let us now together kill the magistrate, choose someone suitable to establish, and join the feudal lords, thus preserving our homes and families. Otherwise, both fathers and sons will be slaughtered, and it will be for naught." The elders then led the youths to kill the magistrate of Pei together, opened the city gates to welcome Emperor Gaozu, and wished to make him the magistrate of Pei. Emperor Gaozu said, "The world is in turmoil, and the feudal lords have risen together. If the appointment of a leader is not done well, we will be utterly defeated. I dare not be selfish, but I fear my abilities are insufficient to protect our fathers, brothers, and sons. This is a great matter; I hope the officials will choose someone capable." Xiao He, Cao Shen, and others were all civil officials who cherished their own safety and feared that if the venture failed, their families would be exterminated by Qin. Thus, they all yielded to Emperor Gaozu. All the elders said, "We have always heard that Liu Ji is extraordinary and destined for greatness. Moreover, divinations have been made, and none is more auspicious than Liu Ji." Emperor Gaozu repeatedly declined. As no one else was willing to take the position, Emperor Gaozu was finally established as the Duke of Pei. They worshipped the Yellow Emperor and offered sacrifices to Chi You in the court of Pei, and they anointed the drums and flags with blood. The banners were all red, because the snake that was killed was the son of the White Emperor, and the killer was the son of the Red Emperor. Thereupon, young and heroic officials like Xiao He, Cao Shen, and Fan Kuai all gathered the youths of Pei, amassing three thousand men.

In the same month, Xiang Liang and his nephew Xiang Yu rose in Wu. Tian Dan and his cousins Tian Rong and Tian Heng rose in Qi and declared themselves the King of Qi. Han Guang declared himself the King of Yan. Wei Jiu declared himself the King of Wei. Zhou Zhang, a general under Chen She, marched west into the pass and reached Xi, where he was repelled and defeated by the Qin general Zhang Han.

In the tenth month of the second year of Qin, the Duke of Pei attacked Huling and Fangyu, then returned to defend Feng. The Qin supervisor Ping of Sishui led troops to besiege Feng. After two days, the Duke of Pei sallied forth to battle and defeated them. He ordered Yong Chi to defend Feng. In the eleventh month, the Duke of Pei led his troops to Xue. The Qin commander Zhuang of Sishui was defeated at Xue, fled to Qi, and was killed by the Duke of Pei's left Sima. The Duke of Pei then returned his army to Kangfu and reached Fangyu. The King of Zhao, Wu Chen, was killed by his own general. In the twelfth month, the King of Chu, Chen She, was killed by his charioteer, Zhuang Jia. Zhou Shi of Wei conquered the lands of Feng and Pei and sent a message to Yong Chi, saying, "Feng was once a relocation site of Liang, and now dozens of cities in Wei have been secured. If Chi submits to Wei now, Wei will make Chi a marquis to defend Feng; if not, Feng will be massacred." Yong Chi had never wished to be subordinate to the Duke of Pei, and when Wei offered him a position, he immediately turned and defended Feng for Wei. The Duke of Pei attacked Feng but could not take it. He returned to Pei, resentful of Yong Chi and the youths of Feng for their betrayal.

In the first month, Zhang Er and others established Zhao Xie, a descendant of Zhao, as the King of Zhao. Ning Jun of Dongyang and Qin Jia established Jing Ju as the King of Chu in Liu. The Duke of Pei went to join them and on the way met Zhang Liang, so they went together to see Jing Ju and requested troops to attack Feng. At that time, Zhang Han had left Chen, and his deputy general Sima Rong led troops north to secure the lands of Chu, massacred Xiang, and reached Dang. Ning Jun of Dongyang and the Duke of Pei led their troops west and engaged in battle west of Xiao, but were unsuccessful, so they gathered their troops and concentrated at Liu. In the second month, they attacked Dang and captured it in three days. They gathered the troops from Dang, amassing six thousand men, and combined with their original forces to make nine thousand. In the third month, they attacked Xiayi and captured it. They then turned back to attack Feng but could not take it. In the fourth month, Xiang Liang killed Jing Ju and Qin Jia and halted at Xue. The Duke of Pei went to see him. Xiang Liang reinforced the Duke of Pei with five thousand soldiers and ten generals of the fifth rank. The Duke of Pei returned, led his troops to attack Feng, and captured it. Yong Chi fled to Wei.

In the fifth month, Xiang Yu captured Xiangcheng and returned. Xiang Liang summoned all his deputy generals. In the sixth month, the Duke of Pei went to Xue and together with Xiang Liang established Xin, the grandson of King Huai of Chu, as King Huai of Chu. Zhang Han defeated and killed King Jiu of Wei and King Tian Dan of Qi at Linji. In the seventh month, there was heavy continuous rain. The Duke of Pei attacked Kangfu. Zhang Han besieged Tian Rong at Dong'a. The Duke of Pei and Xiang Liang together rescued Tian Rong and decisively defeated Zhang Han at Dong'a. Tian Rong returned, and the Duke of Pei and Xiang Yu pursued the fleeing enemy north to Chengyang, where they attacked and massacred the city. Their army was stationed east of Puyang and they engaged Zhang Han in battle again, defeating him once more.

Zhang Han regained his strength and defended Puyang, encircled by water. The Duke of Pei and Xiang Yu left to attack Dingtao. In the eighth month, Tian Rong established Tian Shi, the son of Tian Dan, as the King of Qi. Dingtao had not yet fallen, so the Duke of Pei and Xiang Yu marched west to conquer lands as far as Yongqiu, where they fought the Qin army and inflicted a major defeat, killing Li You, the governor of Sanchuan. They then turned back to attack Waihuang, but Waihuang had not yet fallen.

Xiang Liang defeated the Qin army again and became arrogant. Song Yi advised him, but he did not listen. Qin reinforced Zhang Han with more troops. In the ninth month, Zhang Han launched a night attack on Xiang Liang at Dingtao, inflicting a major defeat and killing Xiang Liang. At that time, continuous rain had persisted from the seventh month to the ninth month. The Duke of Pei and Xiang Yu were just attacking Chenliu when they heard of Liang's death, and their soldiers were frightened. They then led their troops east with General Lü Chen and moved King Huai from Xuyi to Pengcheng. Lü Chen's army was stationed east of Pengcheng, Xiang Yu's army was stationed west of Pengcheng, and the Duke of Pei's army was stationed at Dang. Wei Jiu's younger brother Bao declared himself the King of Wei. In the intercalary ninth month, King Huai took command of the armies of Lü Chen and Xiang Yu himself. He appointed the Duke of Pei as the governor of Dang Commandery, enfeoffed him as the Marquis of Wu'an, and gave him command of the troops of Dang Commandery. He appointed Yu as the Duke of Lu, enfeoffed him as the Marquis of Chang'an. Lü Chen was made the Minister over the Masses, and his father Lü Qing was made the Prime Minister.

Having already defeated Xiang Liang, Zhang Han believed that the troops in the Chu region were not a concern, so he crossed the river north to attack King Xie of Zhao and inflicted a major defeat. Xie defended the city of Julu, where the Qin general Wang Li besieged him. Zhao repeatedly requested aid, so King

Huai appointed Song Yi as the supreme general, Xiang Yu as the second general, and Fan Zeng as the last general, and sent them north to rescue Zhao.

Initially, King Huai had made a pact with his generals that the first to secure the Guanzhong region would be made king. At that time, the Qin army was strong and often pursued victories aggressively, so none of the generals saw an advantage in being the first to enter the pass. Only Xiang Yu, resentful of Qin for defeating Xiang Liang, was eager and willing to join the Duke of Pei in marching west into the pass. King Huai's veteran generals all said, "Xiang Yu is a fierce and calamitous individual. When he attacked Xiangcheng, not a single soul was left alive in the city, and everywhere he passed was utterly destroyed. Moreover, Chu has repeatedly launched offensives, and both the former King Chen and Xiang Liang were defeated. It would be better to send a virtuous elder to carry righteousness westward and to inform and instruct the fathers and brothers of Qin. The fathers and brothers of Qin have long suffered under their ruler. If we indeed send a virtuous elder to go without violence or aggression, it should be possible to bring them to submission. Xiang Yu must not be sent; only the Duke of Pei, who has always been magnanimous and virtuous, should go." Ultimately, they did not permit Xiang Yu and instead sent the Duke of Pei west to gather the scattered soldiers of King Chen and Xiang Liang. He then traveled from Dang to Yangcheng and Gangli, attacked the Qin army's fortifications, and defeated two of their armies.

In the tenth month of the third year of Qin, the Qi general Tian Du rebelled against Tian Rong and led troops to assist Xiang Yu in rescuing Zhao. The Duke of Pei attacked and defeated the commandant of Dong Commandery at Chengwu. In the eleventh month, Xiang Yu killed Song Yi, took command of his troops, crossed the river, and declared himself the supreme general, with all the generals, including Qing Bu, under his command. In the twelfth month, the Duke of Pei led his troops to Li, encountered the Marquis of Gangwu, seized his army of more than four thousand men, merged them with his own forces, and joined with the armies of the Wei generals Huang Xin and Wu Man to attack the Qin army, defeating them. The former King Jian of Qi's grandson, Tian An, descended from Jibei and followed Xiang Yu to rescue Zhao. Xiang Yu inflicted a major defeat on the Qin army at Julu, captured Wang Li, and drove Zhang Han away.

In the second month, the Duke of Pei marched north from Dang to attack Changyi and encountered Peng Yue. Yue assisted in the attack on Changyi, but it did not fall. The Duke of Pei then traveled west past Gaoyang, where Li Yiji, the village gatekeeper, said, "Many generals have passed through here, but I see that the Duke of Pei is magnanimous." He then sought an audience with the Duke of Pei. The Duke of Pei was sitting with his legs spread on a bed, having two women wash his feet. Li Yiji did not bow but made a long salute, saying, "If Your Lordship truly wishes to eliminate the tyrannical Qin, it is not appropriate to receive an elder in such a posture." Thereupon, the Duke of Pei stood up, adjusted his clothes, apologized, and invited him to take a seat. Li Yiji advised the Duke of Pei to launch a surprise attack on Chenliu. The Duke of Pei appointed him as the Lord of Guangye and made his younger brother Shang a general, commanding the troops of Chenliu. In the third month, they attacked Kaifeng but did not capture it. They then marched west and engaged the Qin general Yang Xiong in battle at Baima, and again east of Quyu, where they inflicted a major defeat. Yang Xiong fled to Yingyang, and the Second Emperor sent an envoy to execute him as a warning. In the fourth month, they attacked Yingchuan to the south and massacred it. With Zhang Liang's assistance, they proceeded to conquer the lands of Han.

At that time, Sima Ang, a deputy general of Zhao, was about to cross the river and enter the pass. The Duke of Pei then attacked Pingyin to the north, cutting off the river crossing. To the south, they fought east of Luoyang, but the army was not successful, so they moved from Huanyuan to Yangcheng to gather the cavalry.

In the sixth month, they engaged the governor of Nanyang, Jiao, in battle east of Chou and inflicted a major defeat. They conquered Nanyang Commandery, and the governor fled, defending the city of Wan. The Duke of Pei led his troops past the west of Wan. Zhang Liang advised, "Although Your Lordship is eager to enter the pass quickly, the Qin army is still numerous and holds strategic positions. If we do not take Wan now, Wan will attack us from behind, and with the strong Qin forces in front, this is a dangerous path." Thereupon, the Duke of Pei led his army back by another route at night, lowered the banners, and at dawn, surrounded the city of Wan in three layers. The governor of Nanyang wanted to commit suicide, but his steward Chen Hui said, "It is not too late to die." He then climbed over the city wall to see the Duke of Pei and said, "I have heard that Your Lordship has made a pact that the first to enter Xianyang will be made king. Now Your Lordship is staying to besiege Wan. Wan has dozens of interconnected cities in its commandery and counties, and its officials and people believe that surrendering will surely lead to death, so they are all steadfastly defending the city. If Your Lordship continues to attack all day, the casualties among the soldiers will surely be many. If you lead the troops away from Wan, Wan will surely follow you. If you proceed forward, you will break the pact to enter Xianyang first, and if you stay, you will face the threat of a strong Wan. For Your Lordship's benefit, it would be best to negotiate a surrender, enfeoff its governor, and then have him cease defending, leading his armored soldiers to join you in marching west. The cities that have not yet fallen will hear of this and compete to open their gates and await Your Lordship, allowing you to pass through without hindrance." The Duke of Pei said, "Good." In the seventh month, the governor of Nanyang, Jiao, surrendered and was enfeoffed as the Marquis of Yin, and Chen Hui was enfeoffed with a thousand households. They led their troops west, and no city failed to surrender. When they reached Danshui, the Marquis of Gaowu, Sai, and the Marquis of Xiang, Wang Ling, surrendered. They turned back to attack Huyang, encountered

Mei Xuan, a deputy general of Fan Jun, and together they attacked Xi and Li, both of which surrendered. Wherever they passed, there was no plundering, and the people of Qin were pleased. They sent Ning Chang, a man of Wei, as an envoy to Qin. That month, Zhang Han led his entire army to surrender to Xiang Yu, who made him the King of Yong. Shen Yang of Xiaqiu descended to Henan.

In the eighth month, the Duke of Pei attacked the Wu Pass and entered Qin. The Qin chancellor Zhao Gao, fearing for his safety, killed the Second Emperor and sent an envoy to propose dividing the kingdom of Guanzhong and ruling jointly, but the Duke of Pei refused. In the ninth month, Zhao Gao installed Ziying, the nephew of the Second Emperor, as the King of Qin. Ziying executed Zhao Gao and sent generals to lead troops to defend the Yao Pass. The Duke of Pei wanted to attack them, but Zhang Liang said, "The Qin army is still strong; we should not act rashly. I suggest first sending men to increase the number of banners on the mountains as a feint, and then sending Li Yiji and Lu Jia to persuade the Qin generals with promises of profit. The Qin generals indeed wanted to make peace, and the Duke of Pei was inclined to agree. Zhang Liang said, "This is just their generals wanting to rebel; they fear their soldiers will not follow. It would be better to take advantage of their laxness and attack them." The Duke of Pei led his troops around the Yao Pass, crossed Kuai Mountain, attacked the Qin army, and inflicted a major defeat south of Lantian. They then reached Lantian and fought again to the north, where the Qin army was utterly defeated.

In the winter of the first year, the tenth month, the five planets gathered in the eastern well. The Duke of Pei arrived at Bashang. The King of Qin, Ziying, in a plain carriage with white horses, tied his neck with a ribbon, and presented the imperial seal, tally, and ceremonial regalia, surrendering by the side of Zhidao Road. Some of the generals suggested executing the King of Qin, but the Duke of Pei said, "When King Huai sent me, it was precisely because I was capable of tolerance. Moreover, the man has already surrendered; killing him would be inauspicious." He then handed him over to the officials. They then entered Xianyang to the west and intended to rest in the palace. Fan Kuai and Zhang Liang advised against it, so they sealed the treasuries containing Qin's precious treasures and wealth and returned to Bashang with the army. Xiao He collected all the maps, records, and documents from the Qin chancellor's office. In the eleventh month, the Duke of Pei summoned the prominent figures from various counties and said, "The elders have long suffered under the harsh laws of Qin. Those who slander are exterminated, and those who conspire are executed in the marketplace. I made a pact with the feudal lords that the first to enter the pass would be made king, and I am to be the king of Guanzhong. I make a pact with the elders: the law shall consist of only three articles: those who kill shall die, those who injure or steal shall be punished accordingly. All other Qin laws shall be abolished. Officials and commoners shall continue their lives as before." All my actions are to eliminate the harm for the elders and brothers, not to invade or harm, so do not be afraid! Moreover, the reason I stationed the army at Bashang is to wait for the feudal lords to arrive and then establish the necessary constraints." He then sent people with Qin officials to travel to the counties, townships, and villages to announce this. The people of Qin were overjoyed and competed to bring cattle, sheep, wine, and food to offer to the soldiers. The Duke of Pei declined to accept, saying, "The granaries are full of grain; I do not wish to burden the people." The people were even more delighted, fearing only that the Duke of Pei would not become the King of Qin.

Someone advised the Duke of Pei, saying, "Qin is ten times richer than the rest of the world, and its terrain is strong. Now that Zhang Han has surrendered to Xiang Yu, and Yu has proclaimed himself the King of Yong, ruling Guanzhong, if he comes, Your Lordship may not be able to hold onto this. You should urgently send troops to guard the Hangu Pass, prevent the feudal lords' armies from entering, gradually recruit soldiers from Guanzhong to strengthen yourself, and resist them." The Duke of Pei agreed with this plan and followed it. In the twelfth month, Xiang Yu indeed led the feudal lords' armies intending to enter the pass from the west, but the pass gates were closed. Upon hearing that the Duke of Pei had already secured Guanzhong, Xiang Yu was furious and sent Ying Bu and others to attack and breach the Hangu Pass, reaching the vicinity of Xi. Cao Wushang, the Left Sima of the Duke of Pei, heard of Xiang Yu's anger and intention to attack the Duke of Pei, so he sent a message to Xiang Yu saying, "The Duke of Pei wishes to be king of Guanzhong, appoint Ziying as his chancellor, and possesses all the treasures." He hoped to gain a fiefdom. Fan Zeng, the Second Father, advised Xiang Yu, saying, "When the Duke of Pei resided east of the mountains, he was greedy for wealth and fond of women. Now that he has entered the pass, he has taken no treasures and favored no women; his ambitions are not small. I have sent people to observe his aura, and it is all dragon-like, forming five colors; this is the aura of an emperor. Attack him quickly; do not miss this opportunity." Thereupon, they feasted the soldiers and prepared to engage in battle the next day. At that time, Xiang Yu's army numbered four hundred thousand, claiming a million. The Duke of Pei's army numbered one hundred thousand, claiming two hundred thousand, and was no match in strength. It happened that Xiang Bo, the Left Yin and uncle of Xiang Yu, was on good terms with Zhang Liang. He rode through the night to see Zhang Liang, fully informed him of the situation, and wanted to leave together with him, not wishing to perish together for nothing. Zhang Liang said, "I am escorting the Duke of Pei on behalf of the King of Han; I cannot leave without informing him, as fleeing would be unrighteous." He then went with Xiang Bo to see the Duke of Pei. The Duke of Pei made a marriage alliance with Xiang Bo, saying, "I entered the pass and dared not take even a hair; I registered the officials and commoners, sealed the treasuries, and awaited the general. The reason I guarded the pass was to prepare against other bandits.

Day and night, I have been looking forward to the general's arrival; how could I dare to rebel? I hope you, Bo, will clearly state that I dare not betray virtue." Xiang Bo agreed and left again that night. He warned the Duke of Pei, saying, "You must come early tomorrow to apologize in person." Xiang Bo returned and fully reported the Duke of Pei's words to Xiang Yu, adding, "If the Duke of Pei had not first defeated the Qin army in Guanzhong, how could you, General, have entered? Moreover, the man has achieved great merit; attacking him would be inauspicious. It would be better to treat him well." Xiang Yu agreed.

The next morning, the Duke of Pei, accompanied by over a hundred horsemen, went to see Xiang Yu at Hongmen and apologized, saying, "I and the general have joined forces to attack Qin. The general fought north of the river, and I fought south of the river. I did not expect to enter the pass first and defeat Qin, and to meet the general again. Now, there are petty men spreading words that have caused a rift between the general and me." Xiang Yu said, "It was your Left Sima, Cao Wushang, who said this; otherwise, why would I have thought of this?" Xiang Yu then invited the Duke of Pei to stay and drink. Fan Zeng repeatedly signaled to Xiang Yu to attack the Duke of Pei, but Xiang Yu did not respond. Fan Zeng stood up, went out, and said to Xiang Zhuang, "Our king is too soft-hearted. You go in and perform a sword dance, and during the dance, attack and kill the Duke of Pei. If you do not, we will all be captured by him." Xiang Zhuang entered and proposed a toast. After the toast, he said, "There is nothing to entertain in the army; I request to perform a sword dance." He then drew his sword and began to dance. Xiang Bo also rose to dance, often shielding the Duke of Pei with his body. Fan Kuai, hearing that the situation was critical, rushed in, filled with anger. Xiang Yu admired his courage and rewarded him with wine. Fan Kuai then reproached Xiang Yu. After a while, the Duke of Pei got up to go to the restroom and called Fan Kuai to come out. He left his carriage and officials, mounted a horse alone, and walked with Fan Kuai, Jin Qiang, Teng Gong, and Ji Cheng, taking a shortcut back to the army, leaving Zhang Liang to stay and apologize to Xiang Yu. Xiang Yu asked, "Where is the Duke of Pei?" Zhang Liang replied, "Hearing that the general intended to hold him accountable, he slipped away and has already returned to the army by a shortcut. Therefore, he sent me to present this jade to you." Xiang Yu accepted it. He also presented a jade vessel to Fan Zeng. Fan Zeng, enraged, smashed the vessel and stood up, saying, "We are now captives of the Duke of Pei!"

The Duke of Pei returned for several days, and Xiang Yu led his troops westward to massacre Xianyang, killing the surrendered King of Qin, Ziying, and burning the Qin palaces. Everywhere they passed, they left destruction in their wake. The people of Qin were greatly disappointed. Xiang Yu sent someone to report back to King Huai, and King Huai said, "As agreed." Xiang Yu resented King Huai for not allowing him to enter the pass westward with the Duke of Pei but instead sending him north to rescue Zhao, thus delaying the fulfillment of the covenant. He then said, "King Huai was established by my family; he has no merit in battle, so how can he arbitrarily decide the covenant? It is the generals and I who have truly pacified the world." In the spring, the first month, he nominally honored King Huai as the Righteous Emperor but did not actually follow his orders.

In the second month, Xiang Yu proclaimed himself the Hegemon King of Western Chu, ruling over nine commanderies in Liang and Chu, with Pengcheng as his capital. He broke the covenant and instead established the Duke of Pei as the King of Han, ruling over forty-one counties in Ba, Shu, and Hanzhong, with Nanzheng as his capital. He divided Guanzhong into three parts and appointed three Qin generals: Zhang Han as the King of Yong, with Feiqiu as his capital; Sima Xin as the King of Sai, with Yueyang as his capital; and Dong Yi as the King of Zhai, with Gaonu as his capital. The Chu general, Shen Yang of Xiaqiu, was made the King of Henan, with Luoyang as his capital. The

Zhao general, Sima Ang, was made the King of Yin, with Chaoge as his capital. The Dangyang Lord, Ying Bu, was made the King of Jiujiang, with Liu as his capital. The pillar of state of King Huai, Gong Ao, was made the King of Linjiang, with Jiangling as his capital. The Lord of Fan, Wu Rui, was made the King of Hengshan, with Zhu as his capital. The grandson of the former King of Qi, Tian An, was made the King of Jibei. The King of Wei, Bao, was moved to become the King of Western Wei, with Pingyang as his capital. The King of Yan, Han Guang, was moved to become the King of Liaodong. The Yan general, Zang Tu, was made the King of Yan, with Ji as his capital. The King of Qi, Tian Shi, was moved to become the King of Jiaodong. The Qi general, Tian Du, was made the King of Qi, with Linzi as his capital. The King of Zhao, Xie, was moved to become the King of Dai. The Zhao chancellor, Zhang Er, was made the King of Changshan. The King of Han resented Xiang Yu for breaking the covenant and wanted to attack him, but the chancellor, Xiao He, advised against it, and he stopped.

In the summer, the fourth month, the feudal lords disbanded from Xi and each returned to their own states. Xiang Yu sent thirty thousand soldiers to follow the King of Han, and tens of thousands of Chu sons and feudal lords who admired him followed, entering through the south of Du into Shizhong. Zhang Liang bid farewell and returned to Han. The King of Han escorted him to Baozhong, and Zhang Liang advised the King of Han to burn and destroy the plank roads to prepare against the bandit armies of the feudal lords, also showing Xiang Yu that he had no intention of moving east.

When the King of Han arrived in Nanzheng, the generals and soldiers all sang songs longing to return east, and many deserted and returned along the way. Han Xin was the Commandant of Grain and also deserted, but Xiao He pursued and brought him back, then recommended him to the King of Han, saying, "If you truly wish to contend for the world, there is no one but Han Xin to discuss strategies with." Thereupon, the King of Han purified himself and set up an altar, appointing Han Xin as the Grand General and asking him for strategies. Han Xin replied, "Xiang Yu broke the covenant and made you, my lord, the King of Han in Nanzheng, which is an exile. The officials and soldiers are all from east of the mountains, longing day and night to return. If we use their sharpness, we can achieve great merit. Now that the world is settled, the people are all at peace and cannot be used again. It would be better to decide on a strategy to move east." He then presented a plan for easily conquering the Three Qins. The King of Han was greatly pleased and followed Han Xin's strategy, deploying the generals. He left Xiao He to collect the taxes from Ba and Shu to supply the army's provisions.

In the fifth month, the King of Han led his troops out from the old road to attack Yong. The King of Yong, Zhang Han, met them in Chencang; the Yong army was defeated and fled. They fought again in Haozhi and were again greatly defeated, fleeing to Feiqiu. The King of Han then secured the land of Yong. He went east to Xianyang, led his troops to besiege the King of Yong in Feiqiu, and sent the generals to conquer other territories.

Tian Rong, hearing that Xiang Yu had moved the King of Qi, Tian Shi, to Jiaodong and established Tian Du as the King of Qi, was furious and led the Qi army to attack Tian Du. Tian Du fled and surrendered to Chu. In the sixth month, Tian Rong killed Tian Shi and proclaimed himself the King of Qi. At that time, Peng Yue was in Juye with over ten thousand men, unaffiliated. Tian Rong gave Peng Yue a general's seal and ordered him to rebel in Liang. Peng Yue killed the King of Jibei, Tian An, and Tian Rong then annexed the lands of the Three Qi. The King of Yan, Han Guang, also refused to move to Liaodong. In the autumn, the eighth month, Zang Tu killed Han Guang and annexed his territory. The King of Sai, Sima Xin, and the King of Zhai, Dong Yi, both surrendered to Han.

Initially, Xiang Liang had established the descendant of the Han royal family, Han Cheng, as the King of Han, with Zhang Liang as the Han Minister of Education. Xiang Yu, because Zhang Liang followed the King of Han and Han Cheng had no merit, did not send him to his state but took him to Pengcheng and killed him. Upon hearing that the King of Han had annexed Guanzhong and that Qi and Liang had rebelled, Xiang Yu was furious and appointed the former magistrate of Wu, Zheng Chang, as the King of Han to resist Han. He ordered the Duke of Xiao, Jiao, to attack Peng Yue, but Peng Yue defeated Jiao's troops. At that time, Zhang Liang was pacifying the Han territory and sent a letter to Xiang Yu, saying, "Han wishes to obtain Guanzhong; if the covenant is fulfilled, it will stop and dare not move east again. "Because of this, Xiang Yu had no intention of moving west and instead attacked Qi in the north.

In the ninth month, the King of Han sent generals Xue Ou and Wang Xi out through the Wu Pass, using Wang Ling's troops to welcome the Grand Duke and Empress Lü from Pei via Nanyang. Xiang Yu, hearing of this, sent troops to block them at Yangxia, preventing them from advancing.

In the winter, the tenth month of the second year, Xiang Yu ordered the King of Jiujiang, Ying Bu, to kill the Righteous Emperor in Chen. Chen Yu also resented Xiang Yu for not making him a king and sought assistance from Tian Rong to attack the King of Changshan, Zhang Er. Zhang Er was defeated and fled, surrendering to Han. The King of Han treated him generously. Chen Yu welcomed the King of Dai, Xie, back to Zhao, and Xie appointed Chen Yu as the King of Dai. Zhang Liang secretly returned to Han from Han, and the King of Han appointed him as the Marquis of Chengxin.

The King of Han went to Shan to pacify the elders outside the pass. The King of Henan, Shen Yang, surrendered, and the Henan Commandery was established. He sent the Grand Commandant of Han, Han Xin, to attack Han, and the King of Han, Zheng Chang, surrendered. In the eleventh month, the Grand Commandant of Han, Han Xin, was established as the King of

Han. The King of Han returned and established his capital in Yueyang, sending the generals to conquer territories, capturing Longxi. Those who surrendered with ten thousand men or a commandery were enfeoffed with ten thousand households. He repaired the fortifications along the river. The former Qin gardens and ponds were opened for the people to cultivate.

In the spring, the first month, Xiang Yu attacked Tian Rong in Chengyang; Tian Rong was defeated and fled to Pingyuan, where the people of Pingyuan killed him. All of Qi surrendered to Chu, but Chu burned their cities, and the people of Qi rebelled again. The generals captured Beidi and captured the younger brother of the King of Yong, Zhang Ping. He pardoned criminals. On the second month, the day Guiwei, he ordered the people to abolish the Qin altars of soil and grain and establish Han altars of soil and grain. He bestowed kindness and virtue, granting the people noble titles. The people of Shu and Han who provided military service were exempted from taxes for two years. Those from Guanzhong who joined the army were exempted from corvée for one year. He selected people over fifty years old who had good conduct and could lead the masses to do good, appointing them as elders of the community, one for each village. From among the village elders, one was chosen as the county elder, who, along with the county magistrate, assistant magistrate, and commandant, would teach the people and were exempted from corvée and garrison duty. In the tenth month, they were bestowed with wine and meat.

In the third month, the King of Han crossed the river from Linjin; the King of Wei, Bao, surrendered and led his troops to follow. They captured Henei and captured the King of Yin, Ang, establishing the Henei Commandery. Arriving at Xiuwu, Chen Ping deserted Chu and surrendered. The King of Han spoke with him, was pleased, and made him a chariot companion to oversee the generals. They crossed the Pingyin Ford to the south and arrived in Luoyang. The elder of Xincheng, Dong Gong, intercepted and advised the King of Han, saying, "I have heard that 'those who follow virtue will prosper, and those who oppose virtue will perish,' and 'military actions without just cause will not succeed.' Therefore, it is said, 'Declare him a thief, and the enemy can be subdued.' Xiang Yu is without principle; he has exiled and killed his lord and is a thief to the world. Benevolence does not rely on bravery, nor righteousness on strength. The masses of the three armies should wear plain mourning clothes and inform the feudal lords, thus marching east to punish, and within the four seas, none will not look up to virtue. This is the action of the three kings." The King of Han said, "Good, without you, I would not have heard this." Thereupon, the King of Han held a funeral for the Righteous Emperor, bared his shoulders, and wept loudly, mourning for three days. He sent envoys to inform the feudal lords, saying, "The world together established the Righteous Emperor and served him as the northern lord. Now Xiang Yu has exiled and killed the Righteous Emperor south of the river, a great act of unprincipledness. I personally have held a funeral, and all my soldiers are in mourning clothes. I am mobilizing all the troops from Guanzhong, gathering the warriors from the three rivers, and floating south along the Jiang and Han rivers to descend. I wish to join the kings and feudal lords in attacking Chu for the killing of the Righteous Emperor."

In the summer, the fourth month, Tian Rong's younger brother, Tian Heng, gathered tens of thousands of men and established Rong's son, Guang, as the King of Qi. Although Xiang Yu heard that Han was moving east, he first attacked Qi, intending to defeat it before attacking Han. The King of Han thus managed to seize the troops of the five feudal lords and marched east to attack Chu. Upon reaching Waihuang, Peng Yue led thirty thousand men to join Han. The King of Han appointed Peng Yue as the Chancellor of Wei and ordered him to pacify Liang. The King of Han then entered Pengcheng, confiscated Xiang Yu's beautiful women and treasures, and held a grand banquet. Xiang Yu, hearing of this, ordered his generals to attack Qi while he personally led thirty thousand elite troops from Lu through Huling to Xiao, launching a dawn attack on the Han army. A great battle ensued east of Lingbi on the Sui River, where the Han army was utterly defeated, with many soldiers killed, so many that the Sui River was blocked. Xiang Yu surrounded the King of Han three times. A great wind rose from the northwest, breaking trees and lifting roofs, scattering sand and stones, turning day into night, throwing the Chu army into chaos, and allowing the King of Han to escape with several dozen horsemen. Passing through Pei, he sent people to search for his family, but they had already fled, and he could not find them. On the road, the King of Han encountered Emperor Hui and Princess Yuan of Lu and took them along. Chu cavalry pursued the King of Han, who, in his haste, pushed the two children out of the carriage. Lord Teng got down, picked them up, and thus they escaped. Shen Yiji followed the Grand Duke and Empress Lü on a secret path but encountered the Chu army. Xiang Yu often kept them in the army as hostages. The feudal lords, seeing Han's defeat, all fled. The King of Sai, Xin, and the King of Zhai, Yi, surrendered to Chu, and the King of Yin, Ang, died.

Empress Lü's brother, Zhou Lühou, led troops stationed at Xiayi, and the King of Han went to join him. Gradually, he gathered his soldiers and stationed them at Dang. The King of Han traveled west through Liang territory to Yu and said to the courtier Sui He, "If you can persuade the King of Jiujiang, Ying Bu, to raise troops and rebel against Chu, King Xiang will surely stay to attack him. If we can delay him for several months, I will surely take the world." Sui He went to persuade Ying Bu and indeed caused him to rebel against Chu.

In the fifth month, the King of Han stationed at Xingyang, and Xiao He sent all the old and weak who had not yet registered from Guanzhong to the army. Han Xin also gathered troops and joined the King of Han, greatly boosting the army's morale. They fought Chu between Jing and Suo south of Xingyang and defeated them. They built a corridor connecting to the river to transport grain from the Ao Granary. The King of Wei, Bao, requested to return to see to his relative's illness. Upon arrival, he cut off the river crossing and turned against Chu.

In the sixth month, the King of Han returned to Yueyang. On the day Renwu, he established the crown prince and pardoned criminals. He ordered the sons of the feudal lords in Guanzhong to gather at Yueyang for defense. He diverted water to flood Feiqiu, and Feiqiu surrendered; Zhang Han committed suicide. Yongzhou was pacified, with over eighty counties, and the regions of Heshang, Weinan, Zhongdi, Longxi, and Shangjun were established. He ordered the ritual officials to sacrifice to the heavens, earth, four directions, gods of the mountains and rivers, and to perform timely sacrifices. He mobilized the soldiers of Guanzhong to garrison the border fortresses. There was a great famine in Guanzhong, with the price of rice reaching ten thousand coins per hu, and people resorted to cannibalism. He ordered the people to seek food in Shu and Han.

In the autumn, the eighth month, the King of Han went to Xingyang and said to Li Yiji, "Go and gently persuade the King of Wei, Bao. If you can make him submit, I will enfeoff you with ten thousand households in Wei territory." Li Yiji went, but Bao did not listen. The King of Han appointed Han Xin as the Left Chancellor, along with Cao Shen and Guan Ying, to attack Wei. When Li Yiji returned, the King of Han asked, "Who is Wei's great general?" He replied, "Bo Zhi." The King said, "He is still wet behind the ears and cannot match Han Xin. Who is the cavalry general?" He said, "Feng Jing." The King said, "He is the son of the Qin general Feng Wuze; although capable, he cannot match Guan Ying. Who is the infantry general?" He said, "Xiang Ta." The King said, "He cannot match Cao Shen. I have no worries." In the ninth month, Han Xin and others captured Bao and sent him to Xingyang. They pacified Wei territory and established the Hedong, Taiyuan, and Shangdang commanderies. Han Xin sent a request for thirty thousand troops, wishing to march north to capture Yan and Zhao, east to attack Qi, and south to cut off

Chu's grain supply route. The King of Han granted his request.

In the winter, the tenth month of the third year, Han Xin and Zhang Er marched east through Jingxing to attack Zhao, killed Chen Yu, and captured the King of Zhao, Xie. They established the Changshan and Dai commanderies. On the day Jiaxu, the last day of the month, there was a solar eclipse. On the day Guimao, the last day of the eleventh month, there was another solar eclipse.

After Sui He persuaded Ying Bu, Bu raised troops to attack Chu. Chu sent Xiang Sheng and Long Ju to attack Bu, but Bu was defeated in battle. In the twelfth month, Bu and Sui He secretly returned to Han. The King of Han divided his troops and together they gathered soldiers to Cheng'ao.

Xiang Yu repeatedly encroached upon the Han corridor, causing the Han army to suffer from food shortages. The King of Han consulted with Li Yiji on how to weaken Chu's power. Li Yiji proposed to establish the descendants of the six states to build alliances. The King of Han had seals carved and was about to send Li Yiji to establish them. He asked Zhang Liang, who raised eight objections. The King of Han stopped eating and spat out his food, saying, "This petty scholar nearly ruined my affairs!" He ordered the seals to be destroyed. He then consulted Chen Ping and followed his plan, giving Ping forty thousand jin of gold to sow discord among the Chu officials and rulers.

In the summer, the fourth month, Xiang Yu besieged Han's Xingyang. The King of Han requested peace, offering to cede the territory west of Xingyang to Han. Yafu urged Xiang Yu to attack Xingyang urgently, causing the King of Han great concern. Chen Ping's plan of sowing discord succeeded, and Xiang Yu indeed became suspicious of Yafu. Yafu left in a rage and died of illness.

In the fifth month, General Ji Xin said, "The situation is critical! I request to deceive Chu, allowing us to escape." That night, Chen Ping sent over two thousand women out of the east gate, and Chu attacked from all sides. Ji Xin then rode in the king's carriage, with a yellow canopy and left banner, declaring, "We are out of food; the King of Han surrenders to Chu." The Chu soldiers all cheered, and while they gathered at the east gate to watch, the King of Han managed to escape with several dozen horsemen through the west gate. He ordered the Imperial Censor Zhou Ke, Wei Bao, and Cong Gong to defend Xingyang. Xiang Yu saw Ji Xin and asked, "Where is the King of Han?" Ji Xin replied, "He has already left." Xiang Yu burned and killed Ji Xin. Zhou Ke and Cong Gong said to each other, "A king who has rebelled against his country is hard to defend the city with." Thus, they killed Wei Bao.

The King of Han left Xingyang and went to Cheng'ao. From Cheng'ao, he entered the pass, gathered troops, and intended to march east again. Yuansheng advised the King of Han, saying, "Han and Chu have been stalemated at Xingyang for several years, and Han has often been in distress. I hope Your Majesty will march out of Wuguan; King Xiang will surely lead his troops south. Your Majesty should fortify your defenses and allow the area between Xingyang and Cheng'ao to rest. Have Han Xin and others pacify the land of Zhao north of the river and connect with Yan and Qi. Then Your Majesty can return to Xingyang. In this way, Chu will have to defend many fronts, and their strength will be divided. Han will be able to rest and then fight again; victory will surely be ours." The King of Han followed this plan and marched his army between Wan and Ye, joining Ying Bu to gather troops.

When Xiang Yu heard that the King of Han was in Wan, he indeed led his troops south. The King of Han fortified his defenses and did not engage in battle. That month, Peng Yue crossed the Sui River and fought Xiang Sheng and Xue Gong at Xiapi, defeating and killing Xue Gong. Xiang Yu sent Zhong Gong to defend Cheng'ao and personally marched east to attack Peng Yue. The King of Han led his troops north, defeated Zhong Gong, and returned to Cheng'ao. In the sixth month, after Xiang Yu had defeated and driven away Peng Yue, he heard that the Han army had returned to Cheng'ao and led his troops west to capture Xingyang, capturing Zhou Ke alive. Xiang Yu said to Zhou Ke, "Serve as my general, and I will appoint you as the Grand General and enfeoff you with thirty thousand households." Zhou Ke cursed, "If you do not quickly surrender to Han, you will be a captive now! You are no match for the King of Han." Xiang Yu executed Zhou Ke and also killed Cong Gong, capturing Han Xin, the King of Han, and then besieged Cheng'ao. The King of Han fled, alone with Teng Gong, escaping through the Yumen Gate of Cheng'ao, crossing the river north, and staying overnight at Xiaoxiuwu. He claimed to be an envoy and rode into the camps of Zhang Er and Han Xin at dawn, taking command of their armies. He then sent Zhang Er north to gather troops in the land of Zhao.

In the autumn, the seventh month, a comet appeared near the Great Horn. The King of Han obtained Han Xin's army, and his forces greatly revived. In the eighth month, he faced south of the river, stationed at Xiaoxiuwu, and intended to fight again. The courtier Zheng Zhong advised the King of Han to stop and fortify his defenses, building high walls and deep trenches to avoid battle. The King of Han heeded his advice and sent Lu Wan and Liu Jia with twenty thousand infantry and several hundred cavalry to cross the Baima Ford into Chu territory, assisting Peng Yue in burning Chu's supplies and defeating the Chu army west of Yan Guo, capturing seventeen cities including Suiyang and Waihuang. In the ninth month, Xiang Yu said to the Marquis of Haichun and Grand Marshal Cao Jiu, "Defend Cheng'ao carefully. Even if the King of Han wishes to challenge you, be cautious and do not engage in battle; just prevent him from advancing east. I will surely pacify the Liang region within fifteen days and then return to join you." Xiang Yu led his troops east to attack Peng Yue.

The King of Han sent Li Yiji to persuade King Tian Guang of Qi to withdraw his defensive troops and make peace with Han. In the winter, the tenth month of the fourth year, Han Xin, following

Kuai Tong's plan, launched a surprise attack and defeated Qi. King Tian Guang of Qi executed Li Yiji and fled east to Gaomi. Upon hearing that Han Xin had defeated Qi and was planning to attack Chu, Xiang Yu sent Long Ju to rescue Qi.

The Han forces indeed repeatedly challenged the Chu army at Cheng'ao to battle, but the Chu army did not come out. After several days of taunting, Grand Marshal Cao Jiu became enraged and led his troops across the Si River. When half the soldiers had crossed, the Han army attacked and utterly defeated the Chu forces, capturing all of Chu's gold, jade, and treasures. Grand Marshal Cao Jiu and Chief Secretary Xin both committed suicide by the Si River. The King of Han led his troops across the river, recaptured Cheng'ao, stationed at Guangwu, and utilized the Ao Granary for provisions.

Xiang Yu captured more than ten cities in the Liang region but, upon hearing of the defeat of the Marquis of Haichun, led his troops back. The Han army was besieging Zhong Limei east of Xingyang and, upon hearing of Xiang Yu's arrival, all fled to difficult terrain. Xiang Yu also stationed at Guangwu and faced off against Han. The able-bodied men suffered from military campaigns, while the old and weak were exhausted from transporting supplies. The King of Han and Xiang Yu faced each other across the Guangwu valley and spoke. Xiang Yu wished to challenge the King of Han to a single combat, but the King of Han enumerated Xiang Yu's faults, saying, "I initially received the mandate from King Huai together with Xiang Yu, stating that whoever first pacified Guanzhong would be king. Xiang Yu broke the agreement and made me king in Shu and Han, which is the first crime. Xiang Yu falsely killed Qingzi, the champion, and exalted himself, which is the second crime. Xiang Yu was supposed to return after rescuing Zhao, but he forcibly took the troops of the feudal lords and entered the pass, which is the third crime. King Huai agreed that entering Qin should be without violence or plunder, but Xiang Yu burned the Qin palaces, excavated the tomb of the First Emperor, and seized their wealth for himself, which is the fourth crime. He also forcibly killed Ziying, the surrendered prince of Qin, which is the fifth crime. He deceitfully buried 200,000 Qin soldiers at Xin'an and made their generals kings, which is the sixth crime. He made all the generals kings in good lands, but exiled the original lords, causing his subordinates to rebel, which is the seventh crime. He expelled the Righteous Emperor from Pengcheng and made it his own capital, seized the land of the King of Han, and made himself king of Liang and Chu, taking much for himself, which is the eighth crime. He secretly had the Righteous Emperor killed south of the river, which is the ninth crime. As a subject, he killed his lord, killed those who had surrendered, governed unjustly, broke the agreed covenants, and was intolerable to the world, committing great treason and being without virtue, which is the tenth crime. I have led the righteous troops with the feudal lords to eliminate the remnants of tyranny, and I have even used criminals to attack you, so why should I trouble myself to challenge you personally?" Xiang Yu was furious and shot the King of Han with a crossbow. The King of Han was wounded in the chest but touched his foot and said, "The enemy has hit my toe!" The King of Han was bedridden due to his injury, but Zhang Liang strongly urged him to rise and inspect the troops to reassure the soldiers and prevent Chu from taking advantage of their victory. The King of Han went out to inspect the army despite his severe illness and then galloped into Cheng'ao.

In the eleventh month, Han Xin and Guan Ying defeated the Chu army, killed the Chu general Long Ju, pursued them to Chengyang, and captured King Tian Guang of Qi. Tian Heng, the prime minister of Qi, proclaimed himself King of Qi and fled to Peng Yue. Han established Zhang Er as the King of Zhao.

The King of Han recovered from his illness and entered the pass to the west, arriving at Yueyang, where he comforted the elders and held a banquet. He displayed the head of the former King Xin of Sai in the market of Yueyang. After staying for four days, he returned to the army, which was stationed at Guangwu. More troops from Guanzhong came out, and Peng Yue and Tian Heng occupied the Liang region, harassing the Chu troops and cutting off their food supplies.

After Han Xin had defeated Qi, he sent a message saying, "Qi borders Chu, and with limited authority, if I am not made an acting king, I fear I cannot stabilize Qi." The King of Han was angry and wanted to attack him, but Zhang Liang said, "It would be better to establish him as king and let him defend himself." In the second month of spring, Zhang Liang was sent with the seal to establish Han Xin as the King of Qi. In the seventh month of autumn, Ying Bu was established as the King of Huainan. In the eighth month, the first head tax was imposed. The northern Mo and the people of Yan sent elite cavalry to assist Han. The King of Han issued an order: for soldiers who unfortunately died in battle, officials were to provide burial clothes and coffins and transport them to their families. The hearts of people from all directions turned towards him.

Xiang Yu realized that he had little support and that his food supplies were exhausted, and Han Xin was advancing to attack Chu, which troubled him. Han sent Lu Jia to persuade Xiang Yu to return the Grand Duke, but Xiang Yu refused. Han then sent Hou Gong to persuade Xiang Yu, and Xiang Yu finally made a pact with Han to divide the world in half, with the area west of the Hong Canal belonging to Han and east to Chu. In the ninth month, the Grand Duke and Empress Lü were returned, and the army all cheered 'Long live!'. Hou Gong was then enfeoffed as the Lord of Pingguo. Xiang Yu disbanded his troops and returned east. The King of Han wished to return west, but Zhang Liang and Chen Ping advised, "Now Han holds more than half of the world, and all the feudal lords have submitted. The Chu troops are exhausted and their food supplies are depleted. This is the time heaven has decreed for their downfall. If we do not take advantage of this opportunity to seize them, it would be like nurturing a tiger to bring future trouble upon ourselves. The

King of Han heeded their advice.

VOLUME 1 PART 2: RECORDS OF EMPEROR GAOZU, PART 2, NO. 1

In the winter of the fifth year, the tenth month, the King of Han pursued Xiang Yu to the south of Yangxia and halted his army. He had planned to meet with the King of Qi, Han Xin, and the Prime Minister of Wei, Peng Yue, to attack Chu, but they did not arrive at Guling. Chu attacked the Han army and inflicted a great defeat. The King of Han retreated into his fortifications, dug deep trenches, and defended. He said to Zhang Liang, "The feudal lords are not following me, what should I do?" Zhang Liang replied, "The Chu army is on the verge of being defeated, but they have not yet been allocated lands, so it is natural that they are not coming. If Your Majesty can share the world with them, they will come immediately. The establishment of the King of Qi, Han Xin, was not Your Majesty's intention, and Han Xin himself is not firmly committed. Peng Yue originally pacified the Liang region, and Your Majesty initially made him Prime Minister because of Wei Bao. Now that Bao is dead, Peng Yue also desires to be king, but Your Majesty has not yet decided. If you can now take the area north of Suiyang to Gucheng and make Peng Yue king there, and give the land from Chen east to the sea to the King of Qi, Han Xin, whose family is in Chu and who desires to recover his former territory, and if you can relinquish these lands to both of them, allowing them to fight for themselves, then Chu will be easily defeated. Thereupon, the King of Han sent envoys to Han Xin and Peng Yue. Upon their arrival, both led their troops to join him.

In the eleventh month, Liu Jia entered Chu territory and besieged Shouchun. Han also sent people to persuade the Grand Marshal of Chu, Zhou Yin. Yin betrayed Chu, used Shu to slaughter Liu, raised the troops of Jiujiang to welcome Ying Bu, and together they slaughtered Chengfu, following Liu Jia and all converging.

In the twelfth month, they besieged Xiang Yu at Gaixia. At night, Xiang Yu heard the Han army singing Chu songs from all sides, realizing that Chu territory was completely lost. Xiang Yu fled with several hundred cavalry, leading to a great defeat. Guan Ying pursued and beheaded Xiang Yu at Dongcheng. The entire Chu territory was pacified, except for Lu, which did not surrender. The King of Han led the troops of the world intending to slaughter it, but because it was a country that upheld integrity and propriety, he held up Xiang Yu's head to show to its elders and brothers, and Lu then surrendered. Initially, King Huai had enfeoffed Xiang Yu as the Duke of Lu, and upon his death, Lu continued to steadfastly defend for him, so Xiang Yu was buried as the Duke of Lu at Gucheng. The King of Han arranged for the funeral, mourned, and then departed. He enfeoffed Xiang Bo and three others as marquises and granted them the surname Liu. All the people who had been displaced in Chu returned. The King of Han returned to Dingtao, galloped into the camp of the King of Qi, Han Xin, and took control of his army. Initially, Gong Ao, the King of Linjiang established by Xiang Yu, had died earlier, and his son Wei succeeded him as king and did not surrender. Lu Wan and Liu Jia were sent to attack and capture Wei.

In the first month of spring, the King of Han posthumously honored his elder brother Bo with the title of Marquis Wu'ai. He issued an order saying, "The Chu territory has been pacified, and after the death of the Righteous Emperor, I wish to comfort the Chu people and establish their lord. The King of Qi, Han Xin, is familiar with Chu customs and is re-established as the King of Chu, ruling north of the Huai River, with his capital at Xiapi.

The Prime Minister of Wei, Peng Yue, the Marquis of Jiancheng, has worked diligently for the people of Wei, humbled himself before his soldiers, often fought against greater numbers, and repeatedly defeated the Chu army. He is hereby made king of the former Wei territory, titled the King of Liang, with his capital at Dingtao. He also said, "The soldiers have not rested for eight years, and the myriad people have suffered greatly. Now that the affairs of the world are concluded, let all under heaven be pardoned except for those sentenced to death."

Thereupon, the feudal lords submitted a memorial saying, "The King of Chu, Han Xin; the King of Han, Han Xin; the King of Huainan, Ying Bu; the King of Liang, Peng Yue; the former King of Hengshan, Wu Rui; the King of Zhao, Zhang Ao; and the King of Yan, Zang Tu, dare to risk death and bow twice to say, Your Majesty the Great King: In the past, Qin was without the Way, and the world rose to execute it. Your Majesty first captured the King of Qin and pacified Guanzhong, contributing the most to the world. You have preserved the perishing, stabilized the endangered, rescued the defeated, and continued the extinguished, bringing peace to the myriad people. Your achievements are grand, and your virtue is profound. Moreover, you have bestowed favors upon the feudal lords who have merited, enabling them to establish their own altars of land and grain. The division of land has been settled, and the titles and ranks are appropriately designated, without distinction of high or low. The greatness of Your Majesty's achievements and virtue should not be hidden from future generations. We dare to risk death and bow twice to offer the honorable title of Emperor." The King of Han said, "I have heard that the title of Emperor is for the virtuous, and empty words without substance are not to be taken. Now that all the feudal lords have elevated me, how should I handle this?" The feudal lords all said, "Your Majesty rose from obscurity, destroyed the chaotic Qin, and your might shook the land. From the remote lands of Hanzhong, you exercised your might and virtue, executed the unjust, established the meritorious, and pacified the land. The meritorious ministers have all received lands and fiefs, not for personal gain. Your Majesty's virtue spreads across the four seas, and the feudal lords cannot adequately express it. It is most fitting for you to occupy the imperial throne. We hope Your Majesty will bring fortune to the world." The King of Han said, "If the feudal lords believe it is beneficial for the people of the world, then it is acceptable. Thereupon, the feudal lords and the Grand Commandant, the Marquis of Chang'an, Chen Wan, along with three hundred others, together with the Erudite Ji Si Jun, Shusun Tong, carefully selected an auspicious day, the second month, day Jiawu, to offer the honorable title. The King of Han ascended the throne as Emperor at the north of the Fan River. He honored the Queen as Empress, the Crown Prince as the Imperial Crown Prince, and posthumously honored his late mother as Lady Zhaoling.

He issued an edict saying, "The former King of Hengshan, Wu Rui, along with his two sons and one nephew, led the troops of Baiyue to assist the feudal lords in executing the tyrannical Qin, achieving great merit, and the feudal lords established him as king. Xiang Yu invaded and seized his lands, calling him the Lord of Fan. Now, with Changsha, Yuzhang, Xiangjun, Guilin, and Nanhai, we establish Lord Fan Rui as the King of Changsha." He also said, "The former King of Yue, Wang Zhu, for generations has performed the sacrifices for Yue, but Qin invaded and seized his lands, preventing his altars from receiving blood offerings. The feudal lords attacked Qin, and Wang Zhu personally led the troops of Minzhong to assist in the destruction of Qin, but Xiang Yu abolished him and did not establish him. Now we make him the King of Minyue, ruling the lands of Minzhong, and ensure he does not lose his position."

The Emperor then moved the capital west to Luoyang. In the summer, the fifth month, all soldiers were dismissed and returned home. An edict was issued saying, "The sons of the feudal lords in Guanzhong are exempted from service for twelve years, and those who return home are exempted for half that time. People who previously gathered to protect the mountains and marshes and were not registered, now that the world is pacified, are ordered to return to their counties, restore their former titles, lands, and residences. Officials are to instruct and inform them according to the law, and they shall not be flogged or humiliated. People who sold themselves into slavery due to hunger are all to be freed and made commoners. Military officers and soldiers who are pardoned, those without crimes but without titles or those below the rank of Daifu, are all to be granted the title of Daifu. Those of the rank of Daifu and above are to be granted one level higher in title. Those of the rank of Qidaifu and above are all to be granted fiefs. Those below the rank of Qidaifu are to be exempted from personal and household service." He also said, "Those of the rank of Qidaifu and Gongcheng and above are all of high rank. The sons of the feudal lords and those who return from military service, many have high ranks. I have repeatedly ordered officials to first grant them lands and residences, and to promptly provide what they should seek from the officials. Those with titles or as lords, whom the Emperor respects and honors, have long stood before officials without decisions being made, which is most unreasonable. In the past, the people of Qin with the title of Gongdafu and above were treated with equal courtesy by magistrates and chancellors. Now, I do not take titles lightly, so how can officials alone take this! Moreover, the law is to grant lands and residences based on merit, yet many minor officials who have never served in the military are fully satisfied, while those with merit are overlooked, betraying the public for private gain. The instructions from the governors and senior officials are most improper. I order all officials to treat those of high rank well, in accordance with my will. Moreover, they are to be investigated for integrity, and those who do not comply with my edict are to be severely punished."

The Emperor held a banquet at the South Palace in Luoyang.

He said, "All generals and marquises, do not dare to hide from me, but speak the truth. Why do I possess the world? Why did the Xiang clan lose the world?" Gao Qi and Wang Ling replied, "Your Majesty is arrogant and insults others, while Xiang Yu is benevolent and respects others. However, Your Majesty sends people to attack cities and seize lands, and those who surrender are given rewards, sharing the benefits with the world. Xiang Yu is jealous of the virtuous and capable, harms those who achieve merit, suspects the virtuous, does not share the rewards of victory, and does not share the benefits of the lands obtained. This is why he lost the world. The Emperor said, "You know one aspect but not the other. In devising strategies within the tent and securing victory a thousand miles away, I am not as good as Zhang Liang. In governing the state, comforting the people, and ensuring the supply of provisions without interruption, I am not as good as Xiao He. In commanding a million troops, ensuring victory in every battle and success in every attack, I am not as good as Han Xin. These three are all outstanding men, and I was able to use them. This is how I gained the world. Xiang Yu had a Fan Zeng but could not use him. This is why he was captured by me." The ministers were convinced.

Initially, Tian Heng returned to Peng Yue. After Xiang Yu was destroyed, Tian Heng feared execution and fled with his guests to the sea. The Emperor, fearing that he would cause trouble for a long time, sent an envoy to pardon Tian Heng, saying, "If Tian Heng comes, he will be made a king if great, a marquis if minor; if he does not come, troops will be sent to execute him." Tian Heng, in fear, took a carriage to Luoyang but committed suicide thirty miles before arriving. The Emperor admired his integrity, shed tears, and sent two thousand soldiers to bury him with royal rites.

A garrison soldier named Lou Jing sought an audience and advised the Emperor, "Your Majesty's way of gaining the world is different from that of the Zhou, and establishing the capital in Luoyang is inconvenient. It would be better to enter the pass and secure the stronghold of Qin." The Emperor consulted Zhang Liang, who also advised him. That day, the imperial carriage moved west to establish the capital in Chang'an. Lou Jing was appointed as Fengchun Jun and granted the surname Liu. On the sixth month, day Renchen, a general amnesty was declared throughout the land.

In the autumn, the seventh month, the King of Yan, Zang Tu, rebelled, and the Emperor personally led the expedition against him. In the ninth month, Zang Tu was captured. An edict was issued for the feudal lords to recognize the most meritorious and establish him as the King of Yan. The King of Jing, Chen Xin, and ten others all said, "The Grand Commandant, the Marquis of Chang'an, Lu Wan, has the most merit. We request that he be established as the King of Yan." The Chancellor, Kuai, was sent to lead troops to pacify the land of Dai.

Li Ji rebelled, and the Emperor personally led the attack to defeat him. Li Ji was a general under Xiang Yu. After Xiang Yu's defeat, Li Ji became the magistrate of Chen and surrendered. The Emperor made him a marquis in Yingchuan. When the Emperor arrived in Luoyang, he summoned Li Ji, who was registered as a marquis, but Li Ji, fearing for his life, rebelled. In the later ninth month, the sons of the feudal lords were relocated to Guanzhong. The construction of the Changle Palace began. In the winter, the tenth month of the sixth year, all counties and cities in the empire were ordered to build walls.

Someone reported that the King of Chu, Han Xin, was plotting a rebellion. The Emperor asked his attendants, who were eager to attack him. Following Chen Ping's strategy, the Emperor pretended to tour Yunmeng. In the twelfth month, he met the feudal lords at Chen, and the King of Chu, Han Xin, came to greet him, whereupon he was seized. An edict was issued: "Now that the world is at peace, the brave and meritorious are to be enfeoffed as marquises. Newly established, we have not yet fully considered their merits. Those who have served in the military for nine years, some unfamiliar with the laws, or who have violated the law due to their circumstances, even if deserving of death, I greatly pity them. A general amnesty is declared throughout the land." Tian Ken congratulated the Emperor, saying, "Excellent, Your Majesty has captured Han Xin and also governs the land of Qin. Qin is a strategically advantageous country, surrounded by rivers and mountains, separated by a thousand miles, with a million soldiers, and Qin possesses one hundred and two of them. The terrain is favorable, and sending troops against the feudal lords is like pouring water from a high roof. As for Qi, it has the wealth of Langya and Jimo in the east, the stronghold of Mount Tai in the south, the barrier of the turbid river in the west, and the benefits of the Bohai Sea in the north. The land spans two thousand miles, with a million soldiers, separated by a thousand miles, and Qi possesses twelve of them. These are the eastern and western Qins. Only one's own sons and brothers can be made kings of Qi." The Emperor said, "Good." He awarded Tian Ken five hundred catties of gold. The Emperor returned to Luoyang, pardoned Han Xin, and enfeoffed him as the Marquis of Huaiyin.

On the day Jiashen, the Emperor began to divide the tallies and enfeoff meritorious officials such as Cao Shen as marquises. An edict was issued: "Qi is an ancient established state, now a commandery and county, it is to be restored as a feudal state. General Liu Jia has repeatedly achieved great merit, and we have chosen a generous and virtuous person to be the king of Qi and Jing." In the spring, on the day Bingwu of the first month, the King of Han, Han Xin, and others petitioned to establish Liu Jia as the King of Jing with the former fifty-three counties of Dongyang, Zhang, and Wu commanderies, and to establish the Emperor's younger brother, Wenxin Jun Jiao, as the King of Chu with the thirty-six counties of Dang, Xue, and Tan commanderies. On the day Renzin, the Emperor's elder brother, Yixin Hou Xi, was established as the King of Dai with the fifty-three counties of Yunzhong, Yanmen, and Dai commanderies. The Emperor's son, Fei, was established as the King of Qi with the seventy-three counties of Jiaodong, Jiaoxi, Linzi, Jibei, Boyang, and Chengyang commanderies. The thirty-one counties of Taiyuan commandery were made the state of Han, and the King of Han, Han Xin, was moved to Jinyang.

The Emperor had already enfeoffed more than thirty great meritorious officials, but the rest were still competing for merit and had not yet been enfeoffed. The Emperor resided in the South Palace and, from the elevated walkway, saw the generals often speaking in pairs. He asked Zhang Liang about this. Zhang Liang said, "Your Majesty, together with these people, took the world. Now that you are the Son of Heaven, those you enfeoff are all old friends you love, and those you execute are all lifelong enemies. Now the military officials are calculating their merits, thinking the world is not enough to enfeoff everyone, and fearing that they might be executed for faults, so they gather to plot rebellion. The Emperor asked, "What should be done?" Zhang Liang replied, "Take one whom Your Majesty has always disliked, whom all the ministers know very well, and enfeoff him first to show the ministers." In the third month, the Emperor held a banquet and enfeoffed Yong Chi, urging the Chancellor to quickly determine the merits and proceed with the enfeoffments. After the banquet ended, all the ministers were pleased, saying, "Even Yong Chi is to be made a marquis, so we have nothing to worry about!"

The Emperor returned to Yueyang and attended court to see his father, the Grand Duke, every five days. The Grand Duke's steward advised the Grand Duke, saying, "Heaven cannot have two suns, and the earth cannot have two kings. The Emperor, though your son, is the ruler; the Grand Duke, though his father, is a subject. How can the ruler bow to a subject? If this continues, authority and dignity will not be maintained." Later, when the Emperor attended court, the Grand Duke held a broom and backed away from the door to greet him. The Emperor was greatly surprised and stepped down to support the Grand Duke.

The Grand Duke said, "Emperor, you are the ruler; how can you disrupt the laws of the world for my sake?" The Emperor then appreciated the steward's words and awarded him five hundred catties of gold. In the summer, on the day Bingwu of the fifth month, an edict was issued: "The closest of human relationships is that between father and son. Therefore, if a father possesses the world, he passes it to his son; if a son possesses the world, he honors his father. This is the ultimate principle of human relations. In the past, the world was in great chaos, arms and conflicts arose, and the people suffered greatly. I personally donned armor and wielded weapons, leading soldiers, facing dangers, quelling rebellions, establishing feudal lords, and bringing peace to the people, resulting in great stability for the world. All this is due to the teachings of the Grand Duke. The kings, marquises, generals, ministers, and officials have already honored me as the Emperor, but the Grand Duke has not yet been given a title. Now, I hereby honor the Grand Duke as the Supreme Emperor."

In the autumn, the ninth month, the Xiongnu besieged the King of Han, Han Xin, at Mayi, and Han Xin surrendered to the Xiongnu.

In the winter, the tenth month of the seventh year, the Emperor personally led an attack against the King of Han, Han Xin, at Tongdi and beheaded his general. Han Xin fled to the Xiongnu and, together with his generals Man Qiu Chen and Wang Huang, established the former Zhao heir, Zhao Li, as king. They gathered Han Xin's scattered troops and, along with the Xiongnu, resisted the Han. The Emperor fought continuously from Jinyang, pursued the enemy northwards, and reached Loufan, where severe cold caused two or three out of ten soldiers to lose fingers. He then arrived at Pingcheng, where he was besieged by the Xiongnu for seven days before escaping using Chen Ping's secret strategy. Fan Kuai was left to pacify the land of Dai.

In the twelfth month, the Emperor returned and passed through

Zhao, but did not show courtesy to the King of Zhao. That month, the Xiongnu attacked Dai, and the King of Dai, Xi, abandoned his state and returned to Luoyang, where he was pardoned and made the Marquis of Heyang. On the day Xinmao, the Emperor's son, Ruyi, was established as the King of Dai. In the spring, it was decreed that officials with crimes punishable by shaving the head or more should be reported. People who gave birth to children were exempted from corvée labor for two years.

In the second month, the Emperor arrived at Chang'an. Xiao He was overseeing the construction of the Weiyang Palace, erecting the east and north gates, the front hall, the armory, and the great granary. When the Emperor saw its grandeur, he was very angry and said to Xiao He, "The world is in turmoil, and the people have suffered for several years, the success or failure is still uncertain. Why is such an excessive construction of palaces being undertaken?" Xiao He replied, "The world is not yet settled, so we can take this opportunity to complete the palace. Moreover, the Son of Heaven takes the four seas as his home; if it is not made grand and magnificent, it will not show his authority, and it will also ensure that future generations have nothing to add." The Emperor was pleased. He moved the capital from Yueyang to Chang'an and established the Zongzheng Palace to order the nine clans. In the summer, the fourth month, he traveled to Luoyang.

In the winter of the eighth year, the Emperor went east to attack the remnants of Han Xin's forces at Dongyuan. On his return, he passed through Zhao. The Chancellor of Zhao, Guan Gao, was ashamed that the Emperor had not shown courtesy to their king and secretly plotted to assassinate the Emperor. The Emperor intended to stay overnight but felt uneasy and asked, "What is the name of this county?" The reply was, "Bairen." The Emperor said, "Bairen means 'pressed by people.'" He left and did not stay overnight.

In the eleventh month, it was decreed that soldiers who died in the army should be given a coffin, returned to their county, and the county should provide burial clothes, a coffin, and burial utensils. A sacrificial offering of a small animal was made, and the local officials attended the burial. In the twelfth month, the Emperor traveled from Dongyuan back.

In the spring, the third month, the Emperor traveled to Luoyang. It was decreed that officials and soldiers who had served in the army at Pingcheng and guarded the city would be exempt from corvée labor for life. Only those with the rank of Gongcheng or higher were allowed to wear the Liu family's crown. Merchants were not allowed to wear embroidered silk, brocade, or fine linen, carry weapons, or ride horses. In the autumn, the eighth month, officials with undiscovered crimes were pardoned. In the ninth month, the Emperor returned from Luoyang, accompanied by the Kings of Huainan, Liang, Zhao, and Chu.

In the winter, the tenth month of the ninth year, the Kings of Huainan, Liang, Zhao, and Chu attended court at the Weiyang Palace, and a banquet was held in the front hall. The Emperor raised a jade cup to toast the Supreme Emperor, saying, "In the past, you often said I was unreliable, unable to manage property, and not as capable as Zhong. Now, whose achievements are greater, mine or Zhong's?" All the ministers in the hall cheered "Long live the Emperor" and laughed heartily.

In the eleventh month, the great clans of Qi and Chu—the Zhao, Qu, Jing, Huai, and Tian families—were relocated to Guanzhong and granted fertile lands and residences. In the twelfth month, the Emperor traveled to Luoyang. The plot of Guan Gao and others was discovered, and they were arrested, along with the King of Zhao, Ao, who was imprisoned. An edict was issued stating that anyone who dared to follow the King would be punished with the extermination of three generations. The officials Tian Shu, Meng Shu, and eight others shaved their heads and bound themselves as the King's slaves, accompanying him to prison. The King truly did not know about the plot. In the spring, the first month, the King of Zhao, Ao, was deposed and made the Marquis of Xuanping. The King of Dai, Ruyi, was moved to Zhao and made the King of Zhao, ruling the state of Zhao. On the day Bingyin, all those previously sentenced to death or less were pardoned.

In the second month, the Emperor returned from Luoyang. The virtuous officials of Zhao, Tian Shu, Meng Shu, and eight others, were summoned and spoken to; no ministers of the Han court could surpass them. The Emperor was pleased and appointed them all as commandery governors and chancellors of feudal states. In the summer, on the last day of the sixth month, Bingwei, there was a solar eclipse. In the winter, the tenth month of the tenth year, the Kings of Huainan, Yan, Jing, Liang, Chu, Qi, and Changsha came to court.

In the summer, the fifth month, the Empress Dowager passed away. In the autumn, on the day Guimao of the seventh month, the Supreme Emperor passed away and was buried at Wannian. Prisoners in Yueyang sentenced to death or less were pardoned. In the eighth month, it was decreed that all feudal kings should establish a temple for the Supreme Emperor in their capitals.

In the ninth month, the Chancellor of Dai, Chen Xi, rebelled. The Emperor said, "Xi once served as my envoy and was very trustworthy. The land of Dai is crucial to me, so I enfeoffed Xi as a marquis and appointed him as Chancellor to guard Dai. Now he has joined forces with Wang Huang and others to plunder Dai! Officials and commoners who are not guilty, if they can leave Xi and Huang and return, will all be pardoned." The Emperor went east and arrived at Handan. He was pleased and said, "Xi did not seize Handan in the south and block the Zhang River; I know he is powerless." The Chancellor of Zhao, Zhou Chang, reported that out of the twenty-five cities in Changshan, twenty had been lost, and he requested the execution of the defending commanders. The Emperor asked,

"Did the defending commanders rebel?" Zhou Chang replied, "No." The Emperor said, "Then it was due to insufficient strength; they are not guilty." The Emperor ordered Zhou Chang to select strong men from Zhao who could be made generals, and four men were presented. The Emperor scolded them, saying, "Can you brats be generals?" The four men were ashamed and prostrated themselves. The Emperor enfeoffed each with a thousand households and appointed them as generals. The attendants remonstrated, saying, "From the campaign in Shu and Han to the conquest of Chu, rewards have not yet been fully distributed. Now, why are you enfeoffing these men? What merit do they have?" The Emperor replied, "This is beyond your understanding. Chen Xi has rebelled, and the lands of Zhao and Dai are under his control. I have issued urgent summons to raise troops from across the land, but none have arrived. Now, the only troops we have are those in Handan. Why should I begrudge four thousand households if it can comfort the sons and brothers of Zhao?" They all said, "Well said." He also inquired, "Does Yue Yi have any descendants?" His grandson, Le Shu, was found and enfeoffed at Lexiang, with the title of Huacheng Jun. When asked about Chen Xi's generals, it was found they were all former merchants. The Emperor said, "I know how to deal with them." He then offered large sums of gold to buy over Chen Xi's generals, and many of them surrendered.

In the winter of the eleventh year, the Emperor was in Handan. Chen Xi's general, Hou Chang, led over ten thousand troops on a campaign, while Wang Huang led over a thousand cavalry to Qu Ni, and Zhang Chun led over ten thousand troops across the river to attack Liaocheng. The Han general Guo Meng, along with the Qi generals, attacked and decisively defeated them. The Grand Commandant Zhou Bo advanced through Taiyuan to pacify the Dai region, reaching Mayi, which did not surrender and was attacked and devastated. Chen Xi's general Zhao Li defended Dongyuan, and the Emperor attacked but could not take it. The soldiers cursed, and the Emperor was enraged. When the city surrendered, the soldiers who had cursed were executed. Those counties that steadfastly refused to surrender to the rebels were exempted from taxes and corvée labor for three years.

In the spring, the first month, the Marquis of Huaiyin, Han Xin, plotted rebellion in Chang'an and was exterminated along with three generations of his family. General Chai Wu executed Han Wang Xin at Canhe.

The Emperor returned to Luoyang and issued an edict: "The land of Dai lies north of Changshan, bordering the barbarians. Zhao is located south of the mountains, distant and frequently harassed by Hu raids, making it difficult to govern as a state. Let us take more of the land south of the mountains, Taiyuan, and attach it to Dai. The region west of Yunzhong in Dai shall become Yunzhong Commandery, thus reducing the border raids on Dai. Let the kings, chancellors, marquises, and officials with a salary of two thousand piculs choose a suitable candidate to be made King of Dai." The King of Yan, Wan, the Chancellor He, and thirty-three others all said, "Your son Heng is virtuous, wise, gentle, and kind. We request that he be made King of Dai, with his capital at Jinyang." A general amnesty was proclaimed throughout the land.

In the second month, an edict was issued: "I greatly desire to reduce taxes. Currently, there is no standard for tributes, and officials often impose excessive taxes to present as tributes, especially among the feudal kings, causing the people great distress. Henceforth, the feudal kings and marquises shall present their tributes in the tenth month, and each commandery shall calculate the amount based on its population, with each person contributing sixty-three coins annually to cover the tribute expenses." It also stated: "I have heard that among kings, none surpassed King Wen of Zhou, and among hegemons, none surpassed Duke Huan of Qi, both of whom achieved fame by relying on worthy men. Are the wise and talented individuals of today any less than those of ancient times? The problem lies in the rulers not engaging with them; how then can scholars advance! Now, by the grace of heaven, I have united the realm with the help of virtuous scholars and officials, making it one family, and I wish for it to endure long, with the ancestral temples never ceasing. The virtuous men have already helped me pacify it; is it acceptable that they do not also help me secure and benefit it? If there are virtuous scholars and officials willing to follow me, I can honor and elevate them. Let this be proclaimed throughout the land so that all may clearly understand my intentions. The Censor-in-Chief, Chang, shall convey this to the Chancellor, the Marquis of Zan, who shall inform the feudal kings. The Deputy Censors shall inform the commandery governors. Those who are known for their virtue must be personally encouraged, provided with carriages, and sent to the Chancellor's office, where their conduct, righteousness, and age shall be recorded. Those who fail to report such individuals, once discovered, shall be dismissed. The elderly and those with chronic illnesses should not be sent."

In the third month, the King of Liang, Peng Yue, plotted rebellion and was exterminated along with three generations of his family. An edict was issued: "Choose a suitable candidate to be made King of Liang and King of Huaiyang." The King of Yan, Wan, and the Chancellor He requested that his son Hui be made King of Liang and his son You be made King of Huaiyang. The commandery of Dong was abolished, and much of its territory was added to Liang; the commandery of Yingchuan was abolished, and much of its territory was added to Huaiyang. In the summer, the fourth month, the Emperor returned from Luoyang. He decreed that all the people of Feng who had been relocated to Guanzhong would be exempt from taxes and corvée labor for life.

In the fifth month, an edict was issued: "The custom of the Yue people is to attack each other. Previously, Qin relocated the people of the central counties to the three southern commanderies, causing them to intermingle with the Baiyue.

When the realm rose against Qin, the Commandant of Nanhai, Tuo, governed the south for a long time with great order and principle, so that the people of the central counties did not diminish, and the Yue custom of attacking each other greatly ceased, all thanks to his efforts. Now, I appoint Tuo as King of Nanyue." He sent Lu Jia to bestow the royal seal and ribbon. Tuo kowtowed and declared himself a subject. In the sixth month, it was decreed that all soldiers who had followed the campaign into Shu, Han, and Guanzhong would be exempt from taxes and corvée labor for life.

In the autumn, the seventh month, the King of Huainan, Bu, rebelled. The Emperor consulted his generals, and the Duke of Teng mentioned that the former Chu Prime Minister, Xue Gong, had strategies. The Emperor summoned Xue Gong, who explained the situation regarding Bu, and the Emperor approved, enfeoffing Xue Gong with a thousand households. An edict was issued for the kings and chancellors to choose a suitable candidate to be made King of Huainan. The ministers requested that his son Chang be made king. The Emperor then mobilized chariots and cavalry from Shangjun, Beidi, and Longxi, as well as the skilled officers of Bashu and thirty thousand troops from the Central Commandant's command to guard the Crown Prince, stationing the army at Bashang. As Xue Gong had predicted, Bu went east, killed King Liu Jia of Jing, seized his troops, crossed the Huai River, and attacked Chu. The King of Chu, Jiao, fled to Xue. The Emperor pardoned all those under the death penalty throughout the land and ordered them to join the army. He summoned the troops of the feudal lords and personally led them to attack Bu.

In the winter, the tenth month of the twelfth year, the Emperor defeated Bu's army at Huifou. Bu fled, and the Emperor ordered other generals to pursue him.

The Emperor returned and passed by Pei, where he stayed and held a banquet at Pei Palace, summoning all his old friends, elders, and young brothers to join in the drinking. He gathered one hundred and twenty boys from Pei and taught them a song. As the wine flowed freely, the Emperor struck the zhu and sang: "A great wind rises, the clouds fly high; my might spreads across the seas, I return to my hometown; how can I find brave warriors to guard the four directions!" He had the boys sing along and practice it. The Emperor then rose to dance, filled with emotion and sorrow, tears streaming down his face. He said to the elders and brothers of Pei: "A wanderer grieves for his hometown. Although I have made my capital in Guanzhong, after ten thousand years, my spirit will still long for and take pleasure in Pei. Moreover, I rose from the position of Duke of Pei to overthrow tyranny and thus gained the realm. Let Pei be my bathing city, and its people shall be exempt from taxes and corvée labor for generations." The elders, mothers, and old friends of Pei drank joyously every day, reminiscing and laughing with great delight. After more than ten days, the Emperor wished to leave, but the elders and brothers of Pei insisted he stay. The Emperor said, "My entourage is large, and the elders and brothers cannot provide for them. Then he departed. The entire county of Pei emptied out and went west to offer tribute. The Emperor stayed and held a banquet for three days. The elders and brothers of Pei kowtowed and said, "Pei is fortunate to be exempt, but Feng has not yet been granted this. We beseech Your Majesty to show compassion." The Emperor said, "Feng is where I grew up; I cannot forget it. I specifically exempted it because of Yong Chi, who rebelled against me for Wei." The elders and brothers of Pei insisted, and so Feng was also exempted, treated the same as Pei.

The Han generals attacked Bu's army north and south of the Tao River, both achieving great victories, and pursued and beheaded Bu at Poyang. Zhou Bo pacified Dai and executed Chen Xi at Dangcheng.

An edict was issued: "Wu is an ancient state. Previously, the King of Jing held its territory, but now he has died without an heir.

I wish to reestablish the King of Wu. Let the suitable candidate be discussed." The King of Changsha, Chen, and others said, "The Marquis of Pei, Bi, is dignified and honest. We request that he be made King of Wu." After the appointment, the Emperor summoned Bi and said, "Your appearance suggests a rebellious nature." He then patted Bi on the back and said, "Fifty years from now, there will be turmoil in the southeast. Could it be you? However, the realm is one family under the same surname. Be careful not to rebel." Bi kowtowed and said, "I dare not."

In the eleventh month, the Emperor returned from Huainan. Passing through Lu, he offered a grand sacrifice to Confucius.

In the twelfth month, an edict was issued: "The Emperor of Qin, the Hidden King of Chu, King Anxi of Wei, King Min of Qi, and King Daoxiang of Zhao all died without heirs. Let twenty households guard the tomb of the First Emperor of Qin, ten households each for Chu, Wei, and Qi, and five households each for Zhao and the son of Wei, Wu Ji. They shall tend to the tombs and be exempt from other duties." A surrendered general of Chen Xi reported that when Xi rebelled, the King of Yan, Lu Wan, had sent people to Xi's camp to conspire. The Emperor sent the Marquis of Piyang, Shen Yiji, to summon Wan, but Wan claimed illness. Shen Yiji reported that there were signs of Wan's rebellion. In the second month of spring, the Emperor sent Fan Kuai and Zhou Bo to lead troops against Wan. An edict was issued: "The King of Yan, Wan, and I have a past relationship, and I loved him like a son. Hearing that he conspired with Chen Xi, I thought it was baseless, so I sent someone to summon him. Wan claimed illness and did not come, making his rebellion clear. The officials and people of Yan are not at fault. Those with a rank of six hundred dan or higher shall each be granted one level of nobility. Those who lived with Wan and left or returned shall be pardoned and also granted one level of nobility." An edict was issued for the feudal kings to discuss a suitable candidate to be made King of Yan. The King of Changsha, Chen, and others requested that his son Jian be made King of Yan.

An edict was issued: "The Marquis of Nanwu, Zhi, is also a descendant of Yue. He shall be made King of Nanhai." In the third month, an edict was issued: "I was established as the Son of Heaven, and the Emperor has ruled the realm for twelve years now. Together with the brave and virtuous of the realm, we have stabilized the realm and brought peace to it. Those who have meritorious service shall be made kings, the next shall be made marquises, and the lesser shall be granted fiefs. The relatives of important ministers, or those made marquises, shall all be allowed to appoint their own officials, collect taxes, and have princesses as wives. Those who are marquises with fiefs shall all wear seals and be granted large residences. Officials with a rank of two thousand dan shall be moved to Chang'an and receive smaller residences. Those who entered Shu and Han and pacified the three Qin shall be exempt from taxes and corvée labor for generations. I have not failed the virtuous and meritorious of the realm. Let all those who act unjustly, rebel against the Son of Heaven, and raise troops without authorization be jointly attacked and executed by the realm. This proclamation is issued to the realm to make my intentions clear."

When the Emperor was attacking Bu, he was hit by a stray arrow and fell ill on the march. The illness worsened, and Empress Lü summoned a skilled physician. The physician entered and was questioned by the Emperor. The physician said, "The illness can be treated." The Emperor then cursed him, saying, "I rose from commoner status with a three-foot sword to gain the realm. Is this not the mandate of heaven? If fate lies with heaven, what good is Bian Que!" He thus refused treatment, awarded the physician fifty catties of gold, and dismissed him. Empress Lü asked, "After Your Majesty's passing, when Chancellor Xiao has also died, who shall replace him?" The Emperor said, "Cao Shen is suitable." Asked who would come next, he said, "Wang Ling is suitable, though he is somewhat obstinate. Chen Ping can assist him. Chen Ping is wise and capable, but it would be difficult for him to take sole responsibility. Zhou Bo is dignified and honest, though lacking in refinement. However, it will be Bo who secures the Liu family. He can be made Grand Commandant." Empress Lü asked who would come after that, and the Emperor said, "After that, it is not for you to know." "

Lu Wan, along with several thousand people, stayed at the border, waiting and hoping for the Emperor's recovery so he could personally come to apologize. On the day Jia Chen in the fourth month of summer, the Emperor passed away in the Changle Palace. Upon hearing the news, Lu Wan fled into the territory of the Xiongnu.

Empress Lü and Shen Yiji conspired, saying, "The generals who once shared commoner status with the Emperor and served as his ministers have always been discontent. Now that they must serve a young ruler, unless their entire clans are eradicated, the realm will not be at peace." For this reason, they did not announce the Emperor's death. Someone heard of this and informed Li Shang. Li Shang went to see Shen Yiji and said, "I have heard that the Emperor has passed away, and for four days the death has not been announced, with the intent to execute the generals. If this is true, the realm is in danger. Chen Ping and Guan Ying command one hundred thousand troops guarding Yingyang, while Fan Kuai and Zhou Bo command two hundred thousand troops pacifying Yan and Dai. If they hear of the Emperor's death and the execution of the generals, they will surely join forces and march back to attack Guanzhong. With ministers rebelling within and generals revolting outside, collapse is imminent." Shen Yiji reported this, and on the day Ding Wei, the death was announced, and a general amnesty was declared throughout the realm.

On the day Bing Yin in the fifth month, the Emperor was buried at Changling. After the burial, the Crown Prince and all the ministers returned to the temple of the Supreme Ancestor. The ministers said, "The Emperor rose from humble beginnings, brought order out of chaos, pacified the realm, and became the founding ancestor of Han. His achievements are the greatest." He was posthumously honored with the title Emperor Gaozu.

Initially, Emperor Gaozu did not engage in literary pursuits, but he was intelligent and open-minded, fond of strategizing, and willing to listen. From gatekeepers to garrison soldiers, he treated them all as old acquaintances. Initially, he complied with the people's wishes and established the Three Articles of Agreement. Once the realm was stabilized, he ordered Xiao He to compile laws and decrees, Han Xin to articulate military strategies, Zhang Cang to establish regulations, Shusun Tong to formulate rituals, and Lu Jia to create new expressions. He also made oaths with meritorious officials, inscribing them on red paper and iron tablets, storing them in golden chests and stone chambers within the ancestral temple. Although there was not a day to spare, his plans and models were grand and far-reaching.

The commentary says: In the Spring and Autumn Annals, the historian Cai Mo of Jin said, "After the decline of the Tao Tang clan, there was Liu Lei, who learned to tame dragons and served Kong Jia. The Fan clan are his descendants." The Grand Master Fan Xuanzi also said, "Our ancestors were the Tao Tang clan before Yu, the Yu Long clan in Xia, the Shi Wei clan in Shang, the Tang Du clan in Zhou, and the Fan clan when Jin led the Xia alliance." The Fan clan served as the Chief Justice of Jin and fled to Qin during the reign of Duke Wen of Lu. Later, they returned to Jin, and those who remained became the Liu clan. Liu Xiang said, "During the Warring States period, the Liu clan was captured by Qin from Wei. When Qin conquered Wei, they moved to Daliang and established their capital in Feng. Hence, Zhou Shi said to Yong Chi, 'Feng is the former migration of Liang.'" Therefore, the ode to Emperor Gaozu states, "The lineage of the Han Emperor originates from the Tang Emperor. Descending to Zhou, in Qin they became Liu. Crossing Wei to the east, they became the Duke of Feng." The Duke of Feng was likely the father of the Supreme Ancestor. Their migration was recent, and their graves in Feng are few. When Emperor Gaozu ascended the throne, he established officials for sacrifices, including shamans from Qin, Jin, Liang, and Jing, who for generations worshipped heaven and earth, connecting them through rituals. How could this not be true? From this, it can be inferred that Han inherited the mandate of Yao, with its virtue and fortune already flourishing. The omen of the severed snake and the red banners harmonized with the fire virtue, a natural response, and obtained the mandate of heaven.

VOLUME 2: RECORDS OF EMPEROR HUI, NO. 2

Emperor Xiaohui was the crown prince of Emperor Gaozu, and his mother was Empress Lü. The Emperor was five years old when Emperor Gaozu first became King of Han. In the second year, he was established as crown prince. In the fourth month of the twelfth year, Emperor Gaozu passed away. On the day Bing Yin in the fifth month, the crown prince ascended the throne as emperor, and the empress was honored as Empress Dowager. The people were granted one rank of nobility. Gentlemen of the Palace and Palace Attendants who had served for six years were granted three ranks of nobility, and those who had served for four years were granted two ranks. Outer Gentlemen who had served for six years were granted two ranks. Gentlemen of the Palace who had served for less than a year were granted one rank. Outer Gentlemen who had served for less than two years were granted ten thousand coins. Palace eunuchs in charge of food were treated similarly to Palace Attendants. Heralds, shield bearers, halberdiers, warriors, and grooms were treated similarly to Outer Gentlemen. The crown prince's charioteer was granted the rank of Grandee, and retainers who had served for five years were granted two ranks. Those who participated in the funeral arrangements were granted twenty thousand coins for officials with a rank of two thousand dan, ten thousand coins for those with a rank of six hundred dan or above, and five thousand coins for those with a rank of five hundred dan or below down to assistant officials. Those who supervised the construction of the mausoleum were granted forty gold pieces for generals, twenty gold pieces for officials with a rank of two thousand dan, six gold pieces for those with a rank of six hundred dan or above, and two gold pieces for those with a rank of five hundred dan or below down to assistant officials. The land tax was reduced to one-fifteenth. Those with the rank of Grandee, officials with a rank of six hundred dan or above, and palace attendants who served the emperor and were well-known, if they committed crimes punishable by being shackled, were all to be treated leniently. Those with the rank of Shangzao or above, and the grandsons and great-grandsons of both the imperial and external families, if they committed crimes punishable by mutilation or by being made to do hard labor, were all to be made to gather firewood and grind rice. People aged seventy or above, or under ten, if they committed crimes punishable by mutilation, were all to be spared. It was also said, "Officials are there to govern the people. If they can fully carry out their governance, the people will rely on them. Therefore, their salaries are made substantial, for the sake of the people. Now, officials with a rank of six hundred dan or above, their parents, wives, and children living with them, as well as former officials who once held the seals of generals or commandants and led troops, or who held the seals of officials with a rank of two thousand dan, their households are only required to provide military levies, and nothing else is demanded of them.

An order was issued for the commanderies and feudal kings to establish high temples.

In the winter month of the first year, Zhao Yinwang Ruyi passed away. Commoners who committed crimes could purchase thirty ranks of nobility to avoid the death penalty. The people were granted nobility, one rank per household.

In the spring month of the first year, the city of Chang'an was built.

In the winter month of the second year, Qi Daohui Wang came to court, offering the city of Chengyang to increase the fief of Princess Luyuan, and the princess was honored as Empress Dowager.

On the day Guiyou in the spring month of the first year, two dragons appeared in the well of a family in Lanling, but by the evening of Yihai, they had disappeared. An earthquake occurred in Longxi.

There was a summer drought. Marquis Heyang Zhong passed away. On the day Xinwei in the seventh month of autumn, Chancellor He passed away.

In the spring of the third year, 146,000 men and women within six hundred li of Chang'an were conscripted to build the city of Chang'an, and the work was completed in thirty days.

A daughter of the imperial clan was made a princess and married to the Xiongnu chieftain.

In the summer month of May, Minyue Jun Yao was established as the King of the Eastern Sea.

In June, twenty thousand servants and laborers from the feudal kings and marquises were conscripted to build the city of Chang'an.

In the autumn month of July, the capital stables suffered a disaster. The King of Nanyue, Zhao Tuo, declared his allegiance and presented tribute.

On the day Renyin in the winter month of October in the fourth year, Empress Zhang was established.

In the spring month of January, those among the people who were filial, fraternal, and diligent in farming were exempted from corvée labor.

On the day Jiazi in the third month, the Emperor was crowned, and a general amnesty was declared throughout the realm. Laws and decrees that hindered officials and the people were abolished; the law prohibiting the possession of books was repealed. The Hongtai Pavilion in the Changle Palace suffered a disaster. In Yiyang, it rained blood.

On the day Yihai in the seventh month of autumn, the icehouse in the Weiyang Palace suffered a disaster; on the day Bingzi, the weaving house suffered a disaster.

In the winter month of October in the fifth year, there was an earthquake; peach and plum trees blossomed, and jujubes bore fruit.

In the spring month of January, 145,000 men and women within six hundred li of Chang'an were again conscripted to build the city of Chang'an, and the work was completed in thirty days.

In the summer, there was a great drought.

On the day Jichou in the eighth month of autumn, Chancellor Can passed away.

In September, the city of Chang'an was completed. The people were granted nobility, one rank per household.

On the day Xinchou in the winter month of October in the sixth year, King Fei of Qi passed away.

The people were allowed to sell their ranks of nobility. Women aged fifteen to thirty who did not marry were taxed five times the usual amount.

In the summer month of June, Marquis Kuai of Wuyang passed away.

The Western Market of Chang'an was established, and the Ao Granary was repaired.

In the winter month of October in the seventh year, chariots, cavalry, and skilled officers were dispatched to Xingyang, commanded by Grand Marshal Guan Ying.

On the day Xinchou in the spring month of January, there was a solar eclipse. On the day Dingmao in the summer month of May, there was another solar eclipse, which was total.

On the day Wuyin in the eighth month of autumn, the Emperor passed away in the Weiyang Palace. On the day Xinchou in September, he was buried in the Anling Mausoleum.

The commentary says: Emperor Xiaohui internally cultivated familial affection, externally respected the chancellor, and showed great favor and respect to Qi Daohui and Zhao Yinwang, demonstrating deep kindness and reverence. He was apprehensive upon hearing the admonitions of Shusun Tong and pleased by the responses of Chancellor Cao, showing that he could be considered a benevolent and lenient ruler. It is lamentable that he suffered the detriment of Empress Dowager Lü's actions to his supreme virtue. Alas!

VOLUME 3: RECORDS OF EMPRESS LÜ, NO. 3

Empress Lü, the mother of Emperor Hui, assisted Emperor Gaozu in stabilizing the realm. Her father and brothers, along with Emperor Gaozu, were enfeoffed as marquises. When Emperor Hui ascended the throne, Empress Lü was honored as Empress Dowager. The Empress Dowager established the daughter of Emperor Hui's elder sister, Princess Luyuan, as empress. Since the empress had no sons, a son of a palace beauty was taken and named as the crown prince. After Emperor Hui's death, the crown prince was established as emperor, but due to his young age, the Empress Dowager assumed regency and issued a general amnesty. She then enfeoffed her nephews Lü Tai, Lü Chan, Lü Lu, and Lü Tong as kings, and six members of the Lü family were made marquises. As recorded in the Biographies of the Imperial Relatives.

In the spring month of January in the first year, an edict was issued: "Previously, Emperor Xiaohui expressed his desire to abolish the punishment of exterminating three generations and the law against seditious speech, but the discussion was unresolved when he passed away. Now, these are abolished." In February, the people were granted nobility, one rank per household. For the first time, one person with a rank of two thousand dan was appointed as a filial and fraternal diligent farmer. On the day Bingshen in the summer month of May, the Congtai Pavilion in the palace of the King of Zhao suffered a disaster. The sons of Emperor Hui's harem were enfeoffed as follows: Qiang as the King of Huaiyang, Buyi as the King of

Hengshan, Hong as the Marquis of Xiangcheng, Chao as the Marquis of Zhi, and Wu as the Marquis of Huguan. In autumn, peach and plum trees blossomed.

In the spring of the second year, an edict was issued: "Emperor Gaozu rectified and regulated the realm, and all those who had merit were enfeoffed as marquises with territories, bringing great peace to the myriad people, all of whom received his benevolent virtue. I, reflecting on the distant past, find that the merits and reputations of these individuals are not prominently recorded, and there is no way to honor their great righteousness for future generations. Now, I wish to rank the merits of the marquises to determine their positions at court, and to record these in the high temple, ensuring they are remembered for generations, with their descendants inheriting their ranks and merits. Let this be discussed and decided upon with the marquises and then reported to me." Chancellor Chen Ping stated: "With the utmost respect, we have discussed with Marquis Jiang Chen Bo, Marquis Quzhou Chen Shang, Marquis Yingyin Chen Ying, and Marquis Anguo Chen Ling, and we find that the marquises have been fortunate to receive meal allowances and fiefs. Your Majesty, in your benevolence, wishes to determine their court positions based on their merits. We humbly request that these be recorded in the high temple." The report was approved. On the day Yimao in the spring month of January, an earthquake occurred, and landslides happened in Qiangdao and Wududao. On the day Bingxu in the summer month of June, there was a solar eclipse. In the autumn month of July, King Hengshan Buyi passed away. The eight-zhu coin was issued.

In the summer of the third year, the Jiang River overflowed, displacing more than four thousand households. In autumn, stars were visible during the day.

In the summer of the fourth year, the young emperor, realizing he was not the empress's son, voiced his grievances, and the

Empress Dowager confined him in the Yong Lane. An edict was issued: "Those who possess the realm and govern the myriad people should cover them like the heavens and contain them like the earth; above, they should have a joyful heart to lead the people, and the people should gladly serve them above, with mutual joy and communication leading to the governance of the realm. Now, the emperor's prolonged illness has not ceased, leading to confusion and disorder, making him unable to continue the ancestral sacrifices and guard the ancestral temple, and thus unfit to govern the realm. The officials were ordered to discuss his replacement." All the ministers said: "The Empress Dowager, for the sake of the realm, has deeply considered the stability of the ancestral temple and the state. We kowtow and respectfully accept the edict." On the day Bingchen in May, King Hengshan Hong was established as emperor.

In the spring of the fifth year, the King of Nanyue, Zhao Tuo, proclaimed himself the Martial Emperor of the South. In the autumn month of August, King Huaiyang Qiang passed away. In September, cavalry from Hedong and Shangdang were dispatched to garrison Beidi.

In the spring of the sixth year, stars were visible during the day. In the summer month of April, a general amnesty was declared. The magistrate of Changling was granted a rank of two thousand dan. In June, the city of Changling was built. The Xiongnu raided Didao and attacked A'yang. The five-fen coin was issued.

In the winter month of December in the seventh year, the Xiongnu raided Didao and captured more than two thousand people. On the day Dingchou in the spring month of January, King You of Zhao died in confinement at his residence. On the day Jichou, there was a solar eclipse, which was total. Lü Chan, the King of Liang, was appointed as Chancellor, and Lü Lu, the King of Zhao, as Grand General. Liu Ze, Marquis of Yingling, was established as the King of Langya. On the day Xinwei in the summer month of May, an edict was issued: "Lady Zhaoling was the consort of the Supreme Emperor; Marquis Wu'ai and Lady Xuan were the elder brother and sister of Emperor Gaozu. Their titles and posthumous names are not fitting; let their honorable titles be discussed." Chancellor Chen Ping and others requested to honor Lady Zhaoling as Empress Zhaoling, Marquis Wu'ai as King Wu'ai, and Lady Xuan as Empress Zhaoling. In June, King Hui of Zhao committed suicide. In the autumn month of September, King Jian of Yan passed away. Nanyue invaded and plundered Changsha, and Marquis Zao of Longlü was sent with troops to attack them.

In the spring of the eighth year, Zhang Shiqing, the Palace Attendant, was enfeoffed as a marquis. All the palace officials and eunuch officials were granted the title of Marquis within the Passes and given fiefs. In summer, the Jiang and Han rivers overflowed, displacing more than ten thousand households.

On the day Xinsi in the autumn month of July, the Empress Dowager passed away in the Weiyang Palace. Her will granted each feudal lord a thousand gold pieces, and the generals, chancellors, marquises, down to the minor officials, were each given varying amounts. A general amnesty was declared.

Grand General Lü Lu and Chancellor Lü Chan, holding military power and governing, knew they had violated Emperor Gaozu's will and feared being executed by the ministers and feudal lords, so they plotted a rebellion. At that time, Zhu Xu, Marquis Zhang, the son of King Daohui of Qi, was in the capital and married to Lü Lu's daughter. Knowing of the plot, he sent someone to inform his elder brother, the King of Qi, to raise troops and march west. Marquis Zhang intended to act as an internal ally with Grand Commandant Bo and Chancellor Ping to eliminate the Lü clan. The King of Qi then raised troops and also deceived Liu Ze, the King of Langya, into mobilizing his state's troops, and together they marched west. Lü Chan and Lü Lu sent Grand General Guan Ying to lead troops against them. Upon reaching Yingyang, Guan Ying sent someone to persuade the King of Qi to ally with him, waiting for the Lü clan's rebellion to jointly eliminate them.

Grand Commandant Bo and Chancellor Ping conspired, knowing that Qu Zhou Marquis Li Shang's son Li Ji was on good terms with Lü Lu, they had someone abduct Li Shang and ordered Li Ji to deceive Lü Lu, saying: "Emperor Gaozu and Empress Lü together stabilized the realm; the Liu clan established nine kings, and the Lü clan established three kings, all decided by the ministers. These matters have been announced to the feudal lords, and the feudal lords consider them appropriate. Now that the Empress Dowager has passed away and the emperor is young, if you do not quickly return to your state to guard your fief but instead remain here as a grand general leading troops, you will be suspected by the ministers and feudal lords. Why not quickly return the general's seal, entrust the troops to the Grand Commandant, and request the King of Liang to also return the Chancellor's seal, then swear an oath with the ministers and return to your state? The Qi troops will certainly withdraw, the ministers will be at ease, and you can rest easy as a king over a thousand li, which is a benefit for ten thousand generations." Lü Lu agreed with the plan and sent someone to report to Lü Chan and the elders of the Lü clan. Some thought it was not convenient, and the plan was hesitant and undecided. Lü Lu trusted Li Ji and went out with him, passing by his aunt Lü Xu. Lü Xu angrily said: "A slave becomes a general and abandons the army; the Lü clan will have no place now!" She then took out all the jewels and precious artifacts and scattered them in the hall, saying: "There is no need to guard them for others!"

On the day Gengshen in August, Marquis Pingyang Cao Zhu acted as the Imperial Censor and went to see Chancellor Lü Chan to discuss matters. The Chief of the Palace Guard Jia Shou, who had returned from Qi, rebuked Lü Chan, saying: "If the king does not return to his state early, even if he wants to go now, is it still possible?" He then fully informed Lü Chan about Guan Ying's alliance with Qi and Chu. Marquis Pingyang Cao

Zhu, upon hearing this, quickly informed Chancellor Ping and Grand Commandant Bo. Bo wanted to enter the Northern Army but could not. Marquis Xiangping Ji Tong, who held the imperial tally, then ordered to take the tally and falsely admit Bo into the Northern Army. Bo then ordered Li Ji and the Diplomat Liu Jie to persuade Lü Lu, saying: "The emperor has ordered the Grand Commandant to guard the Northern Army and wishes for you to return to your state. Quickly return the general's seal and leave. Otherwise, disaster will arise." Lü Lu then took off the seal and entrusted it to the Diplomat, and handed over the troops to Grand Commandant Bo. Bo entered the military gate and issued an order to the army: "Those for the Lü clan, bare your right arm; those for the Liu clan, bare your left arm." The entire army bared their left arms. Bo then took command of the Northern Army. However, there was still the Southern Army, so Chancellor Ping summoned Marquis Zhang of Zhu Xu to assist Bo. Bo ordered Marquis Zhang to guard the military gate and instructed Marquis Pingyang to inform the Commander of the Guards not to admit Chancellor Lü Chan into the palace gates. Lü Chan, unaware that Lü Lu had already left the Northern Army, entered the Weiyang Palace intending to cause chaos. The palace gates did not admit him, and he wandered back and forth. Marquis Pingyang quickly informed Grand Commandant Bo, who was still afraid of not being able to succeed and did not dare to openly declare the execution. He then said to Marquis Zhang of Zhu Xu: "Quickly enter the palace to guard the emperor. Marquis Zhang requested a thousand soldiers from Bo and entered the side gate of the Weiyang Palace, where he saw Lü Chan in the courtyard. At the time of the evening meal, he attacked Lü Chan. Lü Chan fled. A great wind arose, and the officials were in chaos, with no one daring to fight. They pursued Lü Chan and killed him in the latrine of the officials' quarters in the Palace Guard's residence.

After Marquis Zhang had killed Lü Chan, the emperor ordered the Palace Attendant to take the tally and reward Marquis Zhang. Marquis Zhang wanted to seize the tally, but the Palace

Attendant refused, so Marquis Zhang rode with him and, using the tally's authority, quickly killed the Commander of the Guards of Changle Palace, Lü Gengshi. He then returned to the Northern Army and reported back to Grand Commandant Bo. Bo stood up and congratulated Marquis Zhang, saying: "The only concern was Lü Chan, and now that he has been executed, the realm is settled." On the day Xinyou,

they killed Lü Lu and flogged Lü Xu to death. They divided their forces to capture all the male and female members of the Lü clan, and regardless of age, all were executed.

The ministers conspired together, believing that the young emperor and his three younger brothers who were kings were not the sons of Emperor Hui, and they jointly executed them, establishing Emperor Wen. This is recorded in the biographies of Zhou Bo and the Five Kings of Gao.

It is praised: During the reigns of Emperor Hui and Empress Gao, the realm was freed from the suffering of the Warring States, and both the monarch and ministers desired non-action. Thus, Emperor Hui ruled with simplicity, and Empress Gao, as a female ruler, governed from within the palace, yet the realm was peaceful, punishments were rarely used, and the people focused on farming, with food and clothing plentiful.

VOLUME 4: RECORDS OF EMPEROR WEN, NO. 4

Emperor Xiaowen was the middle son of Emperor Gaozu, and his mother was Lady Bo. In the eleventh year of Emperor Gaozu's reign, Chen Xi was executed, and the Dai region was pacified, where he was established as the King of Dai, with his capital at Zhongdu. In the autumn of the seventeenth year, Empress Gao passed away, and the Lü clan plotted a rebellion, intending to endanger the Liu family. Chancellor Chen Ping, Grand Commandant Zhou Bo, Marquis Zhu Xu Liu Zhang, and others jointly executed them and plotted to establish the King of Dai. This is recorded in the Records of Empress Gao and the Biographies of the Five Kings of Gao.

The ministers then sent someone to welcome the King of Dai. The Chief of the Palace Guard Zhang Wu and others discussed, saying: "The Han ministers are all former generals of Emperor Gaozu, experienced in military affairs and full of schemes and deceit. Their intentions are not limited to this; they particularly fear the authority of Emperor Gaozu and Empress Dowager Lü. Now that the Lü clan has been executed and there has been fresh bloodshed in the capital, their claim to welcome the king is not trustworthy. We hope the king will feign illness and not go, to observe the changes." The Commandant Song Chang came forward and said: "The opinions of the ministers are all wrong. When the Qin lost its governance, heroes rose together, and tens of thousands of people thought they could seize the throne, but in the end, it was the Liu family that ascended to the emperor's position, and the realm's hopes were dashed; this is the first point. The sons and brothers of Emperor Gaozu, with their territories interlocking like dog's teeth, form the so-called solid foundation of the clan, and the realm submits to their strength; this is the second point. Since the rise of Han, the oppressive laws of Qin have been abolished, the legal codes simplified, and kindness and favor bestowed, so that everyone is at peace and difficult to shake; this is the third point. Despite Empress Dowager Lü's severity, establishing the three kings of the Lü clan and monopolizing power, Grand Commandant Zhou Bo entered the Northern Army with a single tally, and with one call, the soldiers all bared their left arms for the Liu family, rebelling against the Lü clan, and eventually destroyed them. This is a mandate from heaven, not by human effort. Now, even if the ministers wish to rebel, the common people will not follow them, and their faction cannot remain united. Within, there are the kinship ties of Marquis Zhu Xu and Marquis Dong Mou; without, there is fear of the strength of Wu, Chu, Huainan, Langya, Qi, and Dai. Currently, among the sons of Emperor Gaozu, only the King of Huainan and the King of Dai remain, and the King of Dai is the elder, known throughout the realm for his wisdom, sagacity, benevolence, and filial piety. Therefore, the ministers, aligning with the hearts of the realm, wish to welcome and establish the King of Dai. The King of Dai should not doubt this." The King of Dai reported to the Empress Dowager, but the plan was hesitant and undecided. They consulted the oracle, and the divination resulted in a great horizontal line. The interpretation said: "The great horizontal line is auspicious; I will become the Heavenly King, like Xia Qi who shone." The King of Dai said: "I am already a king; what further kingship is there?" The diviner said: "The so-called Heavenly King is the Son of Heaven." Thereupon, the King of Dai sent his maternal uncle Bo Zhao to see Grand Commandant Bo, and Bo and others fully explained the reasons for welcoming and establishing the king. Bo Zhao returned and reported: "It is true; there is no room for doubt." The King of Dai smiled and said to Song Chang: "It is indeed as you said." He then ordered Song

Chang to ride in the chariot, and Zhang Wu and five others to ride in six carriages to Chang'an. They stopped at Gaoling and sent Song Chang ahead to Chang'an to observe the changes.

Song Chang arrived at the Wei Bridge, and the chancellor and all below came to welcome him. Song Chang returned and reported, and the King of Dai then advanced to the Wei Bridge. The ministers bowed and addressed him as their lord, and the King of Dai bowed in return. Grand Commandant Bo came forward and said: "I wish to speak in private." Song Chang said: "If what you have to say is public, then say it publicly; if it is private, the king has no private matters." Grand Commandant Bo then knelt and presented the imperial seal. The King of Dai declined, saying: "We will discuss this at the residence."

On the day Jiyou of the intercalary month, he entered the Dai residence. The ministers followed him there and presented their proposal: "Chancellor Chen Ping, Grand Commandant Zhou Bo, Grand General Zhang Wu, Imperial Censor Cang, Director of the Imperial Clan Ying, Marquis Zhu Xu Liu Zhang, Marquis Dong Mou Xingju, and Diplomat Jie, we respectfully address Your Highness: The sons of Emperor Hui, such as Hong, are not the sons of Emperor Xiaohui and should not continue the ancestral temple. We humbly request the Marquis of Yin'an, the Queen Dowager of Qing, the King of Langya, the marquises, and the officials of two thousand dan to deliberate. Your Highness, as the son of Emperor Gaozu, should be the heir. We hope Your Highness will ascend to the throne of the Son of Heaven." The King of Dai said: "To continue the ancestral temple of Emperor Gaozu is a weighty matter. I am not worthy and do not deserve it. I wish to invite the King of Chu to deliberate on who is suitable; I dare not presume." The ministers all prostrated themselves and insisted. The King of Dai declined three times facing west and twice facing south. Chancellor Chen Ping and others said: "We have carefully considered it, and Your Highness is the most suitable to continue the ancestral temple of Emperor Gaozu. Even the feudal lords and the myriad people of the realm consider it appropriate. For the sake of the ancestral temple and the state, we dare not be negligent. We hope Your Highness will graciously listen to us. We respectfully present the imperial seal and credentials and bow again." The King of Dai said: "If the imperial clan, generals, ministers, kings, and marquises consider it appropriate for me, I dare not decline." He then ascended to the throne of the Son of Heaven. The ministers served in their respective positions. He sent the Grand Coachman Ying and Marquis Dong Mou Xingju to first cleanse the palace and then, with the imperial chariot, welcome him to the Dai residence. The emperor entered the Weiyang Palace on the same day in the evening. That night, he appointed Song Chang as General of the Guards, commanding the Northern and Southern Armies, and Zhang Wu as Chief of the Palace Guard, managing the palace. He returned to the front hall and issued an edict: "By decree to the Chancellor, Grand Commandant, and Imperial Censor: Recently, the Lü clan monopolized power and plotted a great rebellion, intending to endanger the ancestral temple of the Liu family. Thanks to the generals, ministers, marquises, and imperial clan officials who executed them, all have been punished. As I have just ascended the throne, I hereby pardon the realm, granting the people one rank of nobility, and to each household of women, an ox and wine, with a five-day celebration. "

In the first year, on the day Xinhai of the tenth month in winter, the emperor was presented at the ancestral temple of Emperor Gaozu. He sent General of Chariots and Cavalry Bo Zhao to welcome the Empress Dowager from Dai. An edict was issued: "Previously, Lü Chan appointed himself as the Chancellor of State, and Lü Lu as the Grand General, and they arbitrarily sent General Guan Ying to lead troops to attack Qi, intending to replace the Liu family. Guan Ying remained in Xingyang and conspired with the feudal lords to execute the Lü clan. Lü Chan intended to do evil, and Chancellor Chen Ping and Grand Commandant Zhou Bo plotted to seize the armies of Lü Chan and others. Marquis Zhu Xu Liu Zhang was the first to capture and execute Lü Chan. Grand Commandant Zhou Bo personally led Marquis Xiangping Tong, holding the imperial tally, to enter the Northern Army with the imperial edict. Diplomat Jie seized the seal of Lü Lu. We further grant Grand Commandant Zhou Bo an additional fief of ten thousand households and five thousand jin of gold. Chancellor Chen Ping and General Guan Ying each receive three thousand households and two thousand jin of gold. Marquis Zhu Xu Liu Zhang and Marquis Xiangping Tong each receive two thousand households and one thousand jin of gold. We enfeoff Diplomat Jie as Marquis of Yangxin and grant him one thousand jin of gold. "

In the twelfth month, the son of the late King You of Zhao, Sui, was established as the King of Zhao, and the King of Langya, Ze, was moved to be the King of Yan. The lands of Qi and Chu that the Lü clan had seized were all returned. The laws and decrees regarding the confiscation of property and the punishment of families were completely abolished.

In the first month, the officials requested the early establishment of a crown prince to honor the ancestral temple. An edict was issued: "I am without virtue, and the gods and spirits have not yet accepted my offerings; the people of the realm have not yet found peace. Now, even if I cannot widely seek the virtuous and sagely men of the realm to inherit the throne, to speak of establishing a crown prince in advance is to compound my lack of virtue. What would the realm say? Let it be." The officials said: "Establishing a crown prince in advance is to honor the ancestral temple and the state, and not to forget the realm. The emperor said: "The King of Chu is my uncle, advanced in years, and has seen much of the realm's principles and reasons, and understands the state's system. The King of Wu is my elder brother; the King of Huainan, my younger brother: all uphold virtue to accompany me, how can it not be prepared! Among the feudal kings and the imperial clan brothers, there are many meritorious officials, virtuous and righteous. If we select the virtuous to accompany me to the end, it will be the blessing of the state and the realm's fortune. Now, if we do not select and recommend, but say it must be my son, people will think I have forgotten the virtuous and righteous and focus only on my son, which is not the way to care for the realm. I cannot accept this." The officials insisted: "In ancient times, the states of Yin and Zhou were peaceful and orderly for nearly a thousand years; none who ruled the realm lasted longer, using this principle. Establishing an heir must be a son, a tradition that has long existed. Emperor Gaozu, having just pacified the realm, established the feudal lords, becoming the Great Ancestor of the emperors. The feudal kings and marquises who first received their states also became the ancestors of their states. The descendants inherited the succession, generation after generation without end, which is the great principle of the realm. Therefore, Emperor Gaozu established this to pacify the land within the seas. Now, to abandon what should be established and instead select from the feudal kings and the imperial clan is not the will of Emperor Gaozu. Further discussion is inappropriate. Qi, the eldest son, is sincere, honest, kind, and benevolent; we request to establish him as the crown prince." The emperor then agreed. Consequently, he granted one rank of nobility to the people of the realm who were to succeed their fathers. General Bo Zhao was enfeoffed as the Marquis of Zhi.

In the third month, the officials requested the establishment of an empress. The Empress Dowager said: "Establish the mother of the crown prince, Lady Dou, as the empress."

An edict was issued: "In this time of spring harmony, all living things, including the plants and trees, have their own joy, yet among our people, there are widowers, widows, orphans, and the destitute who may be on the brink of death, and no one is concerned for them. As the parents of the people, what are we to do? Deliberate on how to provide relief and aid." It also said: "The elderly cannot be warm without cloth, nor satisfied without meat. At the beginning of this year, we have not timely sent envoys to inquire after the elders, nor have we bestowed gifts of cloth, silk, wine, and meat. How then can we assist the descendants of the realm in filially caring for their elders? Now, we hear that officials in charge of distributing gruel sometimes give stale grain, which hardly fulfills the intention of caring for the elderly. Make this a decree." The officials requested that the counties and districts be ordered to grant one dan of rice, twenty jin of meat, and five dou of wine per month to those aged eighty and above. For those aged ninety and above, add two bolts of silk and three jin of floss. The distribution of these items and the gruel rice should be overseen by senior officials, with the assistance of the county magistrate or the commandant. For those under ninety, the distribution should be handled by the local officers and clerks. The officials with a salary of two thousand dan should send inspectors to patrol and supervise those who do not comply. Those who are undergoing punishment or have been convicted of crimes requiring penal servitude or more are not subject to this decree.

King Yuan of Chu, Jiao, passed away.
In the fourth month, earthquakes struck Qi and Chu, with twenty-nine mountains collapsing on the same day, and great floods breaking out.

In the sixth month, an order was issued that commanderies and kingdoms should not send tributes. Benefits were bestowed upon the realm, and the feudal lords and the barbarians from all directions were in harmony and joy. Then, the achievements since the return from Dai were reviewed. An edict was issued: "When the great ministers executed the Lü clan and welcomed me, I was hesitant, and all urged me to stop, only Commandant Song Chang encouraged me, and I have been able to preserve the ancestral temple. I have already honored Chang as the General of the Guards, and now I enfeoff him as Marquis Zhuangwu. The six who followed me have all been promoted to the Nine Ministers." It also said: "The sixty-eight marquises who followed

Emperor Gaozu into Shu and Han shall each be granted an additional three hundred households. Officials with a salary of two thousand dan and above who followed Emperor Gaozu, such as the Governor of Yingchuan, Zun, and ten others, shall each receive six hundred households. The Governor of Huaiyang, Shentu Jia, and ten others shall each receive five hundred households. The Commandant of the Guards, Zu, and ten others shall each receive four hundred households." The uncle of the King of Huainan, Zhao Jian, was enfeoffed as the Marquis of Zhouyang; the uncle of the King of Qi, Si Jun, as the Marquis of Jingguo; and the former Chancellor of Changshan, Cai Jian, as the Marquis of Fan.

In the winter of the second year, the tenth month, Chancellor Chen Ping passed away. An edict was issued: "I have heard that in ancient times, the feudal lords established over a thousand states, each guarding their lands, paying tribute in due time, so the people were not toiled, and there was joy between the high and the low, without any violation of virtue. Now, many marquises reside in Chang'an, with their fiefs far away, and the officials and soldiers suffer from the hardship of transportation, while the marquises have no way to instruct their people. Let it be ordered that the marquises return to their states, and those who are officials or have been ordered to stay shall send their crown princes."

On the last day of the eleventh month, Guimao, there was a solar eclipse. An edict was issued: "I have heard that heaven gives birth to the people and appoints a ruler to nurture and govern them. If the ruler is without virtue and the governance is uneven, then heaven shows disasters to warn of misrule. On the last day of the eleventh month, there was a solar eclipse, clearly seen in the sky; what disaster could be greater! I have been able to preserve the ancestral temple, and with my humble person placed above the scholars, people, kings, and lords, the order or chaos of the realm rests with me alone, and the two or three ministers are like my limbs. I, below, cannot govern and nurture the multitude, and above, I burden the brightness of the three luminaries; my lack of virtue is great. When this decree arrives, let all consider my faults and what I have failed to see and know, and earnestly report them to me. And recommend the virtuous, upright, and those capable of speaking frankly and remonstrating to the utmost, to correct my shortcomings. Also, let each be reminded of their duties and responsibilities, striving to reduce labor and expenses for the convenience of the people. Since I cannot extend virtue far, I am thus anxious about the wrongs of outsiders, and therefore the defenses have not ceased. Now, even if we cannot disband the border garrisons, and we must still maintain a strong military defense, let us disband the army of the General of the Guards. The horses seen by the Grand Coachman are sufficient for the remaining needs, and the rest shall be provided for the postal stations."

On the day Dinghai in the first month of spring, an edict was issued: "Agriculture is the foundation of the realm. Let the imperial fields be opened, and I will personally lead the plowing to provide the sacrificial grains for the ancestral temple. All people who have been exiled to work for the county officials and those who have not repaid their loans for seeds and food, or have not fully repaid them, shall all be pardoned."

In the third month, the officials requested that the emperor's sons be established as feudal kings. An edict was issued: "Previously, King You of Zhao died in confinement, and I greatly pitied him, so I have already established his crown prince, Sui, as the King of Zhao. Sui's younger brother, Piqiang, and the sons of Prince Daohui of Qi, Marquis Zhuxu Zhang and Marquis Dongmu Xingju, have rendered meritorious service and may be made kings." Thus, Piqiang was established as the King of Hejian, Zhang as the King of Chengyang, and Xingju as the King of Jibei. Consequently, the emperor's son Wu was established as the King of Dai, Can as the King of Taiyuan, and Ji as the King of Liang.

In the fifth month, an edict was issued: "In ancient times, to govern the realm, the court had banners for advancing good and wooden tablets for criticism, which were means to open the path of governance and invite remonstrance. Now, the law includes crimes of criticism and spreading rumors, which make the ministers dare not express their full feelings, and the ruler has no way to hear of his faults. How then can we attract the virtuous from afar? Let these be abolished. If the people curse the ruler and make agreements only to deceive each other later, the officials consider it a great crime of treason; if they speak otherwise, the officials again consider it criticism. This is the folly of the petty people, who in their ignorance face death, and I do not favor it. From now on, those who commit such offenses shall not be tried."

In the ninth month, for the first time, bronze tiger tallies and bamboo messenger tallies were issued to the commandery governors.

An edict was issued: "Agriculture is the great foundation of the realm, upon which the people rely for their livelihood. Yet some people do not focus on the fundamentals but engage in secondary activities, thus their livelihood is not prosperous. I am concerned about this, so now I personally lead the ministers in agriculture to encourage it. Let half of this year's land tax be exempted for the people of the realm."

In the winter of the third year, on the last day of the tenth month, Dingyou, there was a solar eclipse. On the last day of the eleventh month, Dingmao, there was another solar eclipse.

An edict was issued: "Previously, an edict was issued to send the marquises to their states, but the words have not been acted upon. The chancellor is important to me, so let him lead the marquises to their states." Thus, Chancellor Bo was dismissed and sent to his state. In the twelfth month, the Grand Commandant, Marquis Yingyin Guan Ying, became the chancellor. The position of Grand Commandant was abolished and its duties were assigned to the chancellor.

In the summer, the fourth month, King Chengyang Zhang passed away. The King of Huainan, Chang, killed Marquis Piyang, Shen Yiji.

In the fifth month, the Xiongnu invaded and occupied Beidi and Henan, causing havoc. The emperor went to Ganquan and sent Chancellor Guan Ying to attack the Xiongnu, who then retreated. The Commandant of the Central Army's skilled officers were assigned to the General of the Guards, and the army was stationed in Chang'an.

The emperor went from Ganquan to Gaonu and then to Taiyuan, where he met with the former ministers and bestowed gifts upon them. Merits were recognized and rewards were given, and the people in the villages were granted oxen and wine. The land tax for the people of Jinyang and Zhongdu was exempted for three years. The emperor stayed in Taiyuan for more than ten days.

When the King of Jibei, Xingju, heard that the emperor was going to Dai and intended to attack the Xiongnu himself, he rebelled and raised troops to attack Yingyang. Therefore, an edict was issued to dismiss the chancellor's troops, and Marquis Jipu Chai Wu was appointed as the Grand General, leading four generals with a hundred thousand troops to attack him. Marquis Qi Zeng He was appointed as the general, stationed in Yingyang. In the autumn, the seventh month, the emperor returned from Taiyuan to Chang'an. An edict was issued: "The King of Jibei has turned his back on virtue and rebelled against his ruler, misleading officials and people, committing a great crime of treason. The officials and soldiers of Jibei who stabilize themselves before the troops arrive and those who surrender with their military cities shall all be pardoned and restored to their official positions and titles. Those who have come and gone with King Xingju shall also be pardoned." In the eighth month, the King of Jibei, Xingju, was captured and committed suicide. All those who rebelled with Xingju were pardoned.

In the winter of the fourth year, the twelfth month, Chancellor Guan Ying passed away.

In the summer, the fifth month, the Liu family members who had household registrations were restored, and their families were not involved. Each prince of the feudal lords was granted two thousand households.

In the autumn, the ninth month, seven sons of Prince Daohui of Qi were enfeoffed as marquises.

Marquis Jiang Zhou Bo was accused of a crime and brought to the imperial prison by order of the court.

The Gu Cheng Temple was built.

In the spring of the fifth year, the second month, there was an earthquake.

In the summer, the fourth month, the prohibition against privately minting coins was lifted. A new four-zhu coin was minted.

In the winter of the sixth year, the tenth month, peach and plum trees blossomed.

In the eleventh month, the King of Huainan, Chang, plotted a rebellion, was deposed, and exiled to the strict road in Shu, dying in Yong.

In the winter of the seventh year, the tenth month, it was ordered that the great ladies and ladies of the marquises, the sons of the feudal lords, and officials with a salary of two thousand dan could not arbitrarily arrest people.

On the day Guiyou in the sixth month, a disaster occurred at the eastern gate tower of the Weiyang Palace.

In the summer of the eighth year, the four eldest sons of the King of Huainan, Li, were enfeoffed as marquises.

A long star appeared in the east.

In the spring of the ninth year, there was a great drought.

In the winter of the tenth year, the emperor went to Ganquan.

General Bo Zhao died.

In the winter of the eleventh year, the eleventh month, the emperor went to Dai. In the spring, the first month, the emperor returned from Dai.

In the summer, the sixth month, the King of Liang, Ji, passed away.

The Xiongnu invaded Di Dao.

In the winter of the twelfth year, the twelfth month, the Yellow River breached its banks in Dong Commandery.

In the spring, the first month, each daughter of the feudal lords was granted two thousand households.

In the second month, the beauties from the harem of Emperor Xiaohui were released and allowed to marry.

In the third month, the requirement for passes at the borders was abolished.

An edict was issued: "The way to guide the people lies in focusing on the fundamentals. I have personally led the agriculture of the realm for ten years now, yet the fields have not expanded, and there is a poor harvest every year, with the people showing signs of hunger. This is because the efforts are still insufficient, and the officials have not fully applied themselves. I have issued several edicts, encouraging the people to plant trees every year, yet the achievements have not been realized. This is because the officials have not diligently followed my edicts and have not clearly encouraged the people. Moreover, our farmers are suffering greatly, and the officials have not shown concern for them. How then can we encourage them? Let half of this year's land tax be exempted for the farmers."

Another edict was issued: "Filial piety and fraternal duty are the great order of the realm. Diligent farming is the foundation of livelihood. The three elders are the teachers of the people. Honest officials are the models for the people. I greatly commend the conduct of these two or three officials. Now, in a county of ten thousand households, it is said that there are none who respond to the edicts. Is this truly the sentiment of the people? This is because the officials' method of recommending the virtuous is not yet complete. Let the emissaries be sent to reward and bestow upon the three elders and the filial ones with five bolts of silk each, upon the fraternal and diligent farmers with two bolts each, and upon the honest officials with two hundred dan and above, leading a hundred dan, with three bolts each. And inquire about what the people find inconvenient or unsatisfactory, and based on the household population, establish permanent positions for the three elders, filial ones, fraternal ones, and diligent farmers, and let each lead their intentions to guide the people."

In the spring of the thirteenth year, the second month, on the day Jiayin, an edict was issued: "I personally lead the farming of the realm to supply the sacrificial grains, and the empress personally engages in sericulture to provide the sacrificial garments. Let the rituals be prepared."
In the summer, the secret prayers were abolished, as recorded in the Annals of Suburban Sacrifices. In the fifth month, the corporal punishment laws were abolished, as recorded in the Annals of Penal Laws.

In the sixth month, an edict was issued: "Agriculture is the foundation of the realm, and no task is greater. Now, those who diligently engage in farming are still burdened with land taxes, which means there is no distinction between the fundamental and the secondary, and the way to encourage farming is not yet complete. Let the land taxes be abolished. Bestow upon the widows and orphans of the realm cloth, silk, and wadding, each in specified amounts."

In the winter of the fourteenth year, the Xiongnu invaded the border, killing the Commandant of Beidi, Ang. Three generals were sent to station troops in Longxi, Beidi, and Shangjun. The Commandant of the Central Army, Zhou She, was appointed as the General of the Guards, and the Director of the Palace, Zhang Wu, as the General of Chariots and Cavalry, stationed north of the Wei River with a thousand chariots and a hundred thousand cavalry. The emperor personally visited the army, inspected the troops, reiterated the military orders, and rewarded the officers and soldiers. He intended to personally lead the campaign against the Xiongnu, but the ministers advised against it, and he did not listen. The Empress Dowager firmly insisted, and he finally stopped. Thus, Marquis Dongyang Zhang Xiangru was appointed as the Grand General, Marquis Jiancheng Dong He and the Internal Affairs Officer Luan Bu were both appointed as generals to attack the Xiongnu. The Xiongnu retreated.

In the spring, an edict was issued: "I have been holding the sacrificial animals and jade tablets to serve the ancestral temple of the Supreme Deity for fourteen years now. As the days grow longer, I feel deeply ashamed for being neither wise nor clear-sighted yet continuing to govern the realm for so long. Let the sacrificial altars and jade tablets be widely increased. In the past, the former kings bestowed favors far and wide without seeking rewards, offered sacrifices without praying for blessings, esteemed the virtuous and cherished the relatives, prioritized the people over themselves, reaching the utmost in clarity. Now I hear that the ritual officials in their prayers and blessings all attribute the fortune to me alone, not to the people, and I am deeply ashamed of this. With my lack of virtue, to exclusively enjoy the blessings of fortune while the people are not included, this adds to my lack of virtue. Let the ritual officials pay their respects without making any prayers."

In the spring of the fifteenth year, a yellow dragon appeared in Chengji. The emperor then issued an edict to discuss suburban sacrifices. Gongsun Chen clarified the ceremonial colors, and Xin Yuanping established the Five Temples. This is recorded in the Annals of Suburban Sacrifices. In the summer, the fourth month, the emperor visited Yong and for the first time performed suburban sacrifices to the Five Emperors, pardoned the realm, and restored the sacrifices to the famous mountains and great rivers that had been discontinued. The officials were to perform the rituals at the appropriate times.

In the ninth month, an edict was issued for the princes, dukes, ministers, and commandery governors to recommend those who were virtuous and capable of speaking out and offering bold remonstrations. The emperor personally examined them and listened to their words. This is recorded in the Biography of Chao Cuo.

In the summer of the sixteenth year, the fourth month, the emperor performed suburban sacrifices to the Five Emperors at the north of the Wei River.

In the fifth month, six sons of Prince Daohui of Qi and three sons of Prince Li of Huainan were all enfeoffed as kings.

In the autumn, the ninth month, a jade cup was found, inscribed with the words "The sovereign's longevity is extended." A grand feast was ordered throughout the realm, and the era name was changed the following year.

In the winter of the first year of the later period, the tenth month, Xin Yuanping's deceit was discovered, and he plotted a rebellion, leading to the extermination of his three clans.

In the spring, the third month, Empress Zhang of Emperor Xiaohui passed away.

An edict was issued: "In recent years, there have been consecutive poor harvests, along with disasters of floods, droughts, and epidemics. I am deeply concerned about this. Being foolish and not clear-sighted, I have not understood the cause of these calamities. Could it be that there are faults in my governance and conduct? Or is it that the ways of heaven are not favorable, the benefits of the earth are not obtained, human affairs are often out of harmony, and the spirits and deities are neglected and not worshipped? How have we come to this? Is it because the expenditures for the officials are excessive, or are there too many useless endeavors? Why is the food of the people so scarce and insufficient! The measurement of the fields has not decreased, and the population has not increased. Measuring the land by the number of mouths, there is still more than in ancient times, yet the food is severely insufficient.

Where does the fault lie? Is it because the people are engaged in secondary activities that harm agriculture, or because there is excessive brewing of alcohol that wastes grain, or because the consumption of livestock is too high? The reasoning behind these matters, whether large or small, I have not been able to grasp. Let the chancellor, marquises, officials of two thousand dan, and scholars discuss this. If there are ways to assist the people, let them deliberate deeply and think broadly, concealing nothing." "

In the summer of the second year, the emperor traveled to the Yong Yuyang Palace.

In the sixth month, Prince Can of Dai passed away. The Xiongnu sought peace through marriage. An edict was issued: "I am neither wise nor clear-sighted, and I have not been able to extend virtue far, causing states beyond the borders to be unsettled. The regions beyond the four borders are not at peace, and within the borders, the people toil without respite. The faults in both cases stem from my lack of virtue and inability to reach far. In recent years, the Xiongnu have repeatedly raided the borders, killing many officials and civilians. The border officials and soldiers have not been able to convey their inner intentions, thereby adding to my lack of virtue. The prolonged entanglement of conflicts and continuous warfare, how can the states within and beyond the borders find peace? Now, I rise early and retire late, toiling for the realm, worrying and suffering for the myriad people, feeling distressed and uneasy, not forgetting it for a single day. Therefore, I have sent envoys in succession, their carriages and caps passing each other on the roads, to convey my intentions to the Chanyu. Now, the Chanyu, reversing the ancient ways, considering the safety of the state and the benefit of the myriad people, has newly joined me in abandoning minor faults, following the great way, and establishing the bond of brotherhood, to preserve the countless people of the realm. The peace through marriage is established, beginning this year."

In the spring of the third year, the second month, the emperor traveled to Dai.

In the summer of the fourth year, the fourth month, on the last day of the month (Jia Yin), there was a solar eclipse. In the fifth month, a general amnesty was granted throughout the realm. The government slaves were emancipated and made commoners. The emperor traveled to Yong.

In the spring of the fifth year, the first month, the emperor traveled to Longxi. In the third month, the emperor traveled to Yong. In the autumn, the seventh month, the emperor traveled to Dai.

In the winter of the sixth year, thirty thousand Xiongnu cavalry invaded Shangjun, and another thirty thousand invaded Yunzhong. The Grand Master of the Palace, Ling Mian, was appointed as the General of Chariots and Cavalry and stationed at Feihu. The former Chancellor of Chu, Su Yi, was appointed as a general and stationed at Gouzhu. General Zhang Wu was stationed at Beidi. The Governor of Henei, Zhou Yafu, was appointed as a general and stationed at Xiliu. The Director of the Imperial Clan, Liu Li, was appointed as a general and stationed at Bashang. Marquis Zhuzi, Xu Li, was appointed as a general and stationed at Jimen, all to prepare against the Hu.

In the summer, the fourth month, there was a great drought and a locust plague. The feudal lords were ordered not to bring tribute. The mountains and marshes were opened. The various court expenditures were reduced. The number of officials in the imperial guard was decreased. The granaries were opened to relieve the people. The people were allowed to sell their ranks of nobility.

In the summer of the seventh year, the sixth month, on the day Ji Hai, the emperor passed away in the Weiyang Palace. The imperial edict left behind said: "I have heard that all things under heaven that sprout and grow must inevitably die. Death is the principle of heaven and earth, the natural course of things, so why should there be excessive mourning! In the present age, people all cherish life and detest death, lavish burials that ruin estates, and heavy mourning that harms the living, which I greatly disapprove of. Moreover, I have been lacking in virtue and have not been able to assist the people; now that I have passed away, to have them endure heavy mourning and prolonged observance, suffering the changes of cold and heat, grieving the parents and children, distressing the elders' hearts, reducing their food and drink, and cutting off the sacrifices to the spirits and deities, thereby increasing my lack of virtue, what will the world say! I have been fortunate to preserve the ancestral temple, placing my humble self above the rulers of the world for more than twenty years. Thanks to the divine favor of heaven and the blessings of the state, the land within the borders has been peaceful, without the turmoil of war. I have not been wise, often fearing misdeeds that would shame the legacy of the former emperor; only the long passage of years has made me fear not seeing the end. Now, I am fortunate to have reached the end of my natural life and can be enshrined in the Gao Temple. My lack of clarity and my joy, what cause for mourning and remembrance is there! Let it be ordered that all officials and people of the realm, upon receiving this decree, shall observe three days of mourning, after which all mourning attire shall be removed. There shall be no prohibition on marriages, the worship of ancestors, drinking alcohol, or eating meat. Those who are to provide for the funeral and observe mourning shall not be forced to do so. Mourning belts shall not exceed three inches in width. There shall be no use of cloth-covered vehicles or weapons. The people shall not be compelled to wail in the palace halls. Those in the halls who are to observe mourning shall do so with fifteen cries each at dawn and dusk, and then cease. Except for the times of dawn and dusk, unauthorized wailing is prohibited. From this day forth, the mourning period shall be fifteen days for the great red, fourteen days for the small red, and seven days for the fine, after which mourning attire shall be removed. For matters not included in this decree, they shall be handled by analogy to this decree. Proclaim this throughout the realm, so that all may clearly know my intentions. The mountains and rivers of Baling shall remain as they are, with no changes made. Return the ladies of the palace and below to the junior attendants." The Commandant of the Capital, Yafu, was appointed as the General of Chariots and Cavalry. The Protector of the Dependent States, Han, was appointed as the General of the Garrison. The Chief of the Palace Gentlemen, Zhang Wu, was appointed as the General of Earthworks, mobilizing sixteen thousand soldiers from nearby counties and fifteen thousand soldiers from the capital region, to construct the burial mound and tomb under the command of General Wu. The feudal lords and kings down to the filial and fraternal and those who labored in the fields were granted varying amounts of money and silk. On the day Yi Si, the emperor was buried at Baling.

A eulogy says: Emperor Xiaowen reigned for twenty-three years, during which there were no additions to the palaces, gardens, carriages, or regalia. If there was anything inconvenient, it was relaxed for the benefit of the people. He once wanted to build a terrace and summoned craftsmen to estimate the cost, which came to a hundred pieces of gold. The emperor said, "A hundred pieces of gold is the wealth of ten middle-class families. I have inherited the palaces of the former emperor and often fear shaming them, why should I build a terrace!" He wore coarse silk, and his favored Lady Shen's garments did not drag on the ground. The curtains and hangings were without embroidery, to demonstrate simplicity and set an example for the realm. When constructing Baling, only earthenware was used, and gold, silver, copper, and tin were not used for decoration. The tomb was built following the natural contours of the mountain, without raising a mound. The Commandant of Nanyue, Tuo, declared himself emperor. The emperor summoned Tuo's brothers and honored them, winning them over with virtue, and Tuo subsequently submitted as a subject.

He made peace with the Xiongnu through marriage, but they later broke the treaty and raided. He ordered the borders to be defended but did not send troops deep into enemy territory, fearing to trouble the people. The King of Wu feigned illness and did not attend court, so he was granted a cane. Although the remonstrances of ministers like Yuan Ang were often sharp, he always listened and adopted their advice. Zhang Wu and others were found to have accepted bribes, but instead of punishing them, he increased their rewards to shame them. He focused on transforming the people through virtue, resulting in a prosperous and wealthy nation, with the rise of propriety and righteousness. He adjudicated hundreds of cases, nearly achieving a state where punishments were unnecessary. Ah, how benevolent he was!

VOLUME 5: RECORDS OF EMPEROR JING, NO. 5

Emperor Xiaojing was the crown prince of Emperor Wen. His mother was Empress Dou. In the sixth month of the seventh year of Emperor Wen's reign, Emperor Wen passed away. On the day Ding Wei, the crown prince ascended the throne as emperor, and honored Empress Dowager Bo as the Grand Empress Dowager, and the empress as the Empress Dowager. In the ninth month, a comet appeared in the western sky.

In the winter of the first year, the tenth month, an edict was issued: "It is said that in ancient times, ancestors were honored for their achievements and virtues, and the creation of rites and music had their reasons. Songs are meant to express virtue; dances are meant to display achievements. At the Gao Temple, the Zhou wine offering is accompanied by the dances of Wu De, Wen Shi, and Wu Xing. At the temple of Emperor Xiaohui, the Zhou wine offering is accompanied by the dances of Wen Shi and Wu Xing. Emperor Xiaowen ruled the world, opening the passes and bridges, treating distant regions no differently; he abolished slander laws, removed corporal punishment, rewarded the elderly, cared for the orphaned and widowed, to benefit all living beings. He reduced desires, did not accept tributes, did not punish the families of criminals, did not execute the innocent, and did not seek personal gain; he abolished castration, released the palace women, and took great care to prevent the extinction of families. I am not wise and cannot fully comprehend these actions. These were all things that previous generations did not achieve, yet Emperor Xiaowen personally implemented them.

His virtue was as vast as heaven and earth, and his benefits spread across the four seas, bringing fortune to all. His brilliance was like the sun and moon, yet the temple music does not match, and I am deeply concerned about this. Let the temple of Emperor Xiaowen have the Zhao De dance to display his splendid virtue. Then the merits and virtues of our ancestors will benefit all generations, forever and ever, and I greatly approve of this. Let the Chancellor, the Marquis, the officials of the two thousand bushels, and the ritual officials prepare the rites and submit them." The Chancellor, Chen Jia, and others submitted a memorial: "Your Majesty, in your eternal contemplation of filial piety, established the Zhao De dance to display the great virtue of Emperor Xiaowen, all of which is beyond the understanding of us, your foolish servants. We humbly propose: no achievement in history is greater than that of Emperor Gaozu, and no virtue is more splendid than that of Emperor Xiaowen. The temple of Emperor Gaozu should be the ancestral temple of the founding emperor, and the temple of Emperor Xiaowen should be the temple of the great ancestor. The Son of Heaven should offer sacrifices to the ancestral temple for generations. The feudal lords and kings of the commanderies and states should each establish a temple of the great ancestor for Emperor Xiaowen. The feudal lords, marquises, envoys, and attendants should offer sacrifices at the ancestral temples where the Son of Heaven makes offerings. We request that this be proclaimed throughout the realm." The decree said, "Approved."

In the spring, the first month, an edict was issued: "In recent years, the harvests have been poor, and many people lack food, dying prematurely. I am deeply pained by this. In some commanderies and states, the land is barren, and there is no place for farming, sericulture, or animal husbandry; in others, the land is fertile and vast, with abundant grass and water resources, but people cannot move there. Let it be discussed and allowed for those who wish to move to broad and fertile lands." In the summer, the fourth month, a general amnesty was granted to the realm. The people were granted one rank of nobility.

The Grandee Secretary Qing Di was sent to Dai to make peace with the Xiongnu through marriage. In the fifth month, the land tax was reduced by half.

In the autumn, the seventh month, an edict was issued: "Officials who accept food and drink from those they oversee shall be dismissed, which is severe; those who accept property, buy cheap and sell dear, shall be lightly punished. Let the Commandant of Justice and the Chancellor revise the law and establish it." The Commandant of Justice, Xin, respectfully discussed with the Chancellor and proposed: "Officials and those with ranks who accept food and drink from their subordinates, supervisors, or those they govern, shall calculate the cost and not be punished. For other items, if they buy cheaply or sell dearly, they shall be punished for theft, and the illicit gains shall be confiscated by the state. Officials who are transferred, dismissed, or removed from office and accept property from their former subordinates, supervisors, or those they governed, shall be stripped of their ranks and made common soldiers, and dismissed. Those without ranks shall be fined two catties of gold, and the illicit gains shall be confiscated. Those who can capture and report such offenders shall be given the confiscated property."

In the winter of the second year, the twelfth month, a comet appeared in the southwest. An order was issued that all men in the realm begin their service at the age of twenty. In the spring, the third month, the emperor's sons were enfeoffed as kings: De as the King of Hejian, E as the King of Linjiang, Yu as the King of Huaiyang, Fei as the King of Runan, Pengzu as the King of Guangchuan, and Fa as the King of Changsha. In the summer, the fourth month, on the day Ren Wu, the Grand Empress Dowager passed away. In the sixth month, the Chancellor, Jia, died.

The grandson of the former Chancellor, Xiao He, was enfeoffed as a Marquis. In the autumn, peace was made with the Xiongnu through marriage. In the winter of the third year, the twelfth month, an edict was issued: "Jia, the son of the Marquis of Xiangping, was unfilial and plotted rebellion, intending to kill Jia, which is a great crime and against the Way. Let Jia be pardoned and remain the Marquis of Xiangping, and his wife and children who were implicated shall have their former ranks restored. Punish Hui Shuo and his wife and children according to the law." In the spring, the first month, the main hall of the palace of the King of Huaiyang was destroyed by fire.

The King of Wu, Pi; the King of Jiaoxi, Ang; the King of Chu, Wu; the King of Zhao, Sui; the King of Jinan, Piguang; the King of Zichuan, Xian; and the King of Jiaodong, Xiongqu, all raised armies in rebellion. A general amnesty was granted to the realm. The Grand Commandant, Yafu, and the Grand General, Dou Ying, were sent to lead troops to attack them. The Grandee Secretary, Chao Cuo, was executed to appease the seven states. On the last day of the second month, Ren Zi, there was a solar eclipse.

The generals defeated the seven states, beheading over a hundred thousand people. The King of Wu, Pi, was pursued and killed at Dantu. The King of Jiaoxi, Ang; the King of Chu, Wu; the King of Zhao, Sui; the King of Jinan, Piguang; the King of Zichuan, Xian; and the King of Jiaodong, Xiongqu, all committed suicide. In the summer, the sixth month, an edict was issued: "Previously, the King of Wu, Pi, and others rebelled, raising armies to coerce, misleading officials and people, who had no choice. Now that Pi and others have been eliminated, officials and people who were implicated by Pi and others and those who fled from the army shall all be pardoned. The sons of the King of Chu Yuan, Yi, and others who joined Pi in rebellion, I cannot bear to punish them according to the law. They shall be removed from the register, not to defile the imperial clan." Liu Li, the Marquis of Pinglu, was enfeoffed as the King of Chu to continue the line of King Yuan. The emperor's sons, Duan, was enfeoffed as the King of Jiaoxi, and Sheng as the King of Zhongshan. The people were granted one rank of nobility.

In the spring of the fourth year, the passes were re-established, and travel permits were required for entry and exit. In the summer, the fourth month, on the day Ji Si, the emperor's son Rong was established as the Crown Prince, and Che was enfeoffed as the King of Jiaodong. In the sixth month, a general amnesty was granted to the realm, and the people were granted one rank of nobility. In the autumn, the seventh month, the King of Linjiang, E, passed away. On the last day of the tenth month, Wu Xu, there was a solar eclipse. In the spring of the fifth year, the first month, the city of Yangling was built. In the summer, people were recruited to move to Yangling and were granted two hundred thousand coins.

A princess was sent to marry the Xiongnu Chanyu. In the winter of the sixth year, the twelfth month, there was thunder and continuous rain. In the autumn, the ninth month, Empress Bo was deposed. In the winter of the seventh year, the eleventh month, on the last day of Geng Yin, there was a solar eclipse. In the spring of the first month, Crown Prince Rong was deposed and made the King of Linjiang. In the second month, the office of the Grand Commandant was abolished. In the summer, the fourth month, on the day Yi Si, Empress Wang was established.

On the day Ding Si, the King of Jiaodong, Che, was established as the Crown Prince. The people who were heirs to their fathers were granted one rank of nobility. In the summer of the first year of the Zhongyuan era, the fourth month, a general amnesty was granted to the realm, and the people were granted one rank of nobility. The grandsons of the former Grandee Secretaries, Zhou Ke and Zhou Chang, were enfeoffed as Marquises.

In the spring of the second year, the second month, it was ordered that when a king of a feudal state died, a Marquis was first enfeoffed and went to his state, the Grand Herald would submit the posthumous title, elegy, and eulogy. When a Marquis died and the Grand Tutor of a feudal state was first appointed to office, the Grand Master of Ceremonies would submit the posthumous title, elegy, and eulogy. When a king died, the Grandee of the Imperial Household would be sent to offer condolences, perform the sacrificial rites, and oversee the funeral affairs, thereby establishing the heir. When a Marquis died, the Grand Master of the Palace would be sent to offer condolences and perform the sacrificial rites, oversee the funeral affairs, thereby establishing the heir. For their burial, the state could mobilize people to pull the funeral carriage, dig the grave, and manage the tomb, but no more than three hundred people should be involved to complete the task.

The Xiongnu invaded Yan. The punishment of dismemberment was changed to execution in the marketplace, and dismemberment was no longer to be used. In the third month, the King of Linjiang, Rong, was implicated for encroaching on the land of the temple of the Great Ancestor and was summoned to the Commandant of Justice, where he committed suicide. In the summer, the fourth month, a comet appeared in the northwest. The emperor's son Yue was enfeoffed as the King of Guangchuan, and Ji as the King of Jiaodong. In the autumn, the seventh month, the titles of Commandery Governor were changed to Grand Administrator, and Commandery Commandant to Commandant.

In the ninth month, the sons of four former officials of Chu and Zhao, who had died in service, were enfeoffed as Marquises. On the last day of Jia Xu, there was a solar eclipse. In the winter of the third year, the eleventh month, the office of the Grandee Secretary for the feudal lords was abolished. In the spring, the first month, the Empress Dowager passed away. There was a summer drought, and the sale of alcohol was prohibited. In the autumn, the ninth month, there was a locust plague. A comet appeared in the northwest. On the last day of Wu Xu, there was a solar eclipse.

The emperor's son Cheng was enfeoffed as the King of Qinghe. In the spring of the fourth year, the third month, the construction of the Deyang Palace began. The emperor's son Cheng was enfeoffed as the King of Qinghe. The Grandee Secretary, Wan, submitted a proposal to prohibit horses taller than five feet nine inches and with uneven teeth from passing through the passes. In the summer, there was a locust plague. In the autumn, those sentenced to death for working on the Yangling project were pardoned; those who wished to be castrated were allowed to do so. On the day Wu Wu of the tenth month, there was a solar eclipse.

In the summer of the fifth year, the emperor's son Shun was enfeoffed as the King of Changshan. In the sixth month, a general amnesty was granted to the realm, and the people were granted one rank of nobility. In the autumn, the eighth month, on the day Ji You, the eastern gate tower of the Weiyang Palace was destroyed by fire. The title of Chancellor for the feudal lords was changed to Prime Minister.

In the ninth month, an edict was issued: "Laws and regulations are established to prohibit violence and stop evil. The judiciary is a matter of life and death; the dead cannot be brought back to life. Some officials do not uphold the laws, engaging in bribery, forming cliques, being harsh in their investigations, and severe in their judgments, causing the innocent to lose their positions, which I deeply pity. Those who are guilty do not admit their crimes, and the wicked laws perpetuate violence, which is utterly unreasonable. For all doubtful cases, even if they are legally justified but are not accepted by the people's hearts, they shall be reviewed." "

In the winter of the sixth year, the tenth month, the emperor traveled to Yong to perform the suburban sacrifices at the Five Altars. In the twelfth month, the names of various offices were changed. The law was established to execute those who counterfeit money and gold in the marketplace. In the spring, the third month, there was rain and snow. In the summer, the fourth month, the King of Liang passed away. Liang was divided into five states, and the five sons of King Xiao were all enfeoffed as kings.

In the fifth month, an edict was issued: "Officials are the teachers of the people, and their carriages and clothing should be appropriate. Officials of six hundred bushels and above are all senior officials. Those without rank or who do not wear official attire, entering and leaving neighborhoods, are no different from the common people. Senior officials of two thousand bushels shall have red carriages with two red flags, and those from one thousand to six hundred bushels shall have red carriages with one red flag. If the attendants of carriages and riders do not match their official clothing, or if lower officials enter and leave alleys without the dignity of officials, the two thousand bushel officials shall report their subordinates, and the Three Adjuncts shall report those who do not comply with the laws to the Chancellor and the Grandee Secretary for review." "Previously, many officials had military achievements, and their carriages and clothing were too modest, hence the prohibition was established. Also, considering that harsh officials enforced the law excessively, it was decreed that the relevant authorities should reduce the severity of flogging and establish regulations for caning. This is recorded in the Treatise on Penal Law."

In the sixth month, the Xiongnu invaded Yanmen, reached Wuquan, entered Shangjun, and seized horses from the pastures. Two thousand officials and soldiers died in battle. In the autumn, the seventh month, on the last day of Xin Hai, there was a solar eclipse.

In the spring of the first year of the Houyuan era, the first month, an edict was issued: "Judicial matters are of great importance. People vary in wisdom and folly, and officials have their ranks. Doubtful cases should be reviewed by the relevant authorities. If the authorities cannot decide, they should be transferred to the Commandant of Justice. If a case is reviewed and later found to be incorrect, the reviewer shall not be held at fault. We wish to ensure that those who administer justice prioritize leniency." In the third month, a general amnesty was granted to the realm, and the people were granted one rank of nobility. Officials of two thousand bushels and the Prime Ministers of the feudal lords were granted the rank of Right Common Chief. In the summer, a grand feast was held for five days, and the people were allowed to sell alcohol.

In the fifth month, there was an earthquake. In the autumn, the seventh month, on the last day of Yi Si, there was a solar eclipse. The Marquis of Tiao, Zhou Yafu, was imprisoned and died. In the winter of the second year, the tenth month, the feudal lords were ordered to return to their states. In the spring, the Xiongnu invaded Yanmen, and the Grand Administrator Feng Jing died in battle. Chariots, cavalry, and skilled officers were dispatched to garrison the borders. In the spring, due to a poor harvest, the consumption of horse grain in the interior commanderies was prohibited, and violators would have their grain confiscated.

In the summer, the fourth month, an edict was issued: "Engraving and carving waste the time of farmers; embroidered and woven patterns harm the work of women. If farming is neglected, it leads to famine; if women's work is harmed, it leads to cold. When famine and cold come together, few can avoid wrongdoing. I personally plow, and the Empress personally tends the mulberry trees, to provide offerings and sacrificial garments for the ancestral temples, setting an example for the realm. We do not accept tributes, reduce the expenses of the Grand Provisioner, and lessen corvée and taxes, wishing the realm to focus on farming and sericulture, to accumulate reserves in preparation for disasters. The strong should not bully the weak, the many should not oppress the few, the elderly should live out their lives in peace, and the young and orphaned should be able to grow up. This year's harvest may be poor, and the people's food is scarce. Where does the fault lie?

Some deceitful individuals become officials, and officials engage in bribery, plundering the people and exploiting the masses. The county magistrates, who are senior officials, collude with thieves and violate the law, which is utterly unreasonable. We order the officials of two thousand bushels to fulfill their duties; those who neglect their duties and cause chaos shall be reported by the Chancellor, and their crimes shall be investigated." "Proclaim this to the realm, so that all may clearly understand Our intentions."

In the fifth month, an edict was issued: "People should not worry about their lack of knowledge, but about their deceitfulness; not about their lack of courage, but about their violence; not about their lack of wealth, but about their insatiability. Only the incorruptible are content with little. Now, those with a wealth of ten or more are eligible for office, but the incorruptible do not necessarily need much wealth. Those with a market registration cannot hold office, and those without wealth cannot hold office either, which I deeply regret. Those with a wealth of four shall be eligible for office, so that the incorruptible do not long remain unemployed, and the greedy do not perpetually benefit. "

In the autumn, there was a severe drought.

In the spring of the third year, the first month, an edict was issued: "Agriculture is the foundation of the realm. Gold, pearls, and jade cannot be eaten when hungry, nor worn when cold, and their use as currency is not understood. In years of poor harvests, it is often because there are too many engaged in secondary pursuits and too few in farming. We order the commanderies and states to encourage agriculture and sericulture, and to increase the planting of trees, so that clothing and food can be obtained. Officials who force the people to labor or extract gold, pearls, and jade shall be punished as thieves. If officials of two thousand bushels allow this, they shall be equally guilty." "

The Crown Prince came of age, and those among the people who succeeded their fathers were granted one rank of nobility. On the day of Jia Zi, the Emperor passed away in the Weiyang Palace. His will bestowed upon the feudal lords and marquises two teams of horses, officials of two thousand bushels two catties of gold, and each household of officials and commoners one hundred coins. Palace women were sent home and exempted from taxes for life. On the day of Gui You in the second month, he was buried at Yangling.

The eulogy states: Confucius said, "These people are why the three dynasties could follow the straight path," and indeed, it is true! The flaws of the Zhou and Qin dynasties were their excessive laws and harsh writings, which led to an overwhelming number of wrongdoers. With the rise of the Han dynasty, burdensome regulations were swept away, and the people were allowed to rest. By the time of Emperor Xiaowen, with his added humility and frugality, and Emperor Xiaojing's adherence to these principles, within fifty or sixty years, customs were transformed, and the common people became honest and sincere. The Zhou spoke of Cheng and Kang, and the Han of Wen and Jing—what a splendid era!

VOLUME 6: RECORDS OF EMPEROR WU, PART 6

Emperor Xiaowu was the middle son of Emperor Jing, and his mother was Lady Wang. At the age of four, he was enfeoffed as the Prince of Jiaodong. At seven, he was made the Crown Prince, and his mother was made Empress. At sixteen, in the first month of the third year of the later era, Emperor Jing passed away. On the day of Jia Zi, the Crown Prince ascended the throne, and the Empress Dowager Dou was honored as the Grand Empress Dowager, while the Empress was honored as the Empress Dowager. In the third month, the Empress Dowager's brothers, Tian Fen and Sheng, were both enfeoffed as marquises.

In the winter of the first year of the Jianyuan era, the tenth month, an edict was issued for the Chancellor, the Imperial Censor, marquises, officials of two thousand bushels, and the Prime Ministers of the feudal lords to recommend worthy, virtuous, upright, and outspoken individuals who could offer forthright advice. The Chancellor, Wan, memorialized: "Some of the recommended worthies study the teachings of Shen, Shang, Han Fei, Su Qin, and Zhang Yi, which disturb the governance of the state. I request that they all be dismissed." The memorial was approved.

In the spring, the second month, a general amnesty was granted to the realm, and the people were granted one rank of nobility. Those aged eighty were exempted from two poll taxes, and those aged ninety were exempted from military service. The three-zhu coin was issued.

In the summer, the fourth month, on the day of Ji Si, an edict was issued: "In ancient times, the establishment of education was based on age in the villages and on rank in the court, to guide the world and lead the people, and nothing was better than virtue. Thus, in the villages, the elderly were honored first, and the high-aged were respected, which is the ancient way. Now, the filial sons and obedient grandsons of the realm wish to exert themselves to serve their parents, but they are burdened by public duties and lack resources, so their filial piety is deficient. I deeply lament this. For those among the people aged ninety and above, there is already a law for receiving gruel, and they are to be exempted from the service of their sons or grandsons, so that they may personally lead their wives and concubines in fulfilling their duties of support. "

In the fifth month, an edict was issued: "Rivers and seas moisten a thousand li; let the sacrificial officials repair the temples of the mountains and rivers, and perform the annual rites with added ceremony." A pardon was granted to the families of the seven states of Wu and Chu who were in official service. In the autumn, the seventh month, an edict was issued: "The guards are rotated and stationed with twenty thousand men for transport and reception; reduce this by ten thousand. Discontinue the pasture horses and bestow them upon the poor people."

Discussions were held on establishing the Bright Hall. Envoys were sent with comfortable carriages and wheeled palanquins, bearing bundles of silk and jade, to summon Master Shen of Lu. In the winter of the second year, the tenth month, the Imperial Censor, Zhao Wan, was imprisoned for requesting that matters not be reported to the Grand Empress Dowager, and the Chief of the Palace Guard, Wang Zang, also imprisoned, both committed suicide. The Chancellor, Ying, and the Grand Commandant, Fen, were dismissed. In the spring, the second month, on the day of Bing Xu, the first day of the month, there was a solar eclipse. In the summer, the fourth month, on the day of Wu Shen, there was something like a night sun. The prefecture of Maoling was first established.

In the spring of the third year, the Yellow River overflowed into the plains, causing a great famine, and people resorted to cannibalism. Those who moved to Maoling were granted two hundred thousand coins per household and two qing of land. The construction of the Bianmen Bridge began. In the autumn, the seventh month, a comet appeared in the northwest. The Prince of Jichuan, Ming, was deposed and exiled to Fangling for killing his Grand Tutor and Central Tutor.

The Minyue besieged Dong'ou, and Dong'ou urgently sought help. The court dispatched the Grand Master of the Palace, Yan Zhu, with credentials to mobilize troops from Kuaiji and sail across the sea to rescue them. Before they arrived, Minyue retreated, and the troops returned. In the ninth month, on the day of Bing Zi, the last day of the month, there was a solar eclipse. In the summer of the fourth year, there was a wind as red as blood. In the sixth month, there was a drought. In the autumn, the ninth month, a comet appeared in the northeast. In the spring of the fifth year, the three-zhu coin was abolished, and the half-tael coin was issued. The Five Classics Doctorate was established.

In the summer, the fourth month, the Lord of Pingyuan passed away. In the fifth month, there was a great plague of locusts. In the autumn, the eighth month, the Prince of Guangchuan, Yue, and the Prince of Qinghe, Cheng, both passed away. In the spring of the sixth year, the second month, on the day of Yi Wei, the ancestral temple in Liaodong suffered a disaster. In the summer, the fourth month, on the day of Ren Zi, a fire broke out in the side hall of the Gao Garden. The Emperor wore plain clothes for five days. In the fifth month, on the day of Ding Hai, the Grand Empress Dowager passed away. In the autumn, the eighth month, a comet appeared in the east, stretching across the entire sky.

The King of Minyue, Ying, attacked Nanyue. The court dispatched the Grand Herald, Wang Hui, to lead troops from

Yuzhang, and the Grand Minister of Agriculture, Han Anguo, to lead troops from Kuaiji, to attack him. Before they arrived, the Yue people killed Ying and surrendered, and the troops returned. In the winter of the first year of the Yuanguang era, the eleventh month, it was first ordered that each commandery and state recommend one person of filial piety and integrity. The Commandant of the Guards, Li Guang, was appointed as the General of Valiant Cavalry and stationed in Yunzhong, while the Commandant of the Capital, Cheng Bushi, was appointed as the General of Chariots and Cavalry and stationed in Yanmen. In the sixth month, they were dismissed.

In the summer, the fourth month, a general amnesty was granted to the realm, and the eldest sons of the people were granted one rank of nobility. The ancestral lines of the seven states that had previously been severed were restored.

In the fifth month, an edict was issued to the worthy and virtuous: "I have heard that in the times of Yao and Shun, people did not transgress even when images were drawn, and under the light of the sun and moon, all followed their lead. In the eras of Cheng and Kang of the Zhou, punishments were set aside and not used, virtue extended even to birds and beasts, and teachings spread throughout the four seas. Beyond the seas, there was reverence; in the north, the Qu Sou were pacified, and the Di and Qiang came to submit. Comets did not appear, the sun and moon were not eclipsed, mountains and hills did not collapse, rivers and valleys were not blocked; the unicorn and phoenix were in the suburbs and marshes, and the Yellow River and Luo River produced charts and books. Alas, what deeds have led to this! Now that I have the honor of serving the ancestral temple, I rise early to seek and ponder at night, as if wading through deep waters, uncertain of how to cross. Oh, how great and marvelous! What actions can I take to manifest the grand achievements and splendid virtues of the former emperors, to match Yao and Shun above and the three kings below! I am not wise and cannot extend virtue far, as you, my ministers, have witnessed. The worthy and virtuous, who understand the essence of ancient and modern royal affairs, receive my inquiries and respond in writing, compiling them into volumes for me to personally review. " Thus, Dong Zhongshu, Gongsun Hong, and others came forth.

In the autumn, the seventh month, on the day of Gui Wei, there was a solar eclipse. In the winter of the second year, the tenth month, the Emperor traveled to Yong and performed sacrifices at the Five Altars.

In the spring, an edict was issued to the high officials: "I have adorned my daughters to marry the Xiongnu Chanyu, and have given him lavish gifts of gold coins and embroidered silks, yet the Chanyu treats our commands with increasing disrespect and continues to invade and plunder without end. Our border regions suffer greatly, and I deeply lament this. Now, I wish to raise an army to attack him. What do you think?" The Grand Herald, Wang Hui, suggested that it was appropriate to strike. In the summer, the sixth month, the Imperial Censor, Han Anguo, was appointed as the General of the Protecting Army; the Commandant of the Guards, Li Guang, as the General of Valiant Cavalry; the Grand Coachman, Gongsun He, as the General of Light Chariots; the Grand Herald, Wang Hui, as the General of Garrisoned Troops; and the Grand Master of the Palace, Li Xi, as the General of Skilled Officers. They led a force of three hundred thousand men to station in the valley of Mayi, aiming to lure the Chanyu and launch a surprise attack. The Chanyu entered the frontier, but upon realizing the trap, he fled. In the sixth month, the army was disbanded. General Wang Hui was imprisoned and executed for being the chief planner who failed to advance.

In the autumn, the ninth month, the people were ordered to hold a grand feast for five days. In the spring of the third year, the Yellow River shifted its course, flowing from Dunqiu southeast into the Bohai Sea. In the summer, the fifth month, the descendants of five meritorious officials of Emperor Gaozu were enfeoffed as marquises. The Yellow River breached at Puyang, flooding sixteen commanderies. A force of one hundred thousand soldiers was dispatched to repair the breach. The construction of the Longyuan Palace began. In the winter of the fourth year, the Marquis of Weiji, Dou Ying, was found guilty and executed in the marketplace. In the spring, the third month, on the day of Yi Mao, the Chancellor, Fen, passed away.

In the summer, the fourth month, frost fell and killed the grass. In the fifth month, there was an earthquake. A general amnesty was granted to the realm. In the spring of the fifth year, the first month, the Prince of Hejian, De, passed away. In the summer, laborers from Ba and Shu were conscripted to construct roads in the southern barbarian regions, and an additional ten thousand soldiers were sent to fortify the dangerous passes at Yanmen. In the autumn, the seventh month, a great wind uprooted trees. On the day of Yi Si, Empress Chen was deposed. Those involved in witchcraft and sorcery were captured and beheaded. In the eighth month, there was a plague of locusts.

Officials and commoners who were knowledgeable about current affairs and skilled in the teachings of the ancient sages were summoned, provided with food along the way by the counties, and ordered to travel with the census takers. In the winter of the sixth year, the first tax on merchant carts was implemented. In the spring, a canal was dug to connect to the Wei River.

The Xiongnu invaded Shanggu, killing and plundering officials and commoners. The General of Chariots and Cavalry, Wei Qing, was dispatched to Shanggu; the General of Cavalry, Gongsun Ao, to Dai; the General of Light Chariots, Gongsun He, to Yunzhong; and the General of Valiant Cavalry, Li Guang, to Yanmen. Wei Qing reached Longcheng and captured seven hundred enemy heads. Li Guang and Gongsun Ao lost their troops and returned. An edict was issued: "The barbarians have been without righteousness for a long time. Recently, the Xiongnu have repeatedly raided our borders, so I sent generals to pacify them. In ancient times, when training troops and mobilizing armies, it was because the enemy was about to invade. The newly assembled officers and soldiers were not yet cohesive. The General of Dai, Ao, and the General of Yanmen, Guang, were incompetent, and the colonels acted treacherously and recklessly, abandoning the army and fleeing north, while junior officers violated prohibitions. The principles of using troops are: if they are not diligent and not trained, it is the fault of the commanders; if the orders are clear but the soldiers do not exert themselves, it is the crime of the soldiers. The generals have been handed over to the Minister of Justice to be dealt with justly, but to also impose penalties on the soldiers is to apply both measures simultaneously, which is not the heart of a benevolent and sage ruler. I pity the masses who have been ensnared and wish to erase the shame and change their ways, to once again uphold righteousness, but there is no path to do so. Therefore, I pardon the soldiers of Yanmen and Dai who did not follow the law."

In the summer, there was a great drought and a plague of locusts. In the sixth month, the Emperor traveled to Yong. In the autumn, the Xiongnu raided the border. General Han Anguo was dispatched to station troops at Yuyang.

In the winter of the first year of the Yuanshuo era, the eleventh month, an edict was issued: "The high officials and grandees are appointed to oversee strategies, unify categories, broaden education, and beautify customs. To root in benevolence and originate in righteousness, to praise virtue and reward the worthy, to encourage goodness and punish evil, these are the ways by which the Five Emperors and Three Kings flourished. I rise early and retire late, desiring to lead the scholars of the realm to this path. Therefore, I honor the elderly, restore filial piety and respect, select the talented and outstanding, discuss literature and learning, examine and participate in governance, seek to advance the hearts of the people, deeply instruct those in charge, promote integrity and filial piety, hoping to establish a trend and continue the glorious legacy of the sages. In a village of ten households, there must be loyalty and trust; among three people walking together, there is my teacher. Now, it happens that an entire commandery may not recommend a single person, which means the transformation does not reach down, and virtuous gentlemen are blocked from being known to the higher authorities. The officials with a salary of two thousand dan are in charge of the moral order of human relations. How can they assist me in illuminating the obscure, encouraging the masses, inspiring the common people, and honoring the teachings of the local communities? Moreover, to recommend the worthy is to receive the highest reward, and to obscure the worthy is to suffer public execution, which are the ways of antiquity. Let the officials with a salary of two thousand dan, the ritual officers, and the scholars discuss the punishment for those who do not recommend worthy individuals." The officials proposed: "In ancient times, when feudal lords recommended scholars, once was called favoring virtue, twice was called honoring the worthy, and thrice was called meritorious, and they were granted the nine bestowals; if they did not recommend scholars, once would result in the loss of rank, twice in the loss of territory, and thrice in the loss of both rank and territory. Those who fawn on the subordinates and deceive the superiors shall die; those who fawn on the superiors and deceive the subordinates shall be punished; those who participate in state affairs but do not benefit the people shall be dismissed; those who are in high positions but cannot recommend the worthy shall be removed. This is the way to encourage goodness and eliminate evil. Now, the edict proclaims the glorious legacy of the former emperor, ordering the officials with a salary of two thousand dan to recommend the filial and incorrupt, in order to transform the masses and change customs. Those who do not recommend the filial, who do not obey the edict, shall be charged with disrespect. Those who do not investigate incorruptibility, who are incompetent, shall be dismissed." The proposal was approved.

In the twelfth month, the Prince of Jiangdu, Fei, passed away.

In the spring, the third month, on the day of Jia Zi, Empress Wei was established. An edict was issued: "I have heard that if heaven and earth do not change, transformation cannot be accomplished; if yin and yang do not change, things cannot flourish. The 'Book of Changes' says, 'Through change, the people are not weary.' The 'Book of Songs' says, 'After nine changes, return to the thread, knowing the selection of words.' I admire the times of Tang and Yu and delight in the eras of Yin and Zhou, using the old to understand the new. I hereby pardon the realm and begin anew with the people. All unpaid debts and lawsuits from before the third year of the Xiaojing era shall not be heard."
""

In the autumn, the Xiongnu invaded Liaoxi, killing the governor; they entered Yuyang and Yanmen, defeating the commandants, and killing or capturing over three thousand people. General Wei Qing was dispatched to Yanmen, and General Li Xi to Dai, capturing several thousand enemy heads. The chieftain of the eastern barbarians, Nanlu, and others, with a population of two hundred and eighty thousand, surrendered, and the Canghai Commandery was established. The Prince of Lu, Yu, and the Prince of Changsha, Fa, both passed away.

In the winter of the second year, the Prince of Huainan and the Prince of Zichuan were granted staffs and canes, exempting them from attending court. In the spring, the first month, an edict was issued: "The Prince of Liang and the Prince of Chengyang are affectionate brothers and wish to divide their fiefs with their younger brothers. I grant their request. When the feudal lords and kings request to share their fiefs with their sons and brothers, I will personally review it, so that they may have their positions." Thus, the fiefdoms began to be divided, and the sons and brothers all became marquises.

The Xiongnu invaded Shanggu and Yuyang, killing or capturing over a thousand officials and commoners. Generals Wei Qing and Li Xi were dispatched to Yunzhong, reaching Gaoque, and then westward to Fuli, capturing several thousand enemy heads. The lands south of the river were counted, and the Shuofang and Wuyuan Commanderies were established. On the last day of the third month, the day of Yi Hai, there was a solar eclipse. In the summer, one hundred thousand people were recruited to relocate to Shuofang. Additionally, the prominent figures from the commanderies and kingdoms, as well as those with wealth exceeding three million, were relocated to Maoling.

In the autumn, the Prince of Yan, Dingguo, committed a crime and committed suicide. In the spring of the third year, the Canghai Commandery was abolished. In the third month, an edict was issued: "Punishments are established to prevent evil, and internal growth in culture is to show love. Because the people have not yet fully received the transformation of education, I am pleased to work with the scholars and officials daily to renew their tasks, reverently and without slack. I hereby pardon the realm."

In the summer, the Xiongnu invaded Dai, killing the governor; they entered Yanmen, killing or capturing over a thousand people. On the day of Geng Wu in the sixth month, the Empress Dowager passed away. In the autumn, the southwestern barbarians were dismissed, and the city of Shuofang was built. The people were ordered to hold a grand feast for five days. In the winter of the fourth year, the Emperor traveled to Ganquan. In the summer, the Xiongnu invaded Dai, Dingxiang, and Shangjun, killing or capturing several thousand people.

In the spring of the fifth year, there was a great drought. The Grand General Wei Qing led more than one hundred thousand soldiers from six generals out of Shuofang and Gaoque, capturing fifteen thousand enemy heads.

In the summer, the sixth month, an edict was issued: "It is heard that guiding the people with rites and influencing them with music is the way. Now, the rites are in disarray and the music is in ruin, and I am deeply grieved. Therefore, I extensively invite the scholars of the realm who are well-informed, and all are recommended to the court. Let the ritual officials encourage learning, discuss and deliberate widely, revive the lost rites, and take the lead for the realm. The Grand Master of Ceremonies shall discuss granting disciples to the scholars, promoting the transformation of the local communities, and encouraging the worthy talents." The Chancellor, Hong, requested to establish disciples for the scholars, and the number of learners greatly increased.

In the autumn, the Xiongnu invaded Dai, killing the commandant. In the spring of the sixth year, the second month, the Grand General Wei Qing led more than one hundred thousand cavalry from six generals out of Dingxiang, beheading over three thousand enemies. Upon returning, the soldiers and horses rested in Dingxiang, Yunzhong, and Yanmen. The realm was pardoned.

In the summer, the fourth month, Wei Qing again led six generals across the desert, achieving a great victory. The former general Zhao Xin's army was defeated, and he surrendered to the Xiongnu. The right general Su Jian lost his army, escaped alone, and was redeemed to become a commoner.

In the sixth month, an edict was issued: "I have heard that the Five Emperors did not repeat the same rites, and the Three Dynasties did not follow the same laws; the paths they took were different, but the virtue they established was the same. It is said that Confucius advised Duke Ding to attract the distant, Duke Ai to discuss ministers, and Duke Jing to economize; not because they were different, but because their urgent tasks were different. Now, the Central Plains are unified, but the northern borders are not yet peaceful, and I am deeply grieved. Recently, the Grand General patrolled Shuofang, attacked the Xiongnu, and beheaded eighteen thousand enemies. Those who were under restrictions and those who had faults all received generous rewards, and were allowed to have their crimes reduced or pardoned. Now, the Grand General has again achieved victory, beheading nineteen thousand enemies. Those who received titles and rewards and wish to transfer or sell them have no place to do so. Let it be discussed and made into a law." The officials proposed to establish military merit reward officials to honor the warriors.

In the winter of the first year of Yuanshou, the tenth month, the Emperor traveled to Yong and performed sacrifices at the Five Altars. A white unicorn was captured, and the "Song of the White Unicorn" was composed. In the eleventh month, the Prince of Huainan, An, and the Prince of Hengshan, Ci, plotted rebellion and were executed. Tens of thousands of their followers were killed. In the twelfth month, there was heavy snow, and many people froze to death. In the summer, the fourth month, the realm was pardoned.

On the day of Ding Mao, the Crown Prince was established. Those with a rank of two thousand bushels were granted the title of Right Shuzhang, and the people who were heirs to their fathers were promoted one rank. An edict was issued: "I have heard that Gao Yao said to Yu, 'The key is in knowing people; knowing people is wisdom, and even the Emperor finds it difficult.' Indeed, the ruler is the heart, and the people are the limbs; if the limbs are injured, the heart grieves. Recently, Huainan and Hengshan cultivated literature and spread bribery. The two states bordered each other, were alarmed by heresies, and committed regicide and usurpation. This is my lack of virtue. The 'Book of Songs' says, 'With a sorrowful heart, I grieve for the nation's suffering.' Having already pardoned the realm, I cleanse and begin anew. I commend filial piety and diligent farming, and I grieve for the elderly, the orphaned, the widowed, and the solitary who lack food and clothing, and I deeply pity them. I will send emissaries to travel throughout the realm, to inquire and bestow gifts. It is said, 'The Emperor sends emissaries to bestow upon the county elders and the filial, five bolts of silk each; to the village elders, the respectful, and the diligent farmers, three bolts of silk each; to those over ninety years old, the widowed, the orphaned, and the solitary, two bolts of silk each, and three catties of cotton; to those over eighty years old, three dan of rice each. If there are grievances or loss of position, the emissaries shall report them. The county and village shall bestow the gifts immediately, without gathering the people together.'" ""

On the last day of the fifth month, the day of Yi Si, there was a solar eclipse. The Xiongnu invaded Shanggu, killing several hundred people. In the winter of the second year, the tenth month, the Emperor traveled to Yong and performed sacrifices at the Five Altars. In the spring, the third month, on the day of Wu Yin, the Chancellor, Hong, passed away. The General of Agile Cavalry, Huo Qubing, was dispatched to Longxi, reaching Gaolan, and beheaded over eight thousand enemies. In the summer, horses were born in the Yu River. Nanyue presented tamed elephants and talking birds.

Generals Huo Qubing and Gongsun Ao marched over two thousand li north of the land, passed Juyan, and beheaded over thirty thousand enemies. The Xiongnu invaded Yanmen, killing or capturing several hundred people. The Commandant of Guards, Zhang Qian, and the Chief of the Palace Gentlemen, Li Guang, were both dispatched to Youbeiping. Li Guang killed over three thousand Xiongnu, but his entire army of four thousand was lost, and he escaped alone. Both Gongsun Ao and Zhang Qian arrived late and were sentenced to death, but were redeemed to become commoners.

The Prince of Jiangdu, Jian, committed a crime and committed suicide. The Prince of Jiaodong, Ji, passed away. In the autumn, the Xiongnu King Hunye killed the King Xiutu and led his combined forces of over forty thousand to surrender. Five dependent states were established to settle them, and their lands were made into the Wuwei and Jiuquan Commanderies.

In the spring of the third year, a comet appeared in the east. In the summer, the fifth month, the realm was pardoned. The youngest son of the Prince of Jiaodong Kang, Qing, was established as the Prince of Liu'an. The great-grandson of the former Chancellor Xiao He, Qing, was enfeoffed as a marquis. In the autumn, the Xiongnu invaded Youbeiping and Dingxiang, killing or capturing over a thousand people. Emissaries were sent to encourage the commanderies affected by floods to plant winter wheat. Officials and commoners who were able to lend to the poor were recommended and their names reported.

The garrisons in Longxi, Beidi, and Shangjun were reduced by half. Exiled officials were dispatched to dig the Kunming Pool. In the winter of the fourth year, the officials reported that the poor people from Guandong who had migrated to Longxi, Beidi, Xihe, Shangjun, and Kuaiji totaled 725,000. The county officials provided them with food and clothing and supported their livelihoods, but the expenses were insufficient. It was requested to collect silver and tin to create white gold and leather currency to meet the needs. The initial tax on money was calculated. In the spring, a comet appeared in the northeast.

In the summer, a long comet appeared in the northwest.

The Grand General Wei Qing led four generals out of Dingxiang, and General Huo Qubing led forces out of Dai, each commanding fifty thousand cavalry. The infantry followed behind the army with several hundred thousand men. Wei Qing reached the north of the desert and surrounded the Chanyu, beheading nineteen thousand enemies, and returned after reaching the Tianyan Mountains. Huo Qubing fought with the Left Sage King, beheading and capturing over seventy thousand enemies, and returned after reaching the Langjuxu Mountains. Tens of thousands of soldiers from both armies died in battle. The former general Guang and the rear general Shiji both arrived late. Guang committed suicide, and Shiji redeemed his death sentence.

In the spring of the fifth year, the third month, on the day of Jia Wu, the Chancellor Li Cai committed a crime and committed suicide. Horses were scarce in the realm, and the price of a stallion was set at two hundred thousand. The half-tael coin was abolished, and the five-zhu coin was introduced. Corrupt officials and commoners from the realm were relocated to the borders. In the winter of the sixth year, the tenth month, gold was bestowed upon officials from the Chancellor down to those with a rank of two thousand bushels, and silk was bestowed upon those with a rank of one thousand bushels down to the attendants. The barbarians received brocade in varying amounts. Rain fell, and there was no ice.

In the summer, the fourth month, on the day of Yi Si, the imperial ancestral temple was established, and the Emperor's sons Hong, Dan, and Xu were enfeoffed as the Princes of Qi, Yan, and Guangling, respectively. The first edict was composed.

In the sixth month, an edict was issued: "Recently, officials have reported that the currency is too light, leading to widespread fraud, harming the farmers while benefiting the merchants. Additionally, the prohibition on mergers has been enforced, hence the currency was changed to regulate this. Examining ancient practices, the current system is appropriate. Although it has been abolished for a month, the people in the mountains and marshes have not yet understood it. Benevolence leads to goodness, and righteousness changes customs. Is it that those who enforce the laws have not clearly guided them? Or is it that the people are content with different paths, and corrupt officials take advantage of the situation to exploit the masses? How chaotic and disruptive this is! Now, I am dispatching six scholars and others to travel throughout the realm, to inquire and assist the widowed, orphaned, disabled, and those who cannot support themselves. Instruct the elders and the filial to serve as models for the people, and recommend solitary gentlemen of virtue to be summoned to the imperial court. I commend the virtuous and delight in knowing them. Widely proclaim their ways, and if there are scholars with special talents, the emissaries shall appoint them. Inquire in detail about those in obscurity without positions, those who have been wronged or lost their positions, the corrupt and harmful, and those who have caused wilderness and harsh governance, and report their findings." The commanderies and states shall report any beneficial measures to the Chancellor and the Imperial Censor for consideration."

In the autumn, the ninth month, the Grand Marshal and General of Agile Cavalry, Huo Qubing, passed away. In the summer of the first year of Yuanding, the fifth month, the realm was pardoned, and a grand feast was held for five days. A tripod was obtained on the Fen River. The Prince of Jidong, Pengli, committed a crime, was deposed, and exiled to Shangyong. In the winter of the second year, the eleventh month, the Imperial Censor Zhang Tang committed a crime and committed suicide. In the twelfth month, the Chancellor Qingdi was imprisoned and died. In the spring, the construction of the Bailiang Terrace began.

In the third month, there was heavy snow. In the summer, there was a great flood, and thousands starved to death in Guandong.

In the autumn, the ninth month, an edict was issued: "Benevolence does not distinguish distance, and righteousness does not shirk difficulty. Although the capital has not had a bountiful year, the abundance of the mountains, forests, and marshes is shared with the people. Now, the floods have moved to Jiangnan, and with the winter solstice approaching, I fear the people will suffer from hunger and cold and not survive. The land of Jiangnan practices slash-and-burn agriculture and water weeding. We have just dispatched grain from Ba and Shu to Jiangling, and are sending scholars and others to travel and instruct, ensuring that the people are not further burdened. Officials and commoners who have rescued the starving and alleviated their distress shall be fully reported to me." "

In the winter of the third year, the Hangu Pass was moved to Xin'an. The old pass was designated as Hongnong County. In the eleventh month, it was decreed that those who reported on tax evasion would receive half of the recovered amount. On the day of Wu Zi in the first month, the Yangling Mausoleum caught fire. In the summer, the fourth month, hail fell, and over ten commanderies and states in Guandong suffered famine, leading to cannibalism. The Prince of Changshan, Shun, passed away. His son Heng succeeded him but committed a crime, was deposed, and exiled to Fangling.

In the winter of the fourth year, the tenth month, the Emperor traveled to Yong and performed sacrifices at the Five Altars. The people were granted one rank of nobility, and women received cattle and wine per hundred households. The journey continued from Xiayang to the east, reaching Fenyin. On the day of Jia Zi in the eleventh month, the Temple of the Earth was established on the mound of Fenyin. After the rituals, the Emperor traveled to Xingyang. Upon returning to Luoyang, an edict was issued: "Having sacrificed to the earth in Jizhou, gazed upon the Yellow River and Luo River, inspected Yuzhou, and observed the Zhou dynasty's ancestral temple, which was distant and without sacrifices, I inquired of the elders and found the illegitimate son Jia. He was enfeoffed as the Lord of Zhou Zinan to continue the sacrifices of the Zhou dynasty."

In the spring, the second month, the Prince of Zhongshan, Sheng, passed away. In the summer, the alchemist Luan Da was enfeoffed as the Marquis of Letong, holding the position of Supreme General. In the sixth month, a precious tripod was obtained beside the Temple of the Earth. In the autumn, horses were born in the Wo Wa waters. Songs of the Precious Tripod and the Heavenly Horses were composed. The son of the Prince of Changshan, Xian, was established as the Prince of Sishui.

In the winter of the fifth year, the tenth month, the Emperor traveled to Yong and performed sacrifices at the Five Altars. Then, crossing Long, he ascended Kongtong and traveled west to the Zuli River before returning.

On the day of Xin Si in the eleventh month, at dawn, the winter solstice occurred. The Great Altar was established at Ganquan. The Son of Heaven personally performed the suburban sacrifices, worshiping the sun in the morning and the moon in the evening. An edict was issued: "I, with my humble self, am entrusted above the princes and marquises, yet my virtue has not been able to bring peace to the people. Some of the people suffer from hunger and cold, hence I have traveled to perform sacrifices to the Earth in hopes of a bountiful year. The soil of Jizhou has revealed a tripod with inscriptions, and I have obtained it."

The tripod was offered in the ancestral temple. Horses emerged from the Wo Wa waters, and I shall ride them. Trembling with fear, I am anxious about my inadequacy and think of illuminating heaven and earth, seeking renewal within. The 'Book of Songs' says: 'The four steeds move gracefully, to subdue the unruly.' I personally inspected the borders, reaching the utmost limits. I beheld Taiyi and studied the celestial patterns. On the night of Xin Mao, there were twelve bright lights like reflections. The 'Book of Changes' says: 'Three days before Jia, three days after Jia.' I deeply ponder that the year's harvest has not yet been abundant, and I disciplined myself with fasting and purification. On Ding You, I performed the suburban sacrifices to seek blessings." "

In the summer, the fourth month, Lü Jia, the chancellor of the King of Nanyue, rebelled and killed the Han envoy along with the king and the queen dowager. The realm was pardoned. On the day of Ding Chou, at the end of the month, there was a solar eclipse. In the autumn, toads and frogs fought.

The Fubo General Lu Bode was dispatched from Guiyang to descend the Huang River; the Louchuan General Yang Pu was sent from Yuzhang to descend the Zhen River; the Guiyi Yuehou Yan was appointed as the Gechuan General, sent from Lingling to descend the Li River; and Jia was appointed as the Xialai General, sent to descend the Cangwu River. All were leading convicts, with a hundred thousand Louchuan troops from the regions south of the Yangtze and Huai Rivers. The Yue Chiyi Hou Yi led separate forces of convicts from Ba and Shu, mobilizing troops from Yelang to descend the Zangke River, all converging at Panyu.

In the ninth month, 106 marquises were stripped of their titles for failing to present gold according to the law for the ancestral temple sacrifices. Chancellor Zhao Zhou was imprisoned and died. The Marquis of Letong, Luan Da, was executed for deception. One hundred thousand Qiang tribesmen rebelled, communicated with the Xiongnu, attacked Gu'an, and besieged Fuhan. The Xiongnu invaded Wuyuan and killed the governor.

In the winter of the sixth year, the tenth month, cavalry from Longxi, Tianshui, and Anding, along with troops from the Central Command and 100,000 soldiers from Henan and Henei, were dispatched. Generals Li Xi and the Chief of the Palace Guards led the expedition against the Qiang tribes and pacified them.

Traveling east, the Emperor intended to visit Goushi but reached Tongxiang in Zuoyi, where he heard of the defeat of Nanyue and established the county of Wenxi. In the spring, arriving at Xinzhongxiang in Ji, he obtained the head of Lü Jia and established the county of Huojia. The troops of the Chiyi Hou had not yet descended when the Emperor ordered the expedition against the southwestern barbarians, which was pacified. Thus, the Yue territory was established as the commanderies of Nanhai, Cangwu, Yulin, Hepu, Jiaozhi, Jiuzhen, Rinan, Zhuya, and Dan'er. The southwestern barbarians were pacified and established as the commanderies of Wudu, Zangke, Yuexi, Shenli, and Wenshan.

In the autumn, the King of Dongyue, Yushan, rebelled, attacked and killed Han generals and officials. The Heng Hai General Han Shuo and the Central Command Wang Wenshu were dispatched from Kuaiji, and the Louchuan General Yang Pu from Yuzhang to attack him. Additionally, the Fu Ju General Gongsun He was sent from Jiuyuan, and the Xionghe General Zhao Ponu from Lingju, each traveling over two thousand li, but they did not encounter the enemy and returned. Consequently, the lands of Wuwei and Jiuquan were divided to establish the commanderies of Zhangye and Dunhuang, and people were relocated to populate them.

In the winter of the first year of the Yuanfeng era, the tenth month, an edict was issued: "Nanyue and Dong'ou have both submitted to their guilt, but the western barbarians and northern tribes are still not in harmony. I shall inspect the borders, select troops, and lead them personally, setting up twelve divisions of generals to command the army." The journey began from Yunyang, passed through Shangjun, Xihe, and Wuyuan, exited the Great Wall, ascended the Chanyu Platform to the north, reached Shuofang, and approached the northern river. Eighteen thousand cavalry were mustered, with banners extending over a thousand li, awing the Xiongnu. An envoy was sent to inform the Chanyu: "The head of the King of Nanyue has already been displayed at the northern gate of Han. If the Chanyu can fight, the Son of Heaven will personally await him at the border; if not, he should quickly come to submit. Why hide in the cold and bitter lands north of the desert?" The Xiongnu were intimidated. Upon returning, sacrifices were made to the Yellow Emperor at Qiaoshan, and then the Emperor returned to Ganquan.

The King of Dongyue, Yushan, was killed and surrendered. An edict was issued: "The treacherous and volatile Dongyue is a future trouble. Its people are to be relocated to the region between the Yangtze and Huai Rivers." Thus, the land was left empty.

In the spring, the first month, the Emperor traveled to Goushi. An edict was issued: "I have conducted affairs at Mount Hua and reached the Central Peak, where I obtained a rare beast and saw the stone of Queen Mother Xia. The next day, I personally ascended Mount Song. The imperial censor and his entourage, along with the officials and soldiers beside the temple, all heard the shout of 'Long live the Emperor' three times. All rituals were answered. Let the temple officials increase the sacrifices at the Taishi Temple, and prohibit the cutting of its trees and plants. Three hundred households at the foot of the mountain are to be designated as the offering estate, named Chonggao, solely for the temple's use, exempt from other duties." "The journey continued, and then proceeded to the eastern tour by the sea."

In the summer, the fourth month, on the day of Gui Mao, the Emperor returned, ascended Mount Tai to perform the Feng and Shan sacrifices, and then descended to sit in the Mingtang. An edict was issued: "I, with my humble self, have received the supreme honor, trembling with the thought of my meager virtue, and my lack of understanding in rites and music. Therefore, I have conducted affairs for the eight deities. By the grace of heaven and earth, auspicious signs have appeared, clearly visible as if heard. Startled by strange phenomena, I wished to stop but dared not, and thus ascended Mount Tai to perform the Feng and Shan sacrifices, reaching Liangfu, and then ascended to perform the Su sacrifice. Renewing myself, I rejoice with the officials and scholars in a new beginning. Let the tenth month be the first year of the Yuanfeng era." The places visited on the journey, including Bo, Fenggao, Sheqiu, Licheng, and Liangfu, had their overdue land taxes and loans remitted. Additionally, those aged seventy and above, who were widowed or orphaned, were granted two bolts of silk each. The four counties were exempt from this year's poll tax. All commoners of the realm were granted one rank of nobility, and women were given one ox and one hundred households of wine."

The journey continued from Mount Tai, proceeding eastward

to tour by the sea, reaching Jieshi. From Liaoxi, passing through the northern borders to Jiuyuan, and then returning to Ganquan. In the autumn, a comet appeared in the eastern well and again in the three terraces. The King of Qi, Hong, passed away.

In the winter of the second year, the tenth month, the Emperor traveled to Yong to sacrifice at the Five Altars. In the spring, he visited Goushi and then proceeded to Donglai. In the summer, the fourth month, he returned to sacrifice at Mount Tai. Upon reaching Huzi, he personally inspected the breach in the Yellow River and ordered all accompanying officials and generals to carry firewood to repair the river embankment, composing the "Huzi Song." He pardoned the convicts along the way and granted rice to the lonely and elderly, four dan per person. Upon returning, he constructed the Ganquan Tongtian Terrace and the Feilian Pavilion in Chang'an.

The King of Korea attacked and killed the Commandant of Liaodong, and thus the realm was called upon to recruit those sentenced to death to attack Korea. In the sixth month, an edict was issued: "Within the Ganquan Palace, a nine-stemmed, connected-leafed auspicious fungus has grown. The Lord on High has broadly descended, no different from the lower chambers, bestowing upon me great blessings. Let the realm be pardoned, and the capital of Yunyang be granted one hundred households of oxen and wine." The "Song of the Auspicious Fungus Chamber" was composed. In the autumn, the Mingtang was constructed at the foot of Mount Tai.

The Louchuan General Yang Pu and the Left General Xun Zhi were dispatched to lead the recruited convicts to attack Korea. Additionally, General Guo Chang and the Palace Attendant Wei Guang were sent to mobilize troops from Ba and Shu to pacify the unsubmissive southwestern barbarians, establishing the Yizhou Commandery. In the spring of the third year, a Juedi performance was held, attracting spectators from within a three-hundred-li radius. In the summer, Korea beheaded its king, Youqu, and surrendered. The land was established as the commanderies of Lelang, Lintun, Xuantu, and Zhenfan.

The Louchuan General Yang Pu was dismissed and reduced to commoner status for losing many troops, and the Left General Xun Zhi was executed in the marketplace for competing over merits. In the autumn, the seventh month, the King of Jiaoxi, Duan, passed away. The Di people of Wudu rebelled and were divided and relocated to the Jiuquan Commandery.

In the winter of the fourth year, the tenth month, the Emperor traveled to Yong to sacrifice at the Five Altars. He opened the Huizhong Road, then exited north through the Xiaoguan Pass, passed through Dulu and Mingze, returned from Dai, and visited Hedong. In the spring, the third month, he sacrificed to the Earth God. An edict was issued: "I personally sacrificed to the Earth God and saw light gather at the spiritual altar, shining three times in one night. At the Zhongdu Palace, light was seen in the hall. Let those sentenced to death and below in Fenyin, Xiayang, and Zhongdu be pardoned, and the three counties and the Yang clan be exempt from this year's land taxes and levies." "

In the summer, there was a great drought, and many people died from the heat. In the autumn, considering the Xiongnu weakened and possibly ready to submit, envoys were sent to persuade them. The Chanyu sent envoys, who died in the capital. The Xiongnu raided the borders, and the Bahu General Guo Chang was dispatched to garrison Shuofang.

In the winter of the fifth year, the Emperor conducted a southern tour, reaching Shengtang, where he performed a distant sacrifice to Emperor Shun at Jiuyi. He ascended Mount Qian Tianzhu, floated down the Yangtze River from Xunyang, personally shot a jiao in the river and captured it. With a fleet stretching a thousand li, he reached Zongyang and composed the "Shengtang Zongyang Song." Then he traveled north to Langya, along the coast, performing rituals at famous mountains and great rivers along the way. In the spring, the third month, he returned to Mount Tai and added to the Feng and Shan sacrifices. On the day of Jiazi, he sacrificed to Emperor Gaozu in the Mingtang, pairing him with the Lord on High, and then received the regional lords and marquises, accepting the accounts from the commanderies and kingdoms. In the summer, the fourth month, an edict was issued: "I have toured Jing and Yang, gathered the essence of the Yangtze and Huai Rivers, and met the energy of the great sea to unite with Mount Tai. Heaven has shown signs, and I have increased the Feng and Shan sacrifices. Let the realm be pardoned. The counties visited shall not pay this year's land taxes and levies, and the widowed, orphaned, and lonely shall be granted silk, while the poor shall be given grain." He then returned to Ganquan to perform the suburban sacrifice at the Tai Altar.

The Grand Marshal and General Qing passed away.

For the first time, thirteen regional inspectorates were established. As the ranks of famous civil and military officials were thinning, an edict was issued: "To achieve extraordinary feats, extraordinary individuals are necessary. Just as a horse that gallops fiercely can cover a thousand li, a scholar burdened by societal scorn can still achieve merit and fame. Horses that run wild and scholars who are unruly can be harnessed and directed. Let the commanderies and prefectures identify officials and commoners of exceptional talent and capability who can serve as generals, ministers, or envoys to distant lands."

In the winter of the sixth year, the Emperor traveled to Huizhong. In the spring, the Shoushan Palace was constructed. In the third month, the Emperor traveled to Hedong to sacrifice to the Earth God. An edict was issued: "I performed rituals at Shoushan, and precious items emerged from the Kun fields, some transforming into gold. During the sacrifice to the Earth God, divine light shone three times. Let those sentenced to death and below in Fenyin be pardoned, and the poor of the realm be granted one bolt of cloth and silk each."

Yizhou and Kunming rebelled, and convicts from the capital were pardoned and conscripted into the army. The Bahu General Guo Chang was dispatched to lead the campaign against them. In the summer, the commoners of the capital watched a Juedi performance at the Shanglin Pinglè Pavilion. In the autumn, there was a severe drought and a plague of locusts. In the winter of the first year of the Taichu era, the tenth month, the Emperor traveled to Mount Tai. On the first day of the eleventh month, Jiazi, at dawn on the winter solstice, he sacrificed to the Lord on High in the Mingtang. On the day of Yiyou, the Bailiang Terrace was destroyed by fire.

In the twelfth month, the Feng and Shan sacrifices were performed at Gaoli, and the Earth God was worshipped. The Emperor traveled east to the Bohai Sea and performed a distant sacrifice to Penglai. In the spring, he returned and received the regional accounts at Ganquan. In the second month, the construction of the Jianzhang Palace began. In the summer, the fifth month, the calendar was reformed, designating the first month as the start of the year. The color yellow was elevated, the number five was emphasized, official titles were standardized, and musical tones were harmonized. The General of Yinyu, Gongsun Ao, was dispatched to build the Shouxiang City beyond the frontier.

In the autumn, the eighth month, the Emperor traveled to Anding. The Ershi General Li Guangli was dispatched to mobilize convicts from across the realm for a western campaign against Dayuan. Locusts flew from the east to Dunhuang. In the spring of the second year, on the day of Wushen in the first month, the Chancellor Qing passed away. In the third month, the Emperor traveled to Hedong to sacrifice to the Earth God. He decreed a five-day grand feast for the realm, five days of offerings at household gates, akin to the La festival.

In the summer, the fourth month, an edict was issued: "I have performed rituals at Jie Mountain and sacrificed to the Earth God, and both were met with luminous responses. Let those sentenced to death and below in Fenyin and Anyi be pardoned." In the fifth month, horses owned by officials and commoners were registered to replenish the cavalry and chariot horses. In the autumn, there was a plague of locusts. The Junji General Zhao Ponu was dispatched with twenty thousand cavalry from Shuofang to attack the Xiongnu, but they did not return. In the winter, the twelfth month, the Imperial Censor Er Kuan passed away.

In the spring of the third year, the first month, the Emperor traveled east to tour the seas. In the summer, the fourth month, he returned and performed the Feng and Shan sacrifices at Mount Tai and Shilü. The Guangluxun Xu Ziwei was dispatched to build a series of fortifications beyond the frontier of Wuyuan, extending northwest to Luqu, where the Youji General Han Yue led troops to garrison them. The Qiangnu Commandant Lu Bode built Juyan.

In the autumn, the Xiongnu invaded Dingxiang and Yunzhong, killing and capturing several thousand people, and destroyed the frontier outposts of the Guangluxun. They also invaded Zhangye and Jiuquan, killing the commandants. In the spring of the fourth year, the Ershi General Guangli beheaded the king of Dayuan and brought back the sweat-blood horses. The "Song of the Heavenly Horses of the Western Extremity" was composed. In the autumn, the construction of the Mingguang Palace began. In the winter, the Emperor traveled to Huizhong.

The commandant of Hongnong was relocated to Wuguan to tax travelers to support the garrison soldiers. In the spring of the first year of the Tianhan era, the first month, the Emperor traveled to Ganquan to perform the suburban sacrifice at the Tai Altar. In the third month, he traveled to Hedong to sacrifice to the Earth God. The Xiongnu returned Han envoys and sent envoys to present tribute. In the summer, the fifth month, a general amnesty was declared. In the autumn, the city gates were closed for a large-scale search. Convicts were conscripted to garrison Wuyuan.

In the spring of the second year, the Emperor traveled to the East Sea and then returned to Huizhong. In the summer, the fifth month, the Ershi General led thirty thousand cavalry out of Jiuquan and fought the Right Wise King at the Tianshan Mountains, beheading and capturing over ten thousand. The General of Yinyu was dispatched to exit the Xi River, and the Cavalry Commandant Li Ling led five thousand infantry out of the northern Juyan to engage the Chanyu, beheading and capturing over ten thousand. Li Ling's forces were defeated, and he surrendered to the Xiongnu.

In the autumn, the practice of witchcraft and roadside sacrifices was prohibited, and a large-scale search was conducted. Envoys from the six states of Quli came to present tribute. Bandits led by Xu Heng in Mount Tai and Langya blocked mountain passes and attacked cities, disrupting travel. The Straight Point Envoy Bao Shengzhi and others, dressed in embroidered robes and wielding axes, were dispatched to various regions to hunt them down. Regional inspectors and commandery governors below were all executed.

In the winter, the eleventh month, an edict was issued to the frontier commandants: "Now, many powerful individuals are forming distant alliances, relying on the bandits in the east. Be vigilant in inspecting travelers." In the spring of the third year, the second month, the Imperial Censor Wang Qing committed a crime and committed suicide. The government monopoly on the sale of alcohol was established.

In the third month, the Emperor traveled to Mount Tai to perform the Feng and Shan sacrifices, worshipped at the Mingtang, and received the regional accounts. He then traveled to Beidi to sacrifice to Changshan and buried a black jade. In the summer, the fourth month, a general amnesty was declared, and the lands passed through were exempted from land taxes. In the autumn, the Xiongnu invaded Yanmen, and the governor, fearing the consequences, was executed in the marketplace.

In the spring of the fourth year, the first month, the Emperor convened the feudal lords at the Ganquan Palace. He mobilized the seven categories of convicts and brave warriors from across the realm, dispatching the Ershi General Li Guangli with sixty thousand cavalry and seventy thousand infantry to exit Shuofang, the General of Yinyu Gongsun Ao with ten thousand cavalry and thirty thousand infantry to exit Yanmen, the Youji General Han Yue with thirty thousand infantry to exit Wuyuan, and the Qiangnu Commandant Lu Bode with over ten thousand infantry to join the Ershi General. Guangli fought the Chanyu on the Yu River for several days, while Ao had an unfavorable battle with the Left Wise King, and both forces withdrew.

In the summer, the fourth month, the Emperor's son Bo was enfeoffed as the Prince of Changyi. In the autumn, the ninth month, it was decreed that those sentenced to death could redeem themselves with five hundred thousand coins to reduce their sentence by one degree. In the spring of the first year of the Taishi era, the first month, the General of Yinyu Ao committed a crime and was executed by waist severing. Officials and powerful individuals from commanderies and states were relocated to Maoling and Yunling. In the summer, the sixth month, a general amnesty was declared. In the spring of the second year, the first month, the Emperor traveled to Huizhong.

In the third month, an edict was issued: "Officials have deliberated and said that in the past, I performed the suburban sacrifice to the Lord on High, ascended the Longshan Mountains in the west, obtained a white qilin to present at the ancestral temple, the Wowa River produced a heavenly horse, and Mount Tai revealed gold. It is appropriate to change the old names. Now, gold shall be renamed 'qilin toes and roe deer hooves' to harmonize with these auspicious signs." Thus, they were distributed as gifts to the feudal lords. In the autumn, there was a drought. In the ninth month, convicts sentenced to death were recruited to redeem themselves with five hundred thousand coins to reduce their sentence by one degree.

The Imperial Censor Du Zhou passed away. In the spring of the third year, the first month, the Emperor traveled to the Ganquan Palace to host foreign guests. In the second month, a five-day grand feast was decreed for the realm. The Emperor traveled to the East Sea, captured a red wild goose, and composed the "Song of the Red Wild Goose." He visited Langya, performed rituals at Chengshan, ascended Zhifu, and sailed the great sea. The mountains hailed him with cries of "Long live!" In the winter, households along the Emperor's route were granted five thousand coins, and widowers, widows, orphans, and the childless were each given a bolt of silk.

In the spring of the fourth year, the third month, the Emperor traveled to Mount Tai. On the day of Renwu, he sacrificed to Emperor Gaozu at the Mingtang, pairing him with the Lord on High, and received the regional accounts. On the day of Guiwei, he sacrificed to Emperor Xiaojing at the Mingtang. On the day of Jiashen, he performed the Feng sacrifice. On the day of Bingxu, he performed the Shan sacrifice at Shilü. In the summer, the fourth month, he visited Buqi and sacrificed to the divine beings at the Jiaomen Palace, as if they were seated and bowing. He composed the "Song of Jiaomen." In the summer, the fifth month, he returned to the Jianzhang Palace, held a grand feast, and declared a general amnesty.

In the autumn, the seventh month, in Zhao, a snake entered the city from outside the walls and fought with a group of snakes from the city beneath the temple of Emperor Xiaowen, resulting in the death of the city's snakes. In the winter, the tenth month, on the day of Jiayin, there was a solar eclipse. In the twelfth month, the Emperor traveled to Yong, sacrificed at the Five Altars, and went west to Anding and Beidi. In the spring of the first year of the Zhenghe era, the first month, he returned and traveled to the Jianzhang Palace. In the third month, the King of Zhao, Pengzu, passed away.

In the winter, the eleventh month, cavalry from the three capital regions were dispatched for a large-scale search of the Shanglin Park, and the gates of Chang'an were closed for eleven days before being reopened. Witchcraft and curses began to spread. In the spring of the second year, the first month, the Chancellor He was imprisoned and died. In the summer, the fourth month, a great wind destroyed houses and broke trees. In the intercalary month, the Princesses of Zhuyi and Yangshi were implicated in witchcraft and died. In the summer, the Emperor traveled to Ganquan.

In the autumn, the seventh month, the Marquis of Andao Han Yue, the envoy Jiang Chong, and others excavated a curse in the Crown Prince's palace. On the day of Renwu, the Crown Prince and the Empress conspired to execute Chong, and using their authority, they mobilized troops to engage in a great battle with Chancellor Liu Quli in Chang'an, resulting in tens of thousands of deaths. On the day of Gengyin, the Crown Prince fled, and the Empress committed suicide. For the first time, troops were stationed at the city gates. The imperial insignia was altered with the addition of yellow pennants. The Imperial Censor Bao Shengzhi and the Sizhi Tian Ren were implicated for negligence, leading to Shengzhi's suicide and Ren's execution by waist severing. On the day of Xinhai in the eighth month, the Crown Prince committed suicide at Lake Hu.

On the day of Guihai, an earthquake occurred. In the ninth month, the son of King Jing of Zhao, Yan, was enfeoffed as the Prince of Ping. The Xiongnu invaded Shanggu and Wuyuan, killing and capturing officials and commoners.

In the spring of the third year, the first month, the Emperor traveled to Yong, reaching Anding and Beidi. The Xiongnu invaded Wuyuan and Jiuquan, killing two commandants. In the third month, the Ershi General Guangli was dispatched with seventy thousand troops to exit Wuyuan, the Imperial Censor Shangqiu Cheng with twenty thousand troops to exit Xi River, and the Marquis of Chonghe Ma Tong with forty thousand cavalry to exit Jiuquan. Cheng reached the Junji Mountains and engaged the enemy, achieving many beheadings. Tong reached the Tianshan Mountains, and the enemy withdrew, leading to the surrender of Cheshi. All troops were withdrawn. Guangli was defeated and surrendered to the Xiongnu.

In the summer, the fifth month, a general amnesty was declared. In the sixth month, Chancellor Quli was imprisoned and executed by waist severing, and his wife and children were beheaded. In the autumn, there was a locust plague. In the ninth month, the rebels Gongsun Yong and Hu Qian were discovered and executed. In the spring of the fourth year, the first month, the Emperor traveled to Donglai and approached the great sea. In the second month, on the day of Dingyou, two meteorites fell at Yong, their sound heard for four hundred li.

In the third month, the Emperor plowed at Juding. He then traveled to Mount Tai to perform the Feng sacrifice. On the day of Gengyin, he sacrificed at the Mingtang. On the day of Guisi, he performed rituals at Shilü. In the summer, the sixth month, he returned to Ganquan. In the autumn, the eighth month, on the day of Xinyou, there was a solar eclipse. In the spring of the first year of the Houyuan era, the first month, the Emperor traveled to Ganquan, performed the suburban sacrifice at the Tai Altar, and then visited Anding. The Prince of Changyi, Bo, passed away.

In the second month, an edict was issued: "I performed the suburban sacrifice to the Lord on High and toured the northern frontier, where I saw a flock of cranes resting, uncaught by nets, with nothing to offer. I presented them at the Tai Altar, and light and shadow appeared together. Let a general amnesty be declared."

In the summer, the sixth month, the Imperial Censor

Shangqiu Cheng committed a crime and committed suicide. The Attendant Gentleman Mang Heluo and his brother, the Marquis of Chonghe Tong, plotted rebellion. The Attendant Gentleman and Commandant of the Imperial Stables Jin Midi, the Commandant of the Imperial Chariots Huo Guang, and the Commandant of the Cavalry Shangguan Jie suppressed it. In the autumn, the seventh month, an earthquake occurred, and springs often gushed forth. In the spring of the second year, the first month, the feudal lords were convened at the Ganquan Palace, and the imperial clan was rewarded.

In the second month, the Emperor traveled to the Wuzuo Palace in Zhouzhi. On the day of Yichou, the Emperor's son Fuling was established as the Crown Prince. On the day of Dingmao, the Emperor passed away at the Wuzuo Palace and was encoffined in the front hall of the Weiyang Palace. On the day of Jiashen in the third month, he was buried at Maoling.

Commentary: The Han Dynasty inherited the shortcomings of a hundred kings. Emperor Gaozu rectified chaos and restored order, while Emperors Wen and Jing focused on nurturing the people. As for the matters of ancient rituals and culture, there were still many deficiencies. Upon the initial establishment of Emperor Xiaowu, he resolutely dismissed the Hundred Schools and promoted the Six Classics. He then sought advice from across the realm, selected the talented and virtuous, and worked with them to achieve merit. He established the Imperial University, repaired the suburban sacrifices, corrected the calendar, determined the astronomical cycles, harmonized musical tones, composed poetry and music, established the Feng and Shan sacrifices, honored the myriad deities, and continued the legacy of the Zhou Dynasty. His edicts and writings were brilliant and worthy of recounting. The succeeding generations were able to follow his grand achievements, embodying the style of the Three Dynasties. With Emperor Wu's great talent and broad vision, had he not altered the reverence and frugality of Emperors Wen and Jing to benefit the people, even the praises in the Book of Songs and Book of Documents could not have added more!

VOLUME 7: RECORDS OF EMPEROR ZHAO, NO. 7

Emperor Xiaozhao was the youngest son of Emperor Wu. His mother was Lady Zhao Jieyu, who initially gained favor due to her extraordinary qualities, and when she gave birth to the Emperor, it was also considered extraordinary. This is detailed in the Biography of the Maternal Relatives. Towards the end of Emperor Wu's reign, the Crown Prince Li had been defeated, and the Princes of Yan Dan and Guangling Xu had become arrogant and disrespectful. In the second month of the second year of the Houyuan era, when the Emperor fell ill, Emperor Zhao was established as the Crown Prince at the age of eight. The Attendant Gentleman and Commandant of the Imperial Chariots Huo Guang was appointed as the Grand Marshal and Great General, receiving the Emperor's will to assist the young ruler. The next day, Emperor Wu passed away. On the day of Wuchen, the Crown Prince ascended the throne as Emperor and paid homage at the Gao Temple. The Emperor's elder sister, Princess Eyi, was granted additional fiefs for her bath and hair washing, becoming the Princess Eldest, and she was responsible for the care and supervision within the palace. The Great General Guang held the reins of government, overseeing the affairs of the Secretariat, with the General of Chariots and Cavalry Jin Midi and the Left General Shangguan Jie assisting him.

In the summer, the sixth month, a general amnesty was declared. In the autumn, the seventh month, a comet appeared in the east. The King of Jibei, Kuan, committed a crime and committed suicide. The Princess Eldest and the male members of the imperial clan were granted various rewards. Lady Zhao Jieyu was posthumously honored as Empress Dowager, and the Yunling Mausoleum was constructed. In the winter, the Xiongnu invaded Shuofang, killing and capturing officials and commoners. Troops were dispatched to garrison Xihe, and the Left General Jie patrolled the northern frontier.

In the spring of the first year of the Shiyuan era, the second month, yellow swans descended into the Taiye Pond of the Jianzhang Palace. The high officials presented their congratulations. The feudal lords, marquises, and members of the imperial clan were granted varying amounts of money. On the day of Jihai, the Emperor plowed at the Gou Dun Long Field. The King of Yan, the King of Guangling, and the Princess Eldest of Eyi were each granted an additional thirteen thousand households. In the summer, a garden temple was constructed for the Empress Dowager at Yunling.

The counties of Liantou, Guzeng, Zangke, Tanzhi, and Tongbing in Yizhou, totaling twenty-four settlements, all rebelled. The Commandant of the Waterways, Lü Pohu, was dispatched to recruit officials and commoners and to mobilize troops from Qianwei and Shu commanderies to attack Yizhou, achieving a great victory. The officials requested that Henei be assigned to Jizhou and Hedong to Bingzhou. In the autumn, the seventh month, a general amnesty was declared, and the people were granted cattle and wine per hundred households. There was heavy rain, and the Wei Bridge was destroyed.

In the eighth month, Liu Ze, the grandson of the King of Qi Xiaowang, plotted rebellion, intending to kill the Inspector of Qingzhou, Jun Buyi. The plot was discovered, and all involved were executed. Buyi was promoted to the position of Governor of the Capital District and granted a million coins. On the day of Bingzi in the ninth month, the General of Chariots and Cavalry, Jin Midi, passed away. In the intercalary month, the former

Minister of Justice Wang Ping and four others were dispatched with credentials to tour the commanderies and kingdoms, recommending the virtuous and inquiring about the people's hardships, grievances, and unemployment. In the winter, there was no ice.

In the spring of the second year, the first month, the Great General Guang and the Left General Jie were both enfeoffed for their previous merits in capturing and executing the rebel Marquis of Chonghe, Ma Tong. Guang was enfeoffed as the Marquis of Bolu, and Jie as the Marquis of Anyang. Members of the imperial clan who were not in office were recommended, and the talented Liu Piqiang and Liu Changle were both appointed as Court Gentlemen. Piqiang was made the Commandant of the Guards of Chang Palace.

In the third month, envoys were dispatched to provide relief and loans to the poor who lacked seeds and food. In the autumn, the eighth month, an edict was issued: "In previous years, there were many disasters. This year, the silkworms and wheat have been damaged. The seeds and food provided as relief and loans shall not be reclaimed, and the people are exempted from this year's land tax." In the winter, soldiers trained in archery and combat were sent to Shuofang, and former officials were reassigned to garrison and cultivate fields in Zhangye Commandery. In the spring of the third year, the second month, a comet appeared in the northwest.

In the autumn, the people were recruited to relocate to Yunling and were granted money, land, and houses. In the winter, the tenth month, phoenixes gathered in the Eastern Sea, and envoys were dispatched to offer sacrifices at that location. On the first day of the eleventh month, Ren Chen, there was a solar eclipse.

In the spring of the fourth year, the third month, on the day of Jiayin, Empress Shangguan was established. A general amnesty was declared. Legal cases from more than two years prior were not to be heard. In the summer, the sixth month, the Empress visited the Gao Temple. The Princess Eldest, the Chancellor, the Generals, the Marquises, officials of rank two thousand bushels and below, and the members of the imperial clan were granted varying amounts of money and silk. Wealthy families from the Three Capital Regions were relocated to Yunling and were granted money, with each household receiving one hundred thousand coins.

In the autumn, the seventh month, an edict was issued: "In recent years, the harvests have been poor, and the people are short of food. The wandering laborers have not all returned. Previously, the people were ordered to contribute horses, but this is now to be stopped. The provisions for the central officials shall be reduced." In the winter, the Grand Herald Tian Guangming was dispatched to attack Yizhou. The Minister of Justice Li Zhong was executed in the marketplace for the crime of deliberately releasing a capital offender. In the spring of the fifth year, the first month, the Empress Dowager's father was posthumously honored as the Marquis of Shuncheng.

In the summer, a man from Xiayang named Zhang Yannian went to the northern gate, claiming to be the Crown Prince Wei. He was accused of deceit and was executed by being cut in half at the waist. In the summer, the practice of keeping mares at the postal stations and the restrictions on crossbows and horses were abolished throughout the empire. In the sixth month, the father of the Empress, the General of Agile Cavalry Shangguan An, was enfeoffed as the Marquis of Sangle.

An edict was issued: "We, with our humble self, have been able to preserve the ancestral temple, trembling with fear, rising early and retiring late, emulating the affairs of the ancient emperors and kings, mastering the teachings of the classics, the 'Classic of Filial Piety,' the 'Analects,' and the 'Book of Documents,' yet have not yet achieved enlightenment. Let it be ordered that the Three Capital Regions and the Minister of Ceremonies each recommend two virtuous and talented individuals, and each commandery and kingdom recommend one scholar of high achievement. Officials of rank two thousand bushels and below, down to the common people, are to be granted noble ranks as appropriate." The commanderies of Dan'er and Zhenfan were abolished.

In the autumn, the Grand Herald Guangming and the Army Supervisor Wang Ping attacked Yizhou, beheading and capturing more than thirty thousand people, and seizing over fifty thousand heads of livestock. In the spring of the sixth year, the first month, the Emperor plowed at the Shanglin Park. In the second month, an edict was issued ordering the officials to inquire about the hardships of the people as reported by the virtuous and talented scholars recommended by the commanderies and kingdoms. A discussion was held on abolishing the state monopolies on salt, iron, and alcohol.

Su Wu, the former Supervisor of Yi Zhong, who had been sent as an envoy to the Xiongnu and was detained at the court of the Chanyu for nineteen years before returning, was appointed as the Director of Dependent States for his integrity in fulfilling his mission and was granted a million coins. In the summer, there was a drought, and a great rain dance was performed, during which it was permissible to light fires. In the autumn, the seventh month, the officials in charge of the alcohol monopoly were abolished, and the people were allowed to pay taxes according to the law, selling wine at four coins per liter. Due to the vast distances of the border regions, two counties each from Tianshui, Longxi, and Zhangye commanderies were taken to establish Jincheng Commandery.

An edict was issued: "The Marquis of Gou Ding, Wu Bo, led his chieftains and people to attack the rebels, achieving merit in beheading and capturing them. Let Wu Bo be established as the King of Gou Ding. The Grand Herald Guangming, who led the troops to merit, is to be granted the title of Marquis within the Pass and a fief." In the spring of the first year of the Yuanfeng era, the Princess Eldest, who had worked hard in providing care, was granted additional fiefs in Lantian for her bath and hair washing.

The King of Dai of Sishui had passed away earlier, and as he had no heir, his kingdom was abolished. However, a posthumous son, Nuan, was found in the harem. The Chancellor and the Internal History had not reported this, and when the Emperor heard of it, he took pity and established Nuan as the King of Sishui. The Chancellor and the Internal History were both imprisoned.

In the third month, five individuals selected from the commanderies and kingdoms for their virtuous conduct, including Han Fu from Zhuo Commandery, were each granted fifty bolts of silk and sent home. An edict was issued: "We sympathize with the toil of official duties. Let them cultivate filial piety and fraternal duty to teach their local communities. Let the commanderies and counties always grant sheep and wine in the first month. For those who have suffered misfortune, grant them a set of clothes and blankets, and offer sacrifices with a medium-grade animal."

The Di people of Wudu rebelled, and the Commandant of the Capital Guards Ma Shijian, the Marquis of Longqiang Han Zeng, and the Grand Herald Guangming were dispatched with conscripts from the Three Capital Regions and the Minister of Ceremonies, all of whom had been exempted from punishment, to attack them. In the summer, the sixth month, a general amnesty was declared. In the autumn, the seventh month, on the last day of the month, Yihai, there was a total solar eclipse. In the eighth month, the era name was changed from Shiyuan to Yuanfeng.

In the ninth month, the Princess Eldest of Eyi, King Dan of Yan, the Left General Shangguan Jie, Jie's son the General of Agile Cavalry An, and the Imperial Secretary Sang Hongyang all plotted rebellion and were executed. Initially, Jie and his son

An vied for power with the Great General Guang and sought to harm him, falsely sending someone to submit a letter to King Dan of Yan accusing Guang of crimes. At that time, the Emperor was fourteen years old and detected the deceit. Later, when there were those who slandered Guang, the Emperor would angrily say, "The Great General is a loyal minister of the state, entrusted by the late Emperor. Anyone who dares to slander and defame him shall be punished." "Thus, Guang was able to remain loyal to the utmost. The account is found in the biographies of King Yan and Huo Guang."

In the winter, the tenth month, an edict was issued: "The Left General, Marquis of Anyang Jie, the General of Agile Cavalry, Marquis of Sangle An, and the Imperial Secretary Hongyang have all repeatedly used wicked and crooked means to interfere with the regency. The Great General did not heed them, and they harbored resentment, conspiring with King Yan, setting up postal stations for communication and plotting together. King Yan sent the Elder of Shouxi, Sun Zongzhi, and others to bribe the Princess Eldest, Ding Wairen, the Court Attendant Du Yannian, the Chief Clerk of the Great General Gongsun Yi, and others, exchanging private letters, jointly plotting to have the Princess Eldest host a banquet, ambush and kill the Great General Guang, and summon King Yan to be the Son of Heaven, committing great treason and heinous crimes. Therefore, the Inspector of Rice Fields, Yan Cang, discovered it first and informed the Minister of Agriculture Yang, who then told the Admonishing Official Yannian, and Yannian reported it. The Chief Clerk of the Chancellor, Ren Gong, personally captured and beheaded Jie, and the Junior Clerk of the Chancellor, Wang Shou, lured An into the government office, and they have all been executed, bringing peace to the officials and people. Yannian, Cang, Gong, and Shou were all enfeoffed as Marquises." The edict continued, "King Yan was deluded and lost his way, previously conspiring with Liu Ze, the son of the Prince of Qi, and others in rebellion, which was suppressed and not made public, hoping that the King would return to the right path and reform himself. Now, he has conspired with the Princess Eldest and the Left General Jie and others to endanger the ancestral temple. The King and the Princess have both confessed their crimes. We pardon the Crown Prince Jian of the King, the son of the Princess Wenxin, and the sons of the imperial clan who were involved in the conspiracy with King Yan and Shangguan Jie and others, as well as their parents and siblings who should be implicated, and they are all reduced to commoners. The officials who were misled by Jie and others and have not yet been discovered by the officials shall have their crimes forgiven."

In the summer of the second year, the fourth month, the Emperor moved from the Jianzhang Palace to the Weiyang Palace and hosted a grand banquet. The attendants and officials were granted silk, and the sons of the imperial clan were granted two hundred thousand coins each. The officials and people who presented oxen and wine were granted one bolt of silk each.

In the sixth month, a general amnesty was declared. An edict was issued: "We sympathize with the people who are not yet well-provided for. Last year, we reduced the grain transport by three million dan. We have also reduced the number of imperial carriages and horses and the horses in the parks, to supplement the relay horses in the border commanderies and the Three Capital Regions. Let the commanderies and kingdoms not collect the horse tax this year, and the Three Capital Regions and the Minister of Ceremonies' commanderies may use millet to substitute for the taxes." In the spring of the third year, the first month, a large stone on Mount Tai stood up by itself, and a withered willow tree in the Shanglin Park revived and grew.

The taxes from the Zhongmu Park were abolished and given to the poor. An edict was issued: "Recently, the people have suffered from floods and are in great need of food. We have emptied the granaries and sent envoys to relieve the destitute. Let the grain transport be halted for four years. The relief loans issued before the third year, unless requested by the Chancellor or the Imperial Secretary, shall not be collected from the border commanderies that received oxen."

In the summer, the fourth month, the Junior Tutor Xu Ren, the Commandant of Justice Wang Ping, and the Left Administrator of Fengyi Jia Shenghu were all implicated for indulging the rebels. Ren committed suicide, while Ping and Shenghu were executed by waist-cutting. In the winter, the Wuhuan of Liaodong rebelled, and the General of the Household Fan Mingyou was appointed as the General Who Crosses the Liao, leading two thousand cavalry from the seven northern commanderies to attack them.

In the spring of the fourth year, the first month, on the day of Dinghai, the Emperor assumed the cap of manhood and appeared at the Gao Temple. He granted gold, silk, oxen, and wine to the feudal princes, the Chancellor, the Great General, the Marquises, the imperial clan down to the officials and people, each according to their rank. He granted noble titles to those below the rank of two thousand dan and to the people of the empire. The poll tax for the fourth and fifth years was not collected. The unpaid corvée taxes from before the third year were all forgiven. A five-day feast was ordered throughout the empire.

On the day of Jiaxu, the Chancellor Qianqiu passed away.

In the summer, the fourth month, an edict was issued: "The General Who Crosses the Liao, Mingyou, previously as the Colonel of the Qiang Cavalry, led the Qiang kings, lords, and chieftains to attack the rebels in Yizhou, and later led the attack on the rebellious Di in Wudu. Now, he has defeated the Wuhuan, beheading and capturing them, achieving merit. Let Mingyou be enfeoffed as the Marquis of Pingling. The Inspector of Pingle, Fu Jiezi, as an envoy with the imperial credentials, executed King An of Loulan and returned his head to be displayed at the northern gate of the capital. Let him be enfeoffed as the Marquis of Yiyang."

On the day of Dingchou in the fifth month, the main hall of the Filial and Cultured Emperor's temple caught fire, and the Emperor and his ministers all donned plain garments. Two thousand dan officials were dispatched with the five battalions to repair it, and it was completed in six days. The Minister of Ceremonies, the temple officials, and the clerks were all charged with great disrespect, but were pardoned. The Marquis of Liaoyang, De, the Minister of Ceremonies, was reduced to a commoner. In the sixth month, a general amnesty was declared.

In the spring of the fifth year, the first month, the King of Guangling came to court, and his fief was increased by eleven thousand households. He was granted twenty million coins, two hundred catties of gold, two swords, one carriage, and two teams of horses. In the summer, there was a great drought. In the sixth month, unruly youths and officials from the Three Capital Regions and the commanderies and kingdoms who had been reported and accused were conscripted to garrison Liaodong. In the autumn, the Xiangjun was abolished and divided into Yulin and Zangke. In the winter, the eleventh month, there was a great thunderstorm.

On the day of Gengxu in the twelfth month, the Chancellor Xin passed away. In the spring of the sixth year, the first month, conscripts from the commanderies and kingdoms were recruited to build the Xuantu city in Liaodong. In the summer, a general amnesty was declared. An edict was issued: "When grain is cheap, it harms the farmers. Now, the grain in the Three Capital Regions and the Minister of Ceremonies' commanderies is excessively cheap. Let millet be used to substitute for this year's taxes." The Right General Zhang Anshi, who was loyal and diligent in guarding the palace, was enfeoffed as the Marquis of Fuping.

The Wuhuan again invaded the frontier, and the General Who Crosses the Liao, Fan Mingyou, was sent to attack them. In the spring of the Yuanping first year, the second month, an edict was issued: "The empire takes agriculture and sericulture as its foundation. Recently, we have reduced expenditures, abolished non-essential offices, and decreased corvée labor, so that more people are engaged in farming and sericulture. Yet, the people are still not able to provide for their households, and We are deeply concerned. Let the poll tax be reduced." The officials proposed a reduction of thirty percent, and the Emperor approved it.

On the day of Jiashen, in the morning, a meteor as large as the moon appeared, and all the stars followed it westward. In the summer, the fourth month, on the day of Guiwei, the Emperor passed away in the Weiyang Palace. In the sixth month, on the day of Renshen, he was buried at the Pingling Mausoleum.

It is praised: In the past, King Cheng of Zhou succeeded as a child and faced the rebellion of the four states of Guan and Cai spreading slander. Emperor Xiaozhao ascended the throne in his youth and also faced the rebellious plots of Yan, He, and Shangguan. King Cheng did not doubt the Duke of Zhou, and Emperor Xiaozhao entrusted Huo Guang, each achieving fame in their time, how great! Inheriting the legacy of Emperor Wu's extravagance and the exhaustion of the military, the empire was depleted, and the population was halved. Guang understood the crucial issues of the time, reducing corvée and taxes, allowing the people to rest and recuperate. During the periods of Shiyuan and Yuanfeng, peace was made with the Xiongnu, and the people were prosperous. Virtuous and talented scholars were promoted, and the people's grievances were inquired into. The discussions on salt and iron were held, and the monopoly on alcohol was abolished. The posthumous title 'Zhao' was conferred, is it not fitting!

VOLUME 8: RECORDS OF EMPEROR XUAN, NO. 8.

Emperor Xiaoxuan was the great-grandson of Emperor Wu and the grandson of the Crown Prince Li. The Crown Prince married Shi Liangdi, who gave birth to the Imperial Grandson Shi. The Imperial Grandson married Lady Wang, who gave birth to Emperor Xuan, known as the Imperial Great-Grandson. A few months after his birth, the witchcraft affair occurred, and the Crown Prince, Liangdi, the Imperial Grandson, and Lady Wang were all killed. The details are recorded in the biography of the Crown Prince. Although the Great-Grandson was still in swaddling clothes, he was implicated and imprisoned in the commandery prison. Bing Ji, the Commandant of Justice, was investigating the witchcraft affair at the commandery and, pitying the innocent Great-Grandson, had the female convicts Zhao Zhengqing of Huaiyang and Hu Zu of Weicheng take turns nursing him, privately providing food and clothing, treating him with great kindness.

The witchcraft affair dragged on for years without resolution. In the second year of Houyuan, Emperor Wu fell ill and traveled between the Changyang and Wuzuo Palaces. Those who observed the heavens said that there was an imperial aura in the Chang'an prison. The Emperor sent envoys to systematically execute all prisoners in the capital's prisons, regardless of the severity of their crimes. The Palace Attendant Guo Rang arrived at the commandery prison at night, but Bing Ji barred the gate, preventing the envoy from entering, thus saving the Great-Grandson. Following a general amnesty, Bing Ji then transported the Great-Grandson to the home of his grandmother, Shi Liangdi. The details are recorded in the biographies of Bing Ji and the Empress's family.

Later, an edict was issued for the Palace to care for him, and he was registered under the Imperial Clan. At that time, the Palace Administrator Zhang He, who had served the Crown Prince Li, remembered the old kindness and pitied the Great-Grandson, taking great care of him and using his own money to provide for his education. When he came of age, Zhang He arranged for him to marry the daughter of Xu Guanghan, the Overseer of the Prison for Women. The Great-Grandson relied on the support of the Guanghan brothers and his grandmother's family, the Shis. He studied the Book of Songs under the scholar Fu Zhongweng of Donghai, excelling in his studies and loving learning, but he also enjoyed knight-errantry, cockfighting, and horse racing, and was well aware of the corruptions in the villages and the successes and failures of official governance. He frequently visited the imperial tombs, traveling extensively throughout the Three Capital Regions, often finding himself in difficult situations in the salt marshes of Lianshao. He particularly enjoyed the areas between Du and Hu, often staying in Xiadu. When he attended court, he resided in the Shangguan Lane of Chang'an. He had hair on his body and feet, and when he slept, there were often glowing lights. Every time he bought cakes, the vendors he bought from would encounter great enmity, which he found strange.

In the fourth month of the Yuanping first year, Emperor Zhao passed away without an heir. The Grand General Huo Guang requested the Empress to summon the Prince of Changyi. On the day of Bingyin in the sixth month, the Prince received the imperial seal and was honored as Emperor, with the Empress being honored as Empress Dowager. On the day of Guisi, Guang reported that Prince He was licentious and disorderly, and requested his removal. The details are recorded in the biographies of He and Guang.

In the autumn, the seventh month, Guang presented a memorial: "According to the rites, the way of humanity values kinship and thus honors ancestors, and honoring ancestors leads to respecting the clan. The main lineage has no heir, so a virtuous descendant from a collateral branch should be chosen as the heir. The great-grandson of Emperor Xiaowu, Bingyi, was ordered to be cared for in the Palace, and now he is eighteen years old. He has studied the Book of Songs, the Analects, and the Classic of Filial Piety, is of frugal conduct, kind and benevolent, and can be made the heir to Emperor Xiaozhao, to continue the ancestral line and be a father to the people." The memorial was approved. The Imperial Clan Administrator De was sent to the Great-Grandson's residence in Shangguan Lane to prepare him with a bath and to bestow upon him the garments from the imperial wardrobe. The Grand Coachman used a hunting chariot to escort the Great-Grandson to the residence of the Imperial Clan Administrator for purification. On the day of Gengshen, he entered the Weiyang Palace, met with the Empress Dowager, and was enfeoffed as the Marquis of Yangwu. Subsequently, the ministers presented the imperial seal, and he ascended the throne as Emperor, paying homage at the Gao Temple.

On the day of Jisi in the eighth month, the Chancellor Chang passed away. In the ninth month, a general amnesty was declared throughout the empire. On the day of Renzi in the eleventh month, Empress Xu was established. Gifts of money were bestowed upon the princes and below, down to the officials and common people, with varying amounts for the widowed, orphaned, and solitary. The Empress Dowager returned to the Changle Palace. The establishment of garrison guards was initiated.

In the spring of the first year of Benshi, the first month, officials and common people from the commanderies and kingdoms with assets worth a million or more were recruited to move to Pingling. Envoys were dispatched with credentials to instruct the commandery and kingdom governors to diligently nurture the people and promote moral transformation.

The Grand General Guang bowed his head and returned the governance to the Emperor, who modestly declined and continued to entrust him with responsibilities. In recognition of his contribution to the state's stability, the Grand General Guang was granted an additional fief of seventeen thousand households, and the Chariot and Horse General, the Marquis of Fuping, Anshi, was granted ten thousand households. An edict was issued: "The late Chancellor, the Marquis of Anping, Chang, and others, who held their positions and fulfilled their duties, along with the Grand General Guang and the Chariot and Horse General Anshi, proposed and implemented policies to secure the ancestral temple. They passed away before their merits could be rewarded. Therefore, the fiefs of Chang's heir Zhong, the Chancellor the Marquis of Yangping, Yi, the General Who Crosses the Liao, the Marquis of Pingling, Mingyou, the former General the Marquis of Longluo, Zeng, the Grand Coachman the Marquis of Jianping, Yannian, the Minister of Ceremonies the Marquis of Pu, Chang, the Remonstrance Official the Marquis of Yichun, Tan, the Marquis of Dangtu, Ping, the Marquis of Du, Tuqitang, and the Privy Treasurer the Marquis of Guannei, Sheng, shall be increased by varying numbers of households." The Censor-in-Chief Guangming was enfeoffed as the Marquis of Changshui, the Rear General Chongguo as the Marquis of Yingping, the Minister of Agriculture Yannian as the Marquis of Yangcheng, the Privy Treasurer Lecheng as the Marquis of Yuanshi, and the Grandee Secretary Qian as the Marquis of Pingqiu. The Right Assistant Virtue, the Director of Dependent States Wu, the Commandant of Justice Guang, the Imperial Clan Administrator De, the Grand Herald Xian, the Chamberlain for the Palace Administration Ji, the Grandee Secretary Ji, and the Commandant of the Capital District Guanghan were all granted the title of Marquis of Guannei. De and Wu were granted fiefs. [End of edict.]

In the summer, on the day of Gengwu in the fourth month, an

earthquake occurred. An edict was issued for the commanderies and kingdoms within the realm to each recommend one person of high literary achievement.

In the fifth month, phoenixes gathered in Jiaodong and Qiansheng. A general amnesty was declared throughout the empire. Officials with a rank of two thousand piculs, the chancellors of the feudal lords, down to the officials of the capital, eunuch officials, and those with a rank of six hundred piculs were granted varying levels of noble titles, from the Left Adviser to the Fifth Grand Master. All people of the empire were granted one level of noble title, with filial individuals receiving two levels, and women in every hundred households were given oxen and wine. Taxes were exempted.

In the sixth month, an edict was issued: "The late Crown Prince, who was at Hu, has not been given a posthumous title. During the annual sacrifices, a posthumous title should be deliberated, and a garden city should be established." The details are recorded in the biography of the Crown Prince. In the autumn, the seventh month, an edict was issued to establish the Crown Prince Jian of Yanla as the Prince of Guangyang, and the youngest son Hong of the Prince of Guangling Xu as the Prince of Gaomi. In the spring of the second year, funds from the Water Office were used for Pingling, and the people were moved to construct residences.

The Minister of Agriculture, the Marquis of Yangcheng, Tian Yannian, committed a crime and committed suicide.

In the summer, the fifth month, an edict was issued: "I, with my humble self, have inherited the ancestral line, and day and night I ponder how Emperor Xiaowu personally practiced benevolence and righteousness, selected wise generals, and quelled the unsubmissive, causing the Xiongnu to flee far away, and pacified the Di, Qiang, Kunming, and Nanyue, so that all barbarians turned towards our culture, and came to our borders to offer tribute; he established the Imperial University, repaired the suburban sacrifices, fixed the calendar, and harmonized the musical tones; he sealed Mount Tai, blocked the Xuanfang, and auspicious signs responded, with the precious tripod appearing and a white unicorn being captured. His virtues and achievements were abundant and could not be fully proclaimed, yet the temple music did not match. Let it be discussed and reported." The officials requested that an honorific title be added. On the day of Gengwu in the sixth month, the temple of Emperor Xiaowu was honored as the Temple of Shizong, and the dances of Shengde, Wenshi, and Wuxing were performed, with the Son of Heaven offering sacrifices for generations. Temples were established in all the commanderies and kingdoms that Emperor Wu had visited during his tours. The people were granted one level of noble title, and women in every hundred households were given oxen and wine.

The Xiongnu repeatedly invaded the borders and also launched an expedition to the west against the Wusun. The Kunmi of the Wusun and the princess, through the state's envoys, conveyed that the Kunmi was willing to mobilize the elite troops of the state to attack the Xiongnu, and they beseeched the Son of Heaven to take pity and send troops to rescue the princess. In the autumn, a large mobilization was initiated, calling upon light chariots and sharp soldiers from the Guandong region, and selecting officials from the commanderies and kingdoms with a rank of three hundred piculs who were strong and skilled in archery and horsemanship, all of whom joined the army. The Censor-in-Chief Tian Guangming was appointed as the General of Qilian, the Rear General Zhao Chongguo as the General of Pulei, the Grand Administrator of Yunzhong Tian Shun as the General of Tiger Teeth, along with the General Who Crosses the Liao Fan Mingyou and the former General Han Zeng, making a total of five generals with a force of one hundred and fifty thousand cavalry. The Commandant Chang Hui, holding the imperial credentials, was to oversee the Wusun troops, and all were to attack the Xiongnu.

In the spring of the third year, on the day of Guihai in the first month, Empress Xu passed away. On the day of Wuchen, the five generals led their troops from Chang'an. In the summer, the fifth month, the army was disbanded. The General of Qilian Guangming and the General of Tiger Teeth Shun were found guilty and handed over to the officials, both committing suicide. The Commandant Chang Hui led the Wusun troops into the right territory of the Xiongnu, achieving a great victory and capturing much, and was enfeoffed as a Marquis.

There was a severe drought. In the commanderies and kingdoms that were severely affected by the drought, the people were exempted from paying taxes. The people of the three auxiliary regions who moved to cheaper areas were also exempted from conscription until the end of the fourth year. On the day of Jichou in the sixth month, the Chancellor Yi passed away.

In the spring of the fourth year, the first month, an edict was issued: "It is heard that agriculture is the foundation of virtue's prosperity. This year's harvest has failed, and envoys have already been dispatched to provide relief to the destitute. Let the Grand Provisioner reduce the meals and the number of animals slaughtered, and the Music Bureau decrease the number of musicians, sending them back to agriculture. From the Chancellor down to the Directors and Assistants of the Capital, they shall submit reports on the grain, transporting it to the granaries of Chang'an to assist in lending to the poor. People who transport grain into the passes by cart or boat are exempt from needing a permit."

On the day of Yimao in the third month, Empress Huo was established. Gifts of money and silk were bestowed upon the Chancellor down to the court officials and their subordinates, each according to their rank. A general amnesty was declared throughout the empire.

On the day of Renyin in the summer, the fourth month, earthquakes occurred in forty-nine commanderies and kingdoms, with some mountains collapsing and waters gushing forth. An edict was issued: "Disasters and anomalies are warnings from heaven and earth. I, who have inherited the great enterprise, serve the ancestral temple, and am placed above the scholars and people, have not been able to harmonize all living beings. Recently, earthquakes in Beihai and Langya have damaged the ancestral temples, and I am deeply fearful. Let the Chancellor and the Censor, along with the Marquisates and officials of two thousand piculs, broadly inquire among scholars of the classics, to find ways to respond to these changes and assist me in my shortcomings, without any concealment. Let the three auxiliary regions, the Minister of Ceremonies, and the commanderies and kingdoms within the realm each recommend one person who is virtuous and upright. Where there are laws and decrees that can be abolished to bring peace to the people, let them be itemized and reported. In places severely damaged by earthquakes, do not collect taxes." A great amnesty was declared throughout the empire. The Emperor, due to the collapse of the ancestral temple, wore plain clothes and avoided the main hall for five days.

In the fifth month, phoenixes gathered in Anqiu and Chunyu of Beihai. In the autumn, the Prince of Guangchuan Ji committed a crime, was deposed and exiled to Shangyong, where he committed suicide. In the spring of the first year of Dijie, the first month, a comet appeared in the west. In the third month, the commanderies and kingdoms lent land to the poor people.

In the summer, the sixth month, an edict was issued: "It is heard that Yao was close to his nine clans, and thus harmonized the myriad states. I, who have received the bequeathed virtue and am upholding the sacred enterprise, think of the members of the imperial clan who have not been fully included and have been cut off due to crimes. If there are those with virtuous talents who have reformed and encourage good deeds, let them be reinstated, allowing them to make a fresh start." In the winter, the eleventh month, the Prince of Chu Yanshou plotted rebellion and committed suicide. On the last day of the twelfth month, Guihai, there was a solar eclipse.

In the spring of the second year, the third month, on the day of Gengwu, the Grand Marshal and General-in-Chief Guang passed away. An edict was issued: "The Grand Marshal and General-in-Chief, the Marquis of Bolu, who guarded Emperor Xiaowu for over thirty years and assisted Emperor Xiaozhao for more than ten years, faced great calamities, personally upheld righteousness, and led the Three Excellencies, the feudal lords, the Nine Ministers, and the grandees in formulating strategies for eternity, thereby bringing peace to the ancestral temple. The common people of the empire all enjoyed peace and tranquility, and his virtues and achievements were abundant. I greatly commend him. His descendants shall be restored, their fiefs and cities shall be maintained, and they shall be exempt from all obligations for generations. His achievements are akin to those of the Chancellor of State Xiao."

In the summer, the fourth month, phoenixes gathered in the commandery of Lu, and a flock of birds followed them. A great amnesty was declared throughout the empire. In the fifth month, the Grandee Secretary, Marquis of Pingqiu, Wang Qian, committed a crime, was imprisoned, and died.

The Emperor began to personally handle governmental affairs and, thinking to repay the virtues and achievements of the General-in-Chief, reappointed the Marquis of Leping, Shan, to oversee the affairs of the Imperial Secretariat. He ordered the ministers to submit sealed memorials to inform him of the conditions below. Every five days, he would hold an audience to receive reports from officials on their duties, to relay their words, and to test their capabilities and achievements. The Palace Attendants and the Imperial Secretaries, whose merits warranted promotion or who had exceptional virtues, were generously rewarded, and their descendants were permanently exempt from changes. The administration was thorough and meticulous, the regulations were complete, and the hierarchy was harmonious, with no room for negligence.

In the spring of the third year, the third month, an edict was issued: "It is heard that if merit is not rewarded and crimes are not punished, even the times of Tang and Yu could not transform the world. Now, the Chancellor of Jiaodong, Cheng, has been diligent and unwearied in his labors, and the floating population has registered over eighty thousand people, and his governance is of an exceptional level. Let his rank be elevated to two thousand piculs, and he shall be granted the title of Marquis within the Passes."

Furthermore, it was said: "The widowers, widows, orphans, and the elderly who are poor and in distress are those whom I pity. Previously, an edict was issued to lend public fields and provide seeds and food. Let there be an additional gift of silk to the widowers, widows, orphans, and the elderly. The officials of two thousand piculs must strictly instruct their subordinates to treat them with care and not to neglect their duties." An order was issued for the commanderies and kingdoms within the realm to recommend those who are virtuous and upright and can be close to the people.

In the summer, the fourth month, on the day of Wushen, the Crown Prince was established, and a great amnesty was declared throughout the empire. The Censor-in-Chief was granted the title of Marquis within the Passes, and officials of two thousand piculs were granted the title of Right Common Chief. All those in the empire who were to succeed their fathers were granted one rank. The Prince of Guangling was bestowed with a thousand jin of gold, and fifteen feudal lords were each bestowed with a hundred jin of gold. Eighty-seven marquises in their states were each bestowed with twenty jin of gold.

In the winter, the tenth month, an edict was issued: "On the day of Renshen in the ninth month, there was an earthquake, and I am deeply fearful. If there are those who can admonish me for my faults, as well as those who are virtuous, upright, and forthright in their counsel to assist me in my shortcomings, let them not hesitate to speak out. I, lacking in virtue, have not been able to draw close to those afar, and thus the garrisons on the borders have not ceased. Now, the troops are being ordered to fortify and garrison again, causing prolonged hardship to the people, which is not the way to bring peace to the empire. Let the garrisons of the General of Chariots and Cavalry and the Right General be disbanded. Furthermore, an edict was issued: "The ponds and lakes that have not been visited by the Emperor shall be lent to the poor people. The palaces and lodges in the commanderies and kingdoms shall not be repaired. Those who are returning from being displaced shall be lent public fields and provided with seeds and food, and they shall be exempt from taxation and conscription."

In the eleventh month, an edict was issued: "I, who am inadequate and have not guided the people clearly, rise early in anxiety, pondering the myriad aspects of governance, never forgetting the common people. Fearing that I might disgrace the sage virtue of the late Emperor, I have thus promoted the virtuous and upright to be close to the myriad surnames. Over the years, we have reached this point, yet the transformation of customs is lacking. The classics say: 'Filial piety and fraternal duty are the roots of benevolence!' Let the commanderies and kingdoms each recommend one person who is known for their filial piety, fraternal duty, and righteous conduct in their village." "

In the twelfth month, for the first time, four Justices of the Court were established, with a rank of six hundred piculs. The commandery of Wenshan was abolished and merged into Shu. In the spring of the fourth year, the second month, the Emperor's maternal grandmother was enfeoffed as the Lady of Boping, and the great-grandson of the former Marquis of Zan, Xiao He, Jian Shi, was enfeoffed as a marquis.

An edict was issued: "Guiding the people with filial piety will bring harmony to the empire. Now, there are common people who suffer from mourning clothes and calamities, yet the officials impose corvée labor, preventing them from conducting burials, which grieves the hearts of filial sons. I deeply pity them. From now on, those who have grandparents or parents in mourning shall be exempt from corvée labor, allowing them to carry out the funeral and fulfill their filial duties."

In the summer, the fifth month, an edict was issued: "The affection between father and son, the way of husband and wife, are natural instincts. Even in the face of calamity, they would rather face death to preserve it. Sincere love is bound in the heart, the utmost in benevolence and kindness, how can it be violated! From now on, if a son conceals his parents, a wife conceals her husband, or a grandchild conceals grandparents, they shall not be held accountable. If parents conceal their son, a husband conceals his wife, or grandparents conceal their grandchild, in cases of capital crimes, all shall be reported to the Court of Justice for review." "

The grandson of the late King Hui of Guangchuan, Wen, was established as the King of Guangchuan.

In the autumn, the seventh month, the Grand Marshal Huo Yu plotted rebellion. An edict was issued: "Recently, Zhang She, the Clerk of the Eastern Weaving Workshop, sent the powerful Li Jing of Wei Commandery to inform the Marquis of Guanyang, Huo Yun, of the plot to commit great treason. Out of consideration for the General-in-Chief, I suppressed and did not publicize it, hoping for their self-renewal. Now, the Grand Marshal, Marquis of Bolu, Yu, along with his mother, the Lady Xian of Xuancheng Marquis, and his cousins, the Marquis of Guanyang, Yun, the Marquis of Leping, Shan, their brothers-in-law, General Fan Mingyou of Du Liao, the Junior Tutor of the Empress Dowager, Deng Guanghan, the Commandant of the Gentlemen-of-the-Household, Ren Sheng, the Commandant of

Cavalry, Zhao Ping, and the commoner Feng Yin of Chang'an, have conspired to commit great treason. Previously, Xian had also sent the female court physician Chunyu Yan to administer poison to kill the Empress Gong'ai and plotted to poison the Crown Prince, intending to endanger the ancestral temple. Their treason and disorder are without principle, and all have been found guilty. Those who were misled by the Huo family and have not yet been discovered by the officials are all pardoned and exempted." On the day of Jiyou in the eighth month, the Empress Huo was deposed.

In the ninth month, an edict was issued: "I consider that the people have lost their livelihoods and are not self-sufficient, so I have dispatched envoys to tour the commanderies and kingdoms to inquire about the hardships of the people. There are officials who seek personal gain and cause trouble, disregarding their faults, and I deeply pity this. This year, many commanderies and kingdoms have suffered from floods, and relief has already been provided. Salt is the food of the people, yet the prices are universally high, causing great distress to the populace. Let the price of salt be reduced throughout the empire."

Furthermore, it was said: "By Decree A, the dead cannot be brought back to life, and the punished cannot be restored. This was valued by the late Emperor, yet the officials have not acted accordingly. Now, those imprisoned sometimes die in prison from beatings or from hunger and cold—what is the heart behind such inhumane acts! I am deeply pained by this. Let the commanderies and kingdoms annually report the names, counties, ranks, and villages of those prisoners who have died from beatings or from hunger and cold in prison, and let the Chancellor and the Censor assess the best and worst and report them to me."

In the twelfth month, the King of Qinghe, Nian, committed a crime and was deposed and exiled to Fangling. In the spring of the first year of the Yuankang era, the eastern plain of Du was chosen as the initial mausoleum, and Du County was renamed Duling. The Chancellor, generals, marquises, officials of two thousand piculs, and those with wealth of a million were relocated to Duling.

In the third month, an edict was issued: "Recently, phoenixes gathered on Mount Tai and in Chenliu, and sweet dew descended upon the Weiyang Palace. I have not been able to manifest the splendid achievements of the late Emperor, to harmonize and pacify the people, to accord with heaven and earth, to regulate the sequence of the four seasons, yet I have been graced with auspicious signs, bestowed with these blessings of fortune. Day and night I am vigilant, without any trace of arrogance, reflecting inwardly without respite, eternally mindful of the boundless. Does not the Book say? 'The phoenix comes to grace, and the multitude is in harmony.' Let all exiles in the empire be pardoned, and let diligent officials from two thousand piculs down to six hundred piculs be granted noble ranks, from the Gentlemen-of-the-Household to the Fifth Rank Grandee, assistant officials and above be promoted two ranks, the common people one rank, and every hundred households of women be given an ox and wine." In addition, gifts of silk shall be bestowed upon the widowers, widows, orphans, and the childless, the Three Elders, and the filial and fraternal hardworking farmers. The relief loans provided shall not be collected."

In the summer, the fifth month, the temple of the late Emperor's father was established. The households of the Fengming Garden were increased to form Fengming County. The descendants of the one hundred and thirty-six families of meritorious officials of Emperor Gaozu, such as the Marquis of Jiang, Zhou Bo, were restored, and they were ordered to continue the sacrificial rites, generation after generation without end. For those without heirs, the next in line was restored.

In the autumn, the eighth month, an edict was issued: "I am not versed in the six arts, troubled by the great way, hence the untimeliness of yin and yang, wind and rain. Let there be a broad recommendation of officials and commoners, those who have corrected themselves, are proficient in literature, and understand the methods of the ancient kings, to expound and investigate their meanings, two persons each, and one person each from those of two thousand piculs." In the winter, the Jianzhang Guard Commandant was established.

In the spring of the second year, the first month, an edict was issued: "The Book says 'King Wen made punishments, and those who were punished were not pardoned.' Now, the officials cultivate themselves and uphold the law, yet none have been able to satisfy my intentions, and I am deeply troubled by this. Let the empire be pardoned, and let the officials and gentlemen strive diligently for a new beginning." On the day of Yichou in the second month, Empress Wang was established. Gifts of money and silk were bestowed upon the Chancellor down to the accompanying officials, each according to their rank.

In the third month, as phoenixes and sweet dew descended and gathered, officials throughout the empire were granted two ranks of nobility, the common people one rank, every hundred households of women were given an ox and wine, and the elderly widowers, widows, orphans, and the childless were bestowed with silk.

In the summer, the fifth month, an edict was issued: "Prisons are the fate of the myriad people, established to prohibit violence and stop evil, and to nurture the multitude. If they can make the living not resentful and the dead not hateful, then they can be called cultured officials. Now, this is not the case. In applying the law, some harbor cunning hearts, split the statutes into two ends, with uneven depth and shallowness, adding words to embellish faults, to complete the crime. Memorials are not truthful, and the ruler also has no way to know.

This is my lack of clarity and the officials' lack of merit, how will the people of the four directions look up to us! Let the officials of two thousand piculs each inspect their subordinates and not employ such people. Officials must enforce the law fairly. Some arbitrarily initiate corvée labor, decorate kitchens and guesthouses, claim to exceed in serving envoys and guests, overstep their duties and violate the law, to gain fame and reputation, akin to treading on thin ice while awaiting the daylight, is it not perilous! Now, the empire is greatly afflicted by the disaster of epidemics, and I am deeply troubled by this. Let those commanderies and kingdoms severely affected by the disaster not pay this year's land tax and corvée."

It was also said: "I have heard that the names of the ancient Son of Heaven were difficult to know but easy to avoid. Now, many commoners submit writings that inadvertently violate the taboo and thus commit crimes, and I deeply pity them. Let the taboo be changed to 'Xun.' Those who have violated the taboo before this decree are pardoned." In the winter, Zhao Guanghan, the Governor of the Capital, committed a crime and was executed by waist severing.

In the spring of the third year, as the divine birds gathered several times on Mount Tai, gold was bestowed upon the feudal princes, the Chancellor, generals, marquises, and officials of two thousand piculs, and silk was given to the accompanying officials, each according to their rank. Officials throughout the empire were granted two ranks of nobility, the common people one rank, every hundred households of women were given an ox and wine, and the elderly widowers, widows, orphans, and the childless were bestowed with silk.

In the third month, an edict was issued: "It is heard that when Xiang committed a crime, Shun enfeoffed him. The kinship of flesh and bone is clear yet not severed. Let the former King of Changyi, He, be enfeoffed as the Marquis of Haihun."

It was also said: "In my humble beginnings, the Grandee

Secretary Bing Ji, the General of the Household Gentlemen Shi Zeng, Shi Xuan, the Commandant of the Changle Guard Xu Shun, and the Palace Attendant and Grandee for Splendid Happiness Xu Yanshou all had old kindnesses with me. And the former Director of the Rear Palace Zhang He guided and assisted my person, cultivated literature and the classics, with exceptional kindness and grace, his merit was abundant. Does not the Book of Songs say? 'There is no virtue that is not repaid.' Let Pengzu, the son of He's brother and the Palace Attendant General of the Household Gentlemen, be enfeoffed as the Marquis of Yangdu, and let He be posthumously awarded the title of Marquis Ai of Yangdu. Ji, Zeng, Xuan, Shun, and Yanshou were all made marquises. Old friends down to the repeat offenders in the commandery prison who had the merit of protection all received official positions, salaries, fields, residences, and goods, each according to the depth of their kindness to repay them."

In the summer, the sixth month, an edict was issued: "In the summer of the previous year, the divine birds gathered in Yong. This spring, tens of thousands of colorful birds flew over the subordinate counties, soaring and dancing, wanting to gather but not descending. Let the three regions not be allowed to disturb nests or probe eggs in spring and summer, nor to shoot at flying birds. Make this a decree." The imperial son Qin was established as the King of Huaiyang.

The Grandee for Splendid Happiness Qiang and eleven others were dispatched to travel throughout the empire, to inquire after the widowers and widows, to observe customs and traditions, to inspect the successes and failures of official governance, and to recommend outstanding talents and those of extraordinary character. In the second month, the Inspector of Hedong, Huo Zhengshi, and others plotted rebellion and were executed.

In the third month, an edict was issued: "Recently, the divine birds of five colors, in tens of thousands, gathered in the

Changle, Weiyang, Beigong, Gaoqin, and Ganquan Taizhi Palace halls and the Shanglin Garden. My inadequacy, my scant virtue and generosity, have repeatedly been met with auspicious signs, not by my merit. Let officials throughout the empire be granted two ranks of nobility, the common people one rank, every hundred households of women be given an ox and wine. Additionally, the Three Elders, the filial and fraternal hardworking farmers are to be bestowed with silk, two bolts per person, and the widowers, widows, orphans, and the childless are each to be given one bolt. ."

In the autumn, the eighth month, the son of the former Right Assistant of the Capital, Yin Wenggui, was bestowed with a hundred catties of gold to continue his sacrificial rites. Also, the descendants of meritorious officials were each given twenty catties of gold. On the day of Bingyin, the Grand Marshal and General of the Guards, Anshi, passed away. The year was bountiful, and the price of grain was five coins per peck.

In the spring of the first year of Shenjue, the first month, the emperor traveled to Ganquan to perform the suburban sacrifice at the Taizhi Altar. In the third month, he traveled to Hedong to sacrifice to the Earth God. An edict was issued: "I have inherited the ancestral temple, trembling with fear, only managing myriad affairs, yet not fully illuminating their principles. In the fourth year of Yuankang, auspicious grains and black millet descended upon the commanderies and kingdoms, the divine birds repeatedly gathered, golden mushrooms with nine stems grew in the bronze pool of the Hande Hall, Jiuzhen presented a rare beast, and Nan Commandery captured a white tiger and a majestic phoenix as treasures. My lack of clarity, startled by precious things, I disciplined myself and purified my essence, praying for the sake of the people. Crossing the great river to the east, the weather was clear and calm, and divine fish danced in the river. I visited the Palace of Ten Thousand Years, where the divine birds soared and gathered. My lack of virtue, I fear I am not up to the task. Let the fifth year be the first year of Shenjue.

Officials throughout the empire who are diligent in their duties are granted two ranks of nobility, the common people one rank, every hundred households of women are given an ox and wine, and the elderly widowers, widows, orphans, and the childless are bestowed with silk. The materials for relief and loans shall not be collected." The fields passed by shall not be subject to land tax.

The Western Qiang rebelled, and the conscripted laborers from the three regions and the capital's officials who had their sentences relaxed, along with the recruited archers, the orphaned sons of the Imperial Forest, the cavalry of the Hu and Yue, the skilled officers from Sanhe, Yingchuan, Pei, Huaiyang, and Runan, and the cavalry and Qiang riders from Jincheng, Longxi, Tianshui, Anding, Beidi, and Shang commanderies, were sent to Jincheng. In the summer, the fourth month, the Rear General Zhao Chongguo and the Crossbow General Xu Yanshou were dispatched to attack the Western Qiang.

In the sixth month, a comet appeared in the east. Immediately, the Grand Administrator of Jiuquan, Xin Wuxian, was appointed as the General Who Breaks the Qiang, and he advanced together with the two generals. An edict was issued: "The army is exposed, and the transportation of supplies is burdensome. Let the feudal princes, marquises, and the kings and chieftains of the barbarians who are due to attend court in the second year all be exempted from attending court."

In the autumn, the son of the former Minister of Agriculture, Zhu Yi, was bestowed with a hundred catties of gold to continue his sacrificial rites. The Rear General Chongguo proposed a plan for military agricultural colonies, which is detailed in the biography of Chongguo. In the spring of the second year, the second month, an edict was issued: "On the day of Yichou in the first month, phoenixes and sweet dew descended and gathered in the capital, accompanied by tens of thousands of birds. My lack of virtue has repeatedly been met with heavenly blessings, and I serve with reverence and without negligence. Let the empire be pardoned."

In the summer, the fifth month, the Qiang captives surrendered, and their chief instigator, the great chieftain Yang Yu, and the leader Fei were beheaded. A dependent state of Jincheng was established to settle the surrendered Qiang. In the autumn, the King of Rizhu of the Xiongnu, Xianxian Chan, led more than ten thousand of his people to surrender. The Protector of the Western Regions and Commandant of Cavalry, Zheng Ji, was sent to welcome Rizhu and defeat Cheshi, and all were enfeoffed as marquises. In the ninth month, the Colonel Director of the Imperial Clan, Gai Kuanrao, was found guilty and handed over to the officials, whereupon he committed suicide.

The Chanyu of the Xiongnu sent a renowned king to offer tribute and to celebrate the first month, marking the beginning of peaceful relations. In the spring of the third year, the Leyou Garden was established. On the day of Bingwu in the third month, the Chancellor Xiang passed away. In the autumn, the eighth month, an edict was issued: "If officials are not honest and fair, then the way of governance declines. Now, minor officials are all diligent in their duties, but their salaries are meager, and it is difficult for them not to encroach upon and exploit the people. Let the salaries of officials below one hundred dan be increased by fifteen."

In the spring of the fourth year, the second month, an edict was issued: "Recently, phoenixes and sweet dew descended and gathered in the capital, and auspicious omens appeared together. The sacrifices to Taiyi, the Five Emperors, and the Earth God were performed, praying for blessings and fortune for the people. Tens of thousands of phoenixes flew up, soaring and hovering, gathering and alighting nearby. On the eve of the fasting, divine light was strikingly manifest. On the evening of the offering of aromatic wine, divine light intermingled. Some descended from heaven, some ascended from the earth, and some came from all directions to gather at the altar. The Supreme Deity favored and approved, and the entire realm received blessings. Let the empire be pardoned, the people be granted one rank of nobility, every hundred households of women be given an ox and wine, and the elderly widowers, widows, orphans, and the childless be bestowed with silk."

In the summer, the fourth month, the Grand Administrator of Yingchuan, Huang Ba, was promoted to the rank of two thousand dan for his exceptional governance and was enfeoffed as a Marquis within the Pass, bestowed with a hundred catties of gold. The officials and people of Yingchuan who acted righteously were granted two ranks of nobility, hardworking farmers one rank, and chaste women and obedient daughters were bestowed with silk. An order was issued for the commanderies and kingdoms within the empire to each recommend one virtuous and capable person who could be close to the people. In the fifth month, the Chanyu of the Xiongnu sent his younger brother, King Huliuruo Shengzhi, to attend court.

In the winter, the tenth month, eleven phoenixes gathered at Duling. In the eleventh month, the Grand Administrator of Henan, Yan Yannian, was found guilty and executed in the marketplace. In the twelfth month, phoenixes gathered at Shanglin. In the spring of the first year of Wufeng, the first month, the emperor traveled to Ganquan to perform the suburban sacrifice at the Taizhi Altar.

The Crown Prince came of age. The Empress Dowager bestowed silk upon the Chancellor, generals, marquises, and officials of two thousand dan, one hundred bolts each, and to the great ladies, eighty bolts each. Additionally, the heirs of marquises were granted the rank of Fifth Rank Grandee, and men who were the successors of their fathers were granted one rank of nobility. In the summer, those who were conscripted laborers at Duling were pardoned. On the first day of the twelfth month, Bingyou, a solar eclipse occurred. The Left Assistant of the Capital, Han

Yanshou, was found guilty and executed in the marketplace.

In the spring of the second year, the third month, the emperor traveled to Yong to sacrifice at the Five Altars. In the summer, the fourth month, on the day of Jichou, the Grand Marshal and General of Chariots and Cavalry, Zeng, passed away.

In the autumn, the eighth month, an edict was issued: "The rites of marriage are of great importance in human relationships; the gatherings of wine and food are means to perform rites and music. Now, some officials of two thousand dan in the commanderies and kingdoms arbitrarily impose harsh prohibitions, forbidding the people from holding wine and food gatherings to celebrate weddings. This has led to the abandonment of the rites of the community, causing the people to lose their joy, which is not the way to guide them. Does the Book of Songs not say? 'When the people lose their virtue, even dry provisions become a fault.' Do not implement harsh policies. ."

In the winter, the eleventh month, the Chanyu of the Xiongnu, Huchilei, led his people to surrender and was enfeoffed as a marquis. In the twelfth month, the Marquis of Pingtong, Yang Yun, who had previously served as the Minister of the Household and was found guilty, was dismissed and reduced to a commoner. Unrepentant and harboring resentment, he committed a great act of impiety and was executed by waist severing. In the spring of the third year, the first month, on the day of Guimao, the Chancellor Ji passed away.

In the third month, the emperor traveled to Hedong to sacrifice to the Earth God. An edict was issued: "In the past, the Xiongnu repeatedly raided the borders, and the people suffered from their harm. I have ascended to the supreme position, yet I have not been able to pacify the Xiongnu. The Chanyu Xulü Quanqu requested peace and marriage but fell ill and died. The Right Virtuous King Tuqitang took his place. The flesh-and-blood ministers enthroned the son of Chanyu Xulü Quanqu as

Huhanxie Chanyu, who killed Tuqitang. The various kings each established themselves, dividing into five Chanyus, and attacked each other, resulting in tens of thousands of deaths, the loss of eight or nine out of ten livestock, and the people suffering from hunger, resorting to burning and looting for food, leading to great chaos. The wives and descendants of the Chanyu, his brothers, along with Huchilei Chanyu, renowned kings, the Right Yizhi, Juqu, and Danghu, led over fifty thousand people to surrender and return to righteousness. The Chanyu acknowledged himself as a subject, sending his younger brother to present treasures and celebrate the first month at court, bringing peace to the northern borders, with no military conflicts. I have disciplined myself and fasted, sacrificed to the Supreme Deity in the suburbs, and offered sacrifices to the Earth God. Divine light appeared together, some rising from the valleys, illuminating the palace for over ten moments. Sweet dew descended, and divine birds gathered. I have already ordered the officials to report and offer sacrifices to the Supreme Deity and the ancestral temples. On the day of Xinchou in the third month, phoenixes gathered again on the trees within the eastern gate of the Changle Palace, flew down and alighted on the ground, displaying patterns of five colors, remaining for over ten moments, observed by both officials and people. I am not wise and fear I am not up to the task, yet I have repeatedly been blessed with auspicious signs, receiving this fortune. Does the Book of Documents not say? 'Though at rest, do not rest, and serve with reverence without negligence.' Let the dukes, ministers, and high officials strive diligently." The poll tax for the empire was reduced. Those sentenced to death and below were pardoned. The people were granted one rank of nobility, and every hundred households of women were given an ox and wine. A grand feast was held for five days. Additional silk was bestowed upon the elderly widowers, widows, orphans, and the childless.

A dependent state was established in Xihe and Beidi to settle the surrendered Xiongnu. In the spring of the fourth year, the first month, Prince Xu of Guangling was found guilty and committed suicide. The Chanyu of the Xiongnu acknowledged himself as a subject and sent his younger brother, the King of Guli, to serve at court. With the absence of bandits on the borders, the number of garrison soldiers was reduced by twenty percent. The Grand Minister of Agriculture, Zhongcheng Geng Shouchang, proposed the establishment of ever-normal granaries to supply the northern borders, saving on transportation. He was enfeoffed as a Marquis within the Pass.

In the summer, the fourth month, on the day of Xinchou, the last day of the month, a solar eclipse occurred. An edict was issued: "The heavens have shown an anomaly to warn me, indicating my inadequacy and the incompetence of my officials. Previously, I sent envoys to inquire about the people's hardships, and now I am again dispatching twenty-four assistants of the Chancellor and the Censor to tour the empire, to redress wrongful imprisonments and to investigate those who arbitrarily impose harsh prohibitions and severe punishments without reform." In the spring of the first year of Ganlu, the first month, the emperor traveled to Ganquan to perform the suburban sacrifice at the Taizhi Altar.

The Chanyu of the Xiongnu, Huhanxie, sent his son, the Right Virtuous King Zhulou Qutang, to serve at court. On the day of Dingsi in the second month, the Grand Marshal and General of Chariots and Cavalry, Yanshou, passed away. In the summer, the fourth month, a yellow dragon appeared in Xinfeng. On the day of Bingshen, the temple of the Supreme Emperor caught fire. On the day of Jiachen, the temple of Emperor Wen caught fire. The emperor wore plain clothes for five days. In the winter, the Chanyu of the Xiongnu sent his younger brother, the Left Virtuous King, to attend court and offer congratulations.

In the spring of the second year, the first month, the emperor's son Xiao was established as the King of Dingtao.

An edict was issued: "Recently, phoenixes and sweet dew have descended and gathered, yellow dragons have ascended and flourished, sweet springs have flowed abundantly, withered plants have flourished anew, and divine light has appeared together, all receiving auspicious signs. Let the empire be pardoned. The people's poll tax is reduced by thirty. The feudal lords, the Chancellor, generals, marquises, and officials of two thousand dan are bestowed with varying amounts of gold and money. The people are granted one rank of nobility, every hundred households of women are given an ox and wine, and the elderly widowers, widows, orphans, and the childless are bestowed with silk."

In the summer, the fourth month, the Protectorate Commandant Lu was sent to lead troops to attack Zhuya. In the autumn, the ninth month, the emperor's son Yu was established as the King of Dongping. In the winter, the twelfth month, the emperor traveled to the Fuyang Palace and the Zhuyu Pavilion.

The Chanyu of the Xiongnu, Huhanxie, arrived at the Wuyuan Pass, willing to present the treasures of his state at court in the first month of the third year. An edict was issued for the officials to discuss. All said: "The system of the sage kings is to bestow virtue and perform rites, first the capital and then the various Xia states, first the various Xia states and then the barbarians. The Book of Songs says: 'Following the rites without overstepping, then looking and already acting. The soil is fierce and strong, beyond the seas there is arrival.' Your Majesty's sage virtue fills heaven and earth, and its light reaches the four corners. The Chanyu of the Xiongnu, attracted by the customs and admiring righteousness, unites the whole country in presenting treasures and offering congratulations, which has never happened since ancient times. The Chanyu is not one who has been added by the correct calendar, but is a guest of the king, and the etiquette should be like that of the feudal lords, calling himself a subject and daring to die, bowing twice, and his position should be below the feudal lords." An edict was issued:

"I have heard that the Five Emperors and the Three Kings did not apply rites where they could not reach with governance. Now, the Chanyu of the Xiongnu calls himself a northern vassal and comes to court in the first month. My inadequacy means my virtue cannot be broadly spread. Let him be treated with guest rites, and his position be above the feudal lords."

In the spring of the third year, the first month, the emperor traveled to Ganquan to perform the suburban sacrifice at the Taizhi Altar.

The Chanyu of the Xiongnu, Huhanxie Jihousi, came to court, praised and greeted as a vassal without naming himself. He was bestowed with a seal and ribbon, a crown and belt, robes, a peaceful carriage, four horses, gold, brocade, silk, and cotton. Officials were sent to guide the Chanyu first to his residence in Chang'an, staying at Changping. The emperor stayed at the Chiyang Palace from Ganquan. The emperor ascended the Changping Slope and issued an edict that the Chanyu should not greet. His retinue of Danghu and others were all arranged to watch, and the leaders and kings of the barbarians, tens of thousands in number, lined the road to welcome him. The emperor ascended the Wei Bridge, and all hailed with ten thousand years. The Chanyu went to his residence. A banquet was held at the Jianzhang Palace, feasting and bestowing the Chanyu, displaying treasures. In the second month, the Chanyu departed and returned. The Commandant of Changle, Marquis Gaochang Zhong, the Commandant of Chariots and Cavalry Chang, and the Commandant of Cavalry Hu led sixteen thousand cavalry to escort the Chanyu. The Chanyu resided south of the desert, protecting the Guanglu City. An edict was issued to provide grain to the northern borders. The Chanyu Zhizhi fled far away, and the Xiongnu were thus pacified.

An edict was issued: "Recently, phoenixes gathered in Xincai, and flocks of birds arranged themselves in rows on all sides, all facing the phoenixes, numbering in the tens of thousands.

Let the Prefect of Runan be bestowed with one hundred bolts of silk, and the officials of Xincai, the three elders, the filial and brotherly, the strong and diligent, the widowers, widows, orphans, and the childless be bestowed with varying amounts. The people are granted two ranks of nobility. Let this year's taxes be waived." On the day of Jichou in the third month, the Chancellor Ba passed away.

An edict was issued for scholars to discuss the similarities and differences of the Five Classics. The Grand Tutor of the Heir Apparent, Xiao Wangzhi, and others submitted their discussions, and the emperor personally presided over the decision. Thus, the Liangqiu Yi, the Great and Lesser Xiahou Shangshu, and the Guliang Chunqiu were established as academic chairs. In the winter, the Princess of Wusun returned. In the summer of the fourth year, Prince Haiyang of Guangchuan was found guilty, deposed, and exiled to Fangling. On the day of Dingmao in the winter, the tenth month, the Xuanshi Pavilion of the Weiyang Palace caught fire.

In the spring of the first year of Huanglong, the first month, the emperor traveled to Ganquan to perform the suburban sacrifice at the Taizhi Altar. The Chanyu of the Xiongnu, Huhanxie, came to court, and the rites and bestowals were as before. In the second month, the Chanyu returned to his country.

An edict was issued: "I have heard that in the governance of high antiquity, the ruler and his ministers were of one mind, and their actions, whether right or wrong, each found their proper place. Therefore, harmony prevailed above and below, and peace and prosperity were enjoyed throughout the land. Their virtue was beyond reach. I am not enlightened, and have repeatedly issued edicts to the high officials and grandees to strive for leniency and magnanimity, to comply with the people's hardships and sufferings, intending to match the greatness of the Three Kings and to illuminate the virtue of the Former Emperor. Now, some officials consider the non-prohibition of wickedness as leniency, the release of the guilty as non-severity, and some regard cruelty and evil as virtue. All have lost the middle way. To carry out the edict and propagate transformation in such a manner, is it not erroneous? At present, the empire has few affairs, corvée and taxes are reduced, and military campaigns are not waged, yet the people are mostly poor, and bandits do not cease. Where lies the fault? The submitted account books are mere formalities, striving to deceive and evade their responsibilities. The Three Dukes do not consider this important. What am I to rely on? All requests for edicts to reduce soldiers and laborers for self-support are to cease. The Censorate is to examine the account books, and if they suspect they are not truthful, they are to investigate them, so that truth and falsehood are not confused. "

In the third month, a comet appeared in Wangliang and the Pavilion Road, entering the Purple Palace. In the summer, the fourth month, an edict was issued: "To recommend honest officials is truly to seek the genuine. Officials of six hundred dan rank as grandees, if guilty, must first be requested, their rank and salary are communicated upwards, sufficient to demonstrate their virtuous talents. From now on, it is not permitted to recommend." In the winter, the twelfth month, on the day of Jiaxu, the emperor passed away in the Weiyang Palace. On the day of Guisi, the Empress Dowager was honored as the Grand Empress Dowager.

The eulogy states: The governance of Emperor Xiaoxuan was marked by trustworthy rewards and inevitable punishments, a comprehensive examination of names and realities, and officials, scholars, and legal experts all excelling in their abilities. As for the skills of craftsmen and the quality of instruments, few could match them since the Yuan and Cheng periods, which is enough to know that the officials were competent in their duties and the people were secure in their livelihoods. Encountering the turmoil of the Xiongnu, he pushed the perishing and secured the surviving, establishing trust and authority among the northern barbarians, and the Chanyu, admiring righteousness, bowed his head and called himself a vassal. His achievements glorified his ancestors and his legacy was passed down to his descendants. He can be said to have achieved a revival, matching the virtue of the Yin and Zhou ancestors.

VOLUME 9: RECORDS OF EMPEROR YUAN, NO. 9

Emperor Xiaoyuan was the crown prince of Emperor Xuan. His mother was the Empress Xu of Gong'ai, born to Emperor Xuan when he was still a commoner. At the age of two, Emperor Xuan ascended the throne. At the age of eight, he was established as the crown prince. As he grew up, he was gentle, benevolent, and fond of Confucianism. Seeing that Emperor Xuan employed many legal officials who used strict laws to control the subordinates, and that ministers like Yang Yun and He Kuanrao were executed for their critical remarks, he once casually remarked during a banquet: "Your Majesty applies punishments too severely; it would be better to employ Confucian scholars. Emperor Xuan changed his expression and said: "The Han dynasty has its own system, originally blending the ways of the hegemon and the king. How can we purely rely on moral teachings and employ the policies of the Zhou? Moreover, conventional Confucians do not understand the exigencies of the times; they are fond of antiquity and criticize the present, causing people to be confused by names and realities, not knowing what to adhere to. How can they be entrusted with responsibilities!" He then sighed and said: "The one who will bring chaos to our house is the crown prince!" From then on, he distanced himself from the crown prince and favored the Prince of Huaiyang, saying: "The Prince of Huaiyang is discerning and fond of law; he should be my heir. The mother of the prince, Lady Zhang Jieyu, was especially favored. The emperor had the intention to replace the crown prince with the Prince of Huaiyang, but because he had relied on the Xu family from a young age and both had risen from humble beginnings, he ultimately did not go against this.

In the twelfth month of the first year of Huanglong, Emperor Xuan passed away. On the day of Guisi, the crown prince ascended the throne as emperor and paid homage at the Gao Temple. The Empress Dowager was honored as the Grand Empress Dowager, and the Empress was honored as the Empress Dowager.

In the spring of the first year of Chuyuan, on the day of Xinchou in the first month, Emperor Xiaoxuan was buried at Duling. The feudal lords, princesses, and marquises were bestowed with gold, and officials below two thousand dan were given money and silk, each according to their rank. A general amnesty was proclaimed throughout the land. In the third month, the brother of the Empress Dowager, the Palace Attendant and General of the Gentlemen of the Household Wang Shun, was enfeoffed as the Marquis of Anping. On the day of Bingwu, Empress Wang was established. The public fields and parks of the Three Adjuncts, the Grand Minister of Ceremonies, and the commanderies that could be reduced were used to support the poor. Those with assets less than one thousand coins were provided with seeds and food. The cousin of the maternal grandfather, the Marquis of Ping'en Dai, the Palace Attendant Xu Jia, was enfeoffed as the Marquis of Ping'en to continue the line of the Marquis of Dai.

In the summer, the fourth month, an edict was issued: "I have inherited the sacred legacy of the late emperor and have the honor to serve the ancestral temple, trembling with fear. Recently, the earth has shaken repeatedly and has not calmed, and I am afraid of the warnings of heaven and earth, not knowing the cause. At the time of field work, I am concerned about the common people losing their livelihoods, and I have personally dispatched the Grandee Secretary Bao and eleven others to tour the empire, to inquire after the elderly, widowers, widows, orphans, the childless, the impoverished, and those who have lost their positions, to promote the virtuous and talented, to seek out the obscure and lowly, and to observe the transformation of customs. If the governors of the commanderies and the ministers of the two thousand dan sincerely correct themselves and labor diligently, propagate and clarify education and transformation, to be close to the myriad surnames, then harmony and kinship will prevail within the six directions, and perhaps there will be no worries. Does the Book of Documents not say? 'Good are the thighs and arms, and all affairs are at peace!' Let this be proclaimed throughout the empire, so that all may clearly know my intentions." It also said: "This year in the region east of the pass, the grain harvest has failed, and the people are mostly impoverished and in need. Let the commanderies and kingdoms that have suffered severe disasters be exempt from land taxes and corvée. The lakes, ponds, gardens, and pools that belong to the Shaofu shall be lent to the poor people, and they shall not be taxed. Members of the imperial clan with registered lineage were granted one to eight horses, the Three Elders and the filial were given five bolts of silk, the fraternal and diligent farmers were given three bolts, widowers, widows, orphans, and the childless were given two bolts, and for every fifty households of officials and commoners, an ox and wine were bestowed."

In the sixth month, due to a plague among the people, the high officials were ordered to reduce their meals, the number of musicians in the Music Bureau was decreased, and the horses in the parks were reduced to aid the impoverished and needy. In the autumn, the eighth month, more than ten thousand surrendered Hu people from the Shangjun dependent state fled into the territory of the Xiongnu.

In the ninth month, eleven commanderies and kingdoms in the region east of the pass suffered severe floods and famine, and in some places, people resorted to cannibalism. Funds and grain were transferred from neighboring commanderies to provide relief. An edict was issued: "Recently, yin and yang have been out of harmony, and the common people have been suffering from hunger and cold, with no means to secure governance. My virtue is shallow and insufficient to fill the old residences. Let the palaces and halls that are rarely visited not be repaired, the Grand Provisioner reduce the grain fed to horses, and the Water Office decrease the meat fed to animals."

In the spring of the second year, the first month, the emperor traveled to Ganquan and performed the suburban sacrifice at the Tai Altar. The people of Yunyang were granted one rank of nobility, and for every hundred households of women, an ox and wine were bestowed. The emperor's younger brother Jing was established as the Prince of Qinghe. In the third month, the crown prince of the Prince of Guangling Li, Ba, was established as the prince.

An edict was issued to cease the use of dogs and horses from the Yellow Gate for the imperial carriages, and the forbidden parks of the Water Office, the Lower Park of Yichun, the outer ponds of the Shaofu, and the fields of Yanjing were to be lent to the poor people. The edict stated: "It is heard that when sages and worthies are in positions of authority, yin and yang are in harmony, wind and rain come in due season, the sun and moon shine brightly, the stars and planets are tranquil, and the common people are peaceful and prosperous, fulfilling their destinies. Now I, in reverent acceptance of heaven and earth, placed above the dukes and marquises, with my clarity unable to illuminate and my virtue unable to pacify, disasters and anomalies have come together, unceasing for years. On the day of Wuwu in the second month, an earthquake occurred in Longxi Commandery, destroying the wooden decorations of the temple walls of the Supreme Emperor, damaging the city walls, government buildings, and civilian houses in Huandao County, and killing many people. Mountains collapsed and the earth split, with springs of water gushing forth. Heaven has sent down disasters, startling my people. Governance has been greatly deficient, and thus the calamity has come to this. I am vigilant day and night, not understanding the great changes, deeply pondering with sorrow, and do not know the sequence of events. Recently, the harvests have failed for several years, and the common people are impoverished, unable to endure hunger and cold, falling into the punishments and laws. I am deeply grieved by this. The commanderies and kingdoms that have suffered severe earthquake disasters shall be exempt from land taxes and corvée. A general amnesty is proclaimed throughout the empire. If there are matters that can be abolished or reduced for the convenience of the myriad surnames, let them be presented in detail, and nothing shall be concealed. The Chancellor, the Imperial Secretaries, and the officials of two thousand dan shall recommend scholars of outstanding talent and those who speak frankly and remonstrate vigorously, and I shall personally review them."

In the summer, the fourth month, on the day of Dingsi, the crown prince was established. The Imperial Secretary was granted the title of Marquis within the Pass, the officials of two thousand dan were granted the title of Right Grandee, those in the empire who were to succeed their fathers were granted one rank of nobility, marquises were each given two hundred thousand coins, and those of the fifth rank of nobility were given one hundred thousand coins.

In the sixth month, there was famine in the region east of the pass, and in the land of Qi, people resorted to cannibalism. In the autumn, the seventh month, an edict was issued: "Year after year, disasters have occurred, and the people have the pallor of hunger, which grieves my heart. I have already ordered the officials to empty the granaries and open the treasuries to provide relief and to give clothes to those who are cold. This autumn, the millet and wheat have been severely damaged. In one year, the earth has shaken twice. The waters of the North Sea have overflowed, killing people. Yin and yang are not in harmony; where lies the fault? How do the dukes and ministers plan to address these concerns? Let them fully express my faults without any concealment. "

In the winter, an edict was issued: "When a state is about to prosper, it honors its teachers and values its tutors. Therefore, the former general Wang Zhi tutored me for eight years, guiding me with the classics, and his merit was great. He is hereby granted the title of Marquis within the Pass, with an estate of eight hundred households, and shall attend court on the first and fifteenth days of the month." In the twelfth month, the Secretary of the Central Secretariat Hong Gong, Shi Xian, and others slandered Wang Zhi, causing him to be ordered to commit suicide. In the spring of the third year, it was ordered that the positions of the feudal lords' ministers be below those of the commandery governors.

The people of Shannan County in Zhuya Commandery rebelled, and the emperor consulted with his ministers. The expectant official Jia Juanzhi suggested that Zhuya should be abandoned to save the people from famine. Consequently, Zhuya was abolished.

In the summer, the fourth month, on the last day of Yimao, a fire disaster occurred at the White Crane Pavilion in Maoling. An edict was issued: "Recently, a fire disaster descended upon the garden pavilion of Emperor Xiaowu, and I tremble with fear. I have not illuminated the changes and anomalies, and the fault lies with me. The officials have also been unwilling to fully speak of my faults, leading to this situation. How can I awaken to this! The people have repeatedly encountered calamities, with no means to relieve each other, and are further troubled by oppressive officials, entangled in petty regulations, unable to fulfill their destinies. I am deeply grieved by this. Let a general amnesty be proclaimed throughout the empire."

In the summer, there was a drought. The younger brother of the Prince of Changsha Yang was established as the prince. The son of the former Marquis of Haihun, He, named Daizong, was enfeoffed as a marquis.

In the sixth month, an edict was issued: "It is heard that the way to pacify the people originates from the harmony of yin and yang. Recently, yin and yang have been in disorder, and wind and rain have not come in due season. My lack of virtue has perhaps led the dukes to dare to speak of my faults, but now this is not the case. They flatter and blindly follow, unwilling to speak out fully, and I am deeply grieved by this. I constantly think of the hunger and cold of the masses, who are far from their parents, wives, and children, toiling in tasks that are not their proper occupations, guarding palaces that are not their homes, fearing that this is not the way to assist the harmony of yin and yang. Let the guards of the Ganquan and Jianzhang Palaces be dismissed and ordered to return to farming. All officials shall reduce their expenses. Let matters be presented in detail without concealment. The responsible officials shall strive to avoid violating the prohibitions of the four seasons. The Chancellor and the Imperial Secretaries shall each recommend three individuals from the empire who are knowledgeable about yin and yang and disasters and anomalies." Thereupon, many people came forward to discuss affairs, and some were promoted and summoned for audiences, each feeling that they had gained the emperor's favor.

In the spring of the fourth year, the first month, the emperor traveled to Ganquan and performed the suburban sacrifice at the Tai Altar. In the third month, he traveled to Hedong and sacrificed to the Earth God. A pardon was granted to the exiles of Fenyin. The people were granted one rank of nobility, and for every hundred households of women, an ox and wine were bestowed. The elderly widowers and widows were given silk. No land taxes or corvée were levied on the places he passed through. In the spring of the fifth year, the first month, the Lord of Zhouzinan was made the Marquis of Zhouchengxiu, with a rank below the feudal kings. In the third month, the emperor traveled to Yong and sacrificed at the Five Altars.

In the summer, the fourth month, a comet appeared in the constellation of Shen. An edict was issued: "My inadequacies have led to unclear rankings and positions, and the officials have long been in confusion, not finding the right people. The common people are disappointed, and this has moved the heavens above, causing yin and yang to change, bringing calamity to the myriad people. I am deeply afraid of this. Recently, the region east of the pass has suffered continuous disasters, with hunger, cold, disease, and plagues, and lives are not reaching their natural end. Does the Book of Songs not say? 'When the people are in distress, crawl to their rescue.' Let the Grand Provisioner not slaughter daily, and let all provisions be reduced by half. Let the imperial carriages and horses be fed, but not to the detriment of proper affairs. Let the wrestling contests, the rarely visited palaces and pavilions of Shanglin, the three service offices of Qi, the field offices of Beijia, the salt and iron offices, and the ever-normal granaries be abolished. Let there be no fixed number of scholars in the academy, to broaden learning. Let the members of the imperial clan with registered lineage be given one horse up to two teams, the three elders and the filial be given silk, five bolts per person, the fraternal and the diligent farmers be given three bolts, the widowers, widows, orphans, and the childless be given two bolts, and for every fifty households of officials and common people, an ox and wine be bestowed. "More than seventy penal matters were reduced. The order requiring officials from the Grandee of the Palace down to the Gentleman of the Palace to guarantee their parents and siblings was abolished. Officials serving in the palace and the Sima were allowed to register their grandparents, parents, and brothers.

In the winter, the twelfth month, on the day of Dingwei, the Imperial Secretary Gong Yu passed away. The Wei Sima Gu Ji was sent to the Xiongnu and did not return. In the spring of the first year of Yongguang, the first month, the emperor traveled to Ganquan and performed the suburban sacrifice at the Tai Altar.

A pardon was granted to the exiles of Yunyang. The people were granted one rank of nobility, and for every hundred households of women, an ox and wine were bestowed. The elderly were given silk. No land taxes or corvée were levied on the places he passed through.

In the second month, an edict was issued for the Chancellor and the Imperial Secretaries to recommend individuals who are simple, honest, modest, and virtuous, and for the Grandee of the Palace to annually rank the Gentlemen and accompanying officials based on these criteria.

In the third month, an edict was issued: "The Five Emperors and the Three Kings appointed the virtuous and employed the capable, achieving great peace, and yet now there is no governance. Is it because the people are different? The fault lies in my lack of clarity, in not knowing the virtuous. Therefore, the unworthy are in positions, and the good are obstructed. The failings of the Zhou and Qin have further led the people to gradually adopt shallow customs, abandoning propriety and righteousness, and violating the penal laws. Is this not lamentable! From this perspective, how are the common people at fault? Let a general amnesty be proclaimed throughout the empire, and let all strive diligently to renew themselves, each focusing on farming. Those without land shall all be granted it, and seeds and food shall be loaned as to the poor. Officials of the sixth rank and above shall be granted the title of Grandee of the Fifth Rank, diligent officials shall be granted two ranks, and the eldest sons of the people shall be granted one rank. For every hundred households of women, an ox and wine shall be bestowed, and the widowers, widows, orphans, childless, and the elderly shall be given silk." That month, there was rain and snow, and frost damaged the wheat and crops, leading to a poor autumn harvest.

In the spring of the second year, the second month, an edict was issued: "It is heard that in the times of Tang and

Yu, symbolic punishments were used, and the people did not transgress; in the eras of Yin and Zhou, laws were enforced, and the treacherous submitted. Now that I have inherited the great legacy of Emperor Gaozu and occupy a position above the dukes and marquises, I tremble day and night, constantly thinking of the people's urgent needs, never forgetting them. Yet, yin and yang are not in harmony, and the three lights are dim. The common people are in great distress, wandering the roads, and bandits are rampant. The officials, moreover, foster cruelty and fail in their duty to shepherd the people. All of this is due to my lack of clarity and deficiencies in governance. The fault lies here, and I am deeply ashamed. As the parent of the people, to be so neglectful, what can I say to the people! Let a general amnesty be proclaimed throughout the empire, and let the people be granted one rank of nobility. For every hundred households of women, an ox and wine shall be bestowed, and the widowers, widows, orphans, childless, elderly, the three elders, the filial, fraternal, and diligent farmers shall be given silk." Additionally, the feudal kings, princesses, and marquises were granted gold, and officials from the middle two thousand dan down to the middle capital officials and long-serving officials were given varying amounts. Officials of the sixth rank and above were granted the title of Grandee of the Fifth Rank, and diligent officials were each granted two ranks.

On the first day of the third month, Renxu, there was a solar eclipse. An edict was issued: "I tremble with fear, day and night reflecting on my faults, not daring to be negligent or complacent. It is because yin and yang are not in harmony that I have not illuminated the fault. I have repeatedly admonished the dukes and ministers, daily hoping for effectiveness. Up to now, the officials in charge of governance have not achieved balance, and their prohibitions and restrictions have not aligned with the people's hearts. The customs of violence and ferocity have grown stronger, and the way of harmony has daily declined, leaving the people in sorrow and distress, with no place to turn. Therefore, the ominous influences increase yearly, encroaching upon the sun, and the righteous energy is deeply obscured, gradually dimming the light. On the day of Renxu, there was a solar eclipse. Heaven has shown a great anomaly to warn me, and I am deeply grieved. Let the commanderies and kingdoms within the empire each recommend one talented and exceptional individual, a virtuous and outspoken scholar."

In the summer, the sixth month, an edict was issued: "In recent years, there have been continuous crop failures, and all regions are in distress. The common people toil in farming, yet there is no success, and they are beset by famine, with no means of relief. As the parent of the people, my virtue cannot cover them, and yet I impose punishments, which deeply grieves me. Let a general amnesty be proclaimed throughout the empire."

In the autumn, the seventh month, the Western Qiang rebelled, and the Right General Feng Fengshi was sent to attack them. In the eighth month, the Grand Minister of Ceremonies Ren Qianqiu was appointed as the General of Fierce Might, and he led five separate armies to advance together. In the spring of the third year, the Western Qiang were pacified, and the troops were disbanded. In the third month, Prince Kang was established as the King of Jiyang. In the summer, the fourth month, on the day of Guiwei, the Grand Marshal and General of Chariots and Cavalry, Jie, passed away.

In the winter, the eleventh month, an edict was issued: "Recently, on the day of Jichou, there was an earthquake, heavy rain in midwinter, and dense fog, and bandits rose up together. Why did the officials not enforce prohibitions in a timely manner? Each shall fully express their intentions in response." In the winter, the salt and iron offices and the scholar disciples were reinstated. Due to insufficient resources, many people were exempted from taxes, and there were no means to provide for corvée duties both within and outside the capital.

In the spring of the fourth year, the second month, an

edict was issued: "I bear the weight of the supreme throne, yet I cannot illuminate the governance of the people, repeatedly encountering misfortunes. Additionally, the borders are unsettled, armies are abroad, taxes and transport are burdensome, the common people are in turmoil, impoverished and distressed, and they break the law and incur punishment. When those above lose their way and impose severe punishments on those below, I am deeply pained. Let a general amnesty be proclaimed throughout the empire, and the debts of the poor shall not be collected."

In the third month, the emperor traveled to Yong and offered sacrifices at the Five Altars. In the summer, the sixth month, on the day of Jiaxu, a fire broke out at the eastern gate of the mausoleum of Emperor Xuan.

On the last day of Wuyin, there was a solar eclipse. An edict was issued: "It is heard that when a wise king is on the throne, loyal and virtuous men are appointed to positions, then all living beings are harmonious and joyful, and those beyond the borders receive benefits. Now, I am obscure in the way of kingship, toiling day and night with worry, not comprehending its principles, seeing nothing without dizziness, hearing nothing without confusion, thus many decrees are reversed, the hearts of the people are not won, false doctrines advance in vain, and affairs are without success. This is what is widely known throughout the empire. The dukes, ministers, and great officers have different likes and dislikes, some follow deceit to do evil, encroach and reduce the common people, to whom can the masses turn for their fate? On the last day of the sixth month, there was a solar eclipse. Does the Book of Songs not say? 'Now these people below are in great sorrow!' From now on, let the dukes, ministers, and great officers diligently consider the warnings of heaven, carefully cultivate themselves for eternity, to assist me in my shortcomings. Speak out fully and frankly, without any reservations."

On the day of Wuzi in the ninth month, the gardens of Empress Wei Si and the Lì Garden were abolished. On the day of Yichou in the tenth month of winter, the ancestral temples located in the commanderies and kingdoms were abolished. The various mausoleums were divided and placed under the jurisdiction of the Three Adjuncts. The Shouling Pavilion in the original area of Weicheng was designated as the initial mausoleum. An edict was issued: "It is the nature of the common people to be attached to their land and reluctant to move; it is the wish of human sentiment for flesh and blood to stay together. Recently, officials, based on the principle of loyalty and filial piety, proposed relocating the people of the commanderies and kingdoms to serve the imperial gardens and mausoleums, causing the people to abandon their ancestral graves far away, lose their livelihoods and properties, separate from their relatives, and harbor feelings of longing, with each family feeling unsettled. Thus, the eastern regions suffer the harm of depletion, and within the passes, there are people in distress, which is not a long-term strategy. Does the Book of Songs not say? 'The people are also weary, let them have a little rest, benefit this central kingdom, to pacify the four directions.' As for the initial mausoleum now being established, do not establish counties and towns, but let the whole empire be at peace with their land and content with their work, without any intention to move. Proclaim this to the empire, so that all may clearly understand." Additionally, the fiefs of the parents of the former and current empresses were abolished.

In the spring of the fifth year, the first month, the emperor traveled to Ganquan and performed the suburban sacrifice at the Tai Altar. In the third month, the emperor visited Hedong and offered sacrifices to the Earth God. In the autumn, the waters of Yingchuan overflowed, killing people. Officials and attendants from the affected counties reported the disaster. The soldiers were sent home. In the winter, the emperor visited the Changyang Shooting Bear Pavilion, deployed chariots and cavalry, and conducted a grand hunt. In the twelfth month, on the day of Yiyou, the mausoleum gardens of the Supreme Emperor and Emperor Hui were destroyed.

In the spring of the first year of Jianzhao, the third month, the emperor traveled to Yong and offered sacrifices at the Five Altars. In the autumn, the eighth month, a swarm of white moths flew, blocking the sun, from the Eastern Capital Gate to Zhidao. In the winter, the King of Hejian, Yuan, was found guilty, deposed, and exiled to Fangling. The mausoleum gardens of Empress Dowager Wen and Empress Dowager Zhao were abolished.

In the spring of the second year, the first month, the emperor traveled to Ganquan and performed the suburban sacrifice at the Tai Altar. In the third month, the emperor visited Hedong and offered sacrifices to the Earth God. The rank of the governors of the Three River Commanderies was increased. A population of 120,000 households was considered a large commandery. In the summer, the fourth month, a general amnesty was proclaimed throughout the empire. In the sixth month, Prince Xing was established as the King of Xindu. In the intercalary month, on the day of Dingyou, the Grand Empress Dowager Shangguan passed away. In the winter, the eleventh month, earthquakes occurred in Qi and Chu, accompanied by heavy snow, which broke trees and destroyed houses.

Zhang Bo, the uncle of the King of Huaiyang, and Jing Fang, the governor of Wei Commandery, were accused of spying on the feudal kings with malicious intent and leaking confidential court discussions. Zhang Bo was executed by being cut in two at the waist, and Jing Fang was executed in the market. In the summer of the third year, it was decreed that the commandants of the Three Adjuncts and the commandants of large commanderies should all hold a rank of two thousand dan. On the day of Jiachen in the sixth month, Prime Minister Xuancheng passed away.

In the autumn, the Protector of the Western Regions, Cavalry

Commandant Gan Yanshou, and Deputy Colonel Chen Tang mobilized the troops of the Wuji Colonel's agricultural colonies and the Hu soldiers of the Western Regions to attack the Xiongnu Chanyu Zhizhi. In the winter, they beheaded him and sent his head to the capital, where it was displayed at the gate of the barbarian hostel. In the spring of the fourth year, the first month, the execution of the Chanyu Zhizhi was reported at the suburban and ancestral temple sacrifices. A general amnesty was proclaimed throughout the empire. The ministers offered congratulations and set out wine, and the books and maps were shown to the noble consorts of the rear palace.

In the summer, the fourth month, an edict was issued: "I have inherited the glorious achievements of the late emperor, and I am deeply anxious day and night, fearing that I am not up to the task. Recently, yin and yang have been out of harmony, the five elements have lost their order, and the people have suffered from famine. Due to the unemployment of the masses, I am sending the Grandee Secretary Shang and others, twenty-one in total, to tour the empire, to comfort the elderly, widowed, orphaned, and lonely, and those who are impoverished and unemployed, and to recommend talented and exceptional individuals. The nine ministers shall lead with diligence and not be remiss, so that I may observe the spread of moral education." "

On the day of Jiashen in the sixth month, Prince Jing of Zhongshan passed away. In Lantian, sand and stones blocked the Ba River, and the bank of Anling collapsed, blocking the Jing River, causing the water to flow backward.

In the spring of the fifth year, the third month, an edict was issued: "It is heard that a wise king governs the state by clarifying what is good and what is evil to determine what to pursue and what to avoid, by promoting respect and yielding so that the people will rise and act accordingly, thus laws are established and the people do not violate them, decrees are implemented and the people follow them. Now, I have been able to preserve the ancestral temple, working diligently and conscientiously, not daring to slacken, yet my virtue is thin and my wisdom dim, and my moral education is shallow and insignificant. Does the tradition not say?

'If the people have faults, they are mine alone.' Therefore, I proclaim a general amnesty throughout the empire, grant the people one rank of nobility, and give each hundred households of women oxen and wine, and silk to the elders, filial sons, and diligent farmers." It also said: "This is the time of spring when farming and sericulture flourish, and the people exert themselves to the utmost. Therefore, this month is for encouraging the farmers and urging the people, so that they do not miss the season. Now, there are corrupt officials who investigate minor crimes, summon witnesses, and initiate unnecessary affairs, hindering the people and causing them to lose the opportunity for timely work and the achievement of a year's labor. Let the dukes and ministers clearly examine and enforce this decree." "

In the summer, the sixth month, on the day of Gengshen, the Lì Garden was restored. On the last day of Renshen, there was a solar eclipse. In the autumn, the seventh month, on the day of Gengzi, the mausoleum gardens of the Supreme Emperor, the original temple, Empress Zhao Ling, King Wu Ai, Empress Zhao Ai, and Empress Wei Si were restored.

In the spring of the first year of Jingning, the first month, the Xiongnu Chanyu Huhanxie came to court. An edict was issued: "The Xiongnu Chanyu Zhizhi betrayed the rites and righteousness, and having been punished for his crimes, Chanyu Huhanxie does not forget the kindness and virtue, admires the rites and righteousness, and has restored the ritual of court congratulations, wishing to protect the frontier passes for endless generations, so that the borders may long be free from the affairs of war. Therefore, the era name is changed to Jingning, and the Chanyu is granted the attendant Wang Qiang from the Yeting as his consort."

The crown prince was capped. The sons of the marquises were granted the rank of Grandee, and those throughout the empire who were the eldest sons of their fathers were granted one rank of nobility. In the second month, the Grandee Secretary Yanshou passed away. In the third month, on the day of Guiwei, the mausoleum gardens of Emperor Hui, Empress Dowager Wen, and Empress Dowager Zhao were restored. In the summer, Cavalry Commandant Gan Yanshou was enfeoffed as a marquis. Deputy Colonel Chen Tang was granted the title of Marquis within the Passes and a hundred catties of gold.

On the day of Renchen in the fifth month, the emperor passed away in the Weiyang Palace. The temples of the Supreme Emperor, Emperor Hui, and Emperor Jing were destroyed. The mausoleum gardens of Empress Dowager Wen, Empress Dowager Zhao, Empress Zhao Ling, King Wu Ai, and Empress Zhao Ai were abolished. In the autumn, the seventh month, on the day of Bingxu, he was buried in the Weiling Mausoleum.

The commentary says: My maternal grandfather's brothers served as palace attendants during the reign of Emperor Yuan, and they told me that Emperor Yuan was highly talented and skilled, excelled in historical writings, played the qin and se, blew the dongxiao, composed his own melodies, set them to songs, and meticulously arranged the rhythms, reaching the utmost refinement. He was fond of Confucianism from a young age, and upon ascending the throne, he recruited Confucian scholars and entrusted them with governance. Gong, Xue, Wei, and Kuang took turns serving as chancellors. However, the emperor was constrained by literary meanings, indecisive and leisurely, and the achievements of Emperor Xuan declined. Nevertheless, he was broad-minded and accommodating towards his subordinates, practicing humility and frugality, and his edicts were gentle and elegant, bearing the ancient style and vigor.

VOLUME 10: RECORDS OF EMPEROR CHENG, NO. 10

Emperor Cheng of Filial Piety was the crown prince of Emperor Yuan. His mother was Empress Wang, and he was born in the Jia Guan Painting Hall of the Crown Prince's Palace during Emperor Yuan's reign, as the imperial grandson of the direct line. Emperor Xuan loved him and gave him the courtesy name of Grandson, often keeping him by his side. At the age of three, Emperor Xuan passed away, and Emperor Yuan ascended the throne, with Emperor Cheng becoming the crown prince. In his youth, he was fond of the classics, being broad-minded, knowledgeable, and cautious. Initially residing in the Gui Palace, when the emperor once urgently summoned him, the crown prince exited through the Dragon Tower Gate but dared not cross the imperial road. He went west to the Straight Gate, where he could cross, and then returned through the Workshop Gate. The emperor was delayed and asked the reason, to which the crown prince explained the situation. The emperor was greatly pleased and issued a decree allowing the crown prince to cross the imperial road. Later, he indulged in wine and music, and the emperor did not consider him capable. Meanwhile, Prince Gong of Dingtao was talented, and his mother, Consort Fu, was favored, so the emperor often considered making Prince Gong the heir. However, thanks to the protection of the palace attendant Shi Dan over the crown prince's household and his strong assistance, and also because the late emperor had particularly loved the crown prince, he was not deposed.

In the fifth month of the first year of Jingning, Emperor Yuan passed away. On the day of Jiwei in the sixth month, the crown prince ascended the throne as emperor and paid homage at the Gao Temple. He honored the empress dowager as the Grand Empress Dowager and the empress as the Empress Dowager. He appointed his uncle, the palace attendant and commander of the palace guards, Marquis Yangping Wang Feng, as the Grand Marshal and General, in charge of the affairs of the Secretariat. On the day of Yiwei, the officials reported: "The imperial carriage, oxen, horses, and animals are all not in accordance with the rites and should not be used for burial." The memorial was approved.

In the seventh month, a general amnesty was proclaimed throughout the empire. In the spring of the first year of Jianshi, on the day of Yichou in the first month, a fire broke out at the temple of the emperor's late great-grandfather. The younger brother of the former Prince of Hejian, Liang, the director of the Shangjun treasury, was established as a prince. A comet appeared in the constellation Ying Shi. The imperial prison at Shanglin was abolished. In the second month, the Chief Clerk of the Right General, Yao Yin, and others, on their return from a mission to the Xiongnu, were more than a hundred li from the frontier when a violent wind and fire broke out, burning and killing Yin and six others.

The feudal lords, chancellors, generals, marquises, queen dowagers, princesses, lords, and officials with a rank of two thousand piculs of grain were granted gold. Members of the imperial clan, officials with ranks below one thousand piculs down to two hundred piculs, and those of the imperial clan with registered status, as well as the three elders, filial and fraternal individuals, diligent farmers, widowers, widows, orphans, and the childless were granted varying amounts of money and silk. Officials and commoners in groups of fifty households were given oxen and wine.

An edict was issued: "Recently, a fire disaster descended upon the ancestral temple, and a comet appeared in the east, beginning correctly but then waning. What greater fault could there be! The 'Book of Documents' says: 'Only the former kings corrected their affairs.' All the dukes have been diligent, leading the officials to assist me where I am lacking. Promote leniency and generosity, foster harmony, and in all matters, be forgiving, and do not act harshly. Let there be a great amnesty throughout the land, allowing all to start anew."

The uncle of the emperor, the Grand Master of Imperial Entertainments and Marquis within the Passes, Wang Chong, was enfeoffed as the Marquis of Ancheng. The uncles Wang Tan, Wang Shang, Wang Li, Wang Gen, and Wang Fengshi were granted the title of Marquis within the Passes. In the summer, the fourth month, yellow fog filled the passes on all sides, and the emperor broadly inquired among the dukes, ministers, and grandees, leaving nothing unspoken. In the sixth month, a countless number of blue flies gathered on the seats of the courtiers in the Weiyang Palace. In the autumn, twenty-five rarely visited palaces and lodges in Shanglin were abolished.

In the eighth month, two moons appeared together, seen in the east at dawn. On the day of Wuzi in the ninth month, a meteor shone brightly upon the earth, stretching four or five zhang in length, winding like a snake, and piercing through the Purple Palace. In the twelfth month, the northern and southern suburbs of Chang'an were constructed, and the sacrifices at Ganquan and Fenyin were abolished. On that day, a great wind uprooted more than ten large trees at the Ganquan altar. More than forty percent of the commanderies and kingdoms were affected by disasters, and the land tax was waived.

In the spring of the second year, the first month, the five altars of Yong were abolished. On the day of Xinsi, the emperor began the suburban sacrifices at the southern suburbs of Chang'an. An edict was issued: "Recently, the Tai altar and the Earth God were moved to the southern and northern suburbs, and I personally attended to the suburban sacrifices to the Supreme Deity. The response from the heavens was seen with divine light. The three auxiliary regions have long been without the labor of supplying and conscripting, and I pardon those in the suburban counties of Chang'an, Changling, and the capital officials who are serving sentences for misdemeanors. The tax on the empire is reduced to forty coins per person."

In the intercalary month, the Yanling district of Weicheng was designated as the initial mausoleum. In the second month, an edict was issued for the three auxiliary regions and the inner commanderies to each recommend one virtuous and upright person. In the third month, the well water at the Northern Palace overflowed. On the day of Xinchou, the emperor began to worship the Earth God at the northern suburbs. On the day of Bingwu, Empress Xu was established. The six stables and the official for skilled crafts were abolished. In the summer, there was a great drought. Prince Yu of Dongping committed a crime, and the counties of Fan and Kangfu were taken away from him.

In the autumn, the Crown Prince's Bowang Garden was abolished and bestowed upon members of the imperial clan who attended court. The number of horses in the imperial stables was reduced. In the spring of the third year, the third month, all convicts throughout the empire were pardoned. Those who were filial and fraternal and diligent farmers were granted two ranks of nobility. All unpaid taxes and loans that had been relieved were not to be collected.

In the autumn, there was a great flood within the Passes. In the seventh month, a young girl from Si, Chen Chigong, heard that the great flood was coming and ran into the Hengcheng Gate, then entered the Shangfang Yamen through the side gate, reaching the Gou Dun within the Weiyang Palace. Officials and commoners were alarmed and climbed the city walls. In the ninth month, an edict was issued: "Recently, commanderies and kingdoms have been struck by flood disasters, with people being swept away and killed, numbering up to a thousand. In the capital, there were unfounded rumors of a great flood approaching, causing officials and commoners to panic and run to climb the city walls. It is likely that the harsh and severe officials have not ceased, and there are many among the populace who have been wronged and lost their positions. Dispatch the Grand Master of Remonstrance, Lin, and others to tour the empire and inspect its conditions."

On the first day of the twelfth month, Wushen, at the winter solstice, there was a solar eclipse. At night, an earthquake occurred in the Weiyang Palace. An edict was issued: "It is said that Heaven gives birth to the multitude of people but cannot govern them, thus establishing a ruler to unify and manage them. When the way of the ruler is achieved, even plants, trees, insects, and creatures find their proper place; when the ruler lacks virtue, it is manifested in the heavens and earth, and disasters and anomalies frequently occur as a warning of misrule. I have little experience in the way of governance, and my actions have not been appropriate, hence the solar eclipse and earthquake on the day of Wushen, which I greatly fear. Let the dukes and ministers each consider my faults and clearly state them. 'Do not flatter me to my face and then speak ill behind my back.' The Chancellor, the Censor, the generals, the marquises, officials with a rank of two thousand piculs of grain, and the commanderies and kingdoms within the capital are to recommend virtuous, upright, and capable individuals who can speak frankly and remonstrate to the utmost. Let them come to the Gongche Gate, and I will review their submissions."

Mount Yuexi collapsed. In the spring of the fourth year, the eunuchs of the Central Secretariat were dismissed, and initially, five officials were appointed to the Secretariat. In the summer, the fourth month, it snowed. In the fifth month, the Assistant to the Palace Attendant, Chen Lin, killed the Colonel Director of the Capital, Yuan Feng, within the palace. In the autumn, peaches and plums bore fruit. There was a great flood, and the Yellow

River breached the Jin Dyke in Dong Commandery. In the winter, the tenth month, the Grand Master of Remonstrance, Yin Zhong, committed suicide due to his lack of concern over the breach of the Yellow River.

In the spring of the first year of Heping, the third month, an edict was issued: "The Yellow River breached Dong Commandery, flooding two provinces. Colonel Wang Yanshi repaired the dyke and it was promptly stabilized. Therefore, the era name is changed to Heping. All officials and commoners throughout the empire are granted noble ranks, each according to their status."

On the last day of the fourth month, Jihai, at the summer solstice, there was a total solar eclipse. An edict was issued: "I have been able to preserve the ancestral temple, trembling with fear, and have not been able to fulfill my duties. The classics say: 'If the teachings for men are not cultivated, and the affairs of yang are not managed, then the sun will be eclipsed.' Heaven has shown this anomaly, and the fault lies with me. Let the dukes, ministers, and grandees exert their utmost efforts to assist where I am lacking. Let all officials diligently perform their duties, earnestly appoint virtuous people, and remove and distance themselves from the cruel and wicked. State my faults without any concealment. A great amnesty was proclaimed throughout the empire.

In the sixth month, the Office of the Commandant of Dependent States was abolished and merged with the Chamberlain for Dependencies. In the autumn, the ninth month, the ancestral temple and gardens of the Grand Emperor were restored. In the spring of the second year, the first month, the iron official of Pei Commandery smelted iron that flew. This is recorded in the Treatise on the Five Elements. In the summer, the sixth month, the uncles Tan, Shang, Li, Gen, and Fengshi were all enfeoffed as marquises. In the spring of the third year, the second month, on the day of Bingxu, an earthquake occurred in Qianwei, causing a mountain to collapse and block the Jiang River, making the water flow backward.

On the last day of the eighth month, Yimao, at the autumn equinox, there was a solar eclipse. The Grand Master of Imperial Entertainments, Liu Xiang, collated the books in the imperial library. The Attendant Chen Nong was sent to search for lost books throughout the empire. In the spring of the fourth year, the first month, the Chanyu of the Xiongnu came to court. All convicts throughout the empire were pardoned, and those who were filial and fraternal and diligent farmers were granted two ranks of nobility. All unpaid taxes and loans that had been relieved were not to be collected. In the second month, the Chanyu left and returned to his country. On the first day of the third month, Guichou, there was a solar eclipse.

Dispatch the Grand Master of Imperial Entertainments, Boshi Jia, and eleven others to tour the provinces along the Yellow River and provide financial relief to those who have been injured and impoverished by the flood and cannot sustain themselves. For those who have been swept away and killed by the flood and cannot bury themselves, let the commanderies and kingdoms provide coffins for burial. Those who have already been buried are to be given two thousand coins per person. Those who have fled to other commanderies and kingdoms to escape the flood are to be provided with food where they are, treated with care and reason, and not allowed to lose their positions. Recommend honest, kind, capable, and outspoken individuals.

On the day of Renshen, the banks of the Jing River at Changling collapsed, blocking the Jing River. In the summer, the sixth month, on the day of Gengxu, King Ao of Chu passed away. Fire emerged from stones in Shanyang, and the era name was changed to Yangshuo. The first year of Yangshuo. In the spring, the second month, on the last day of Dingwei, there was a solar eclipse. In the third month, all convicts throughout the empire were pardoned. In the winter, Wang Zhang, the Governor of the

Capital, committed a crime and was imprisoned, where he died.

In the spring of the second year, it was cold. An edict was issued: "In ancient times, Emperor Yao established the offices of Xi and He, commanding them to manage the affairs of the four seasons so that they would not lose their order. Therefore, the 'Book of Documents' says, 'The common people flourished in harmony,' which clearly takes yin and yang as the foundation. Now, some of the dukes, ministers, and grandees do not believe in yin and yang, belittling and minimizing it, and many of their petitions and requests violate the current governance. If this is transmitted without understanding, and yet they wish for the harmony and regulation of yin and yang while traveling throughout the empire, is it not absurd? Let them strive to follow the ordinances of the four seasons and the months."

In the third month, a great amnesty was proclaimed throughout the empire. In the summer, the fifth month, the ranks of officials at eight hundred piculs and five hundred piculs were abolished. In the autumn, there was a great flood east of the Passes, and refugees wishing to enter the Hangu, Tianjing, Hukou, and Wuruan Passes were not to be harshly detained. The Grand Master of Remonstrance and the Erudites were dispatched to inspect the situation. On the day of Jiashen in the eighth month, King Kang of Dingtao passed away.

In the ninth month, those sent on missions were not up to the task. An edict was issued: "In ancient times, the establishment of the Grand Academy was intended to transmit the achievements of the former kings and spread their influence throughout the empire. The officials of the Confucian scholars, being the source of wisdom for all under heaven, should be well-versed in the past and the present, reviewing the old to understand the new, and comprehending the essence of the state. Therefore, they are called Erudites. Otherwise, scholars will have nothing to transmit and will be looked down upon by their inferiors, which is not the way to honor morality. 'A craftsman who wishes to do his work well must first sharpen his tools.' Let the Chancellor and the Censor, together with officials of two thousand piculs and below, jointly recommend those who are qualified to fill the position of Erudite, so that they may be outstanding and commendable. "

In that year, Zhang Zhong, the Grand Master of Remonstrance, passed away. In the spring of the third year, on the day of Renxu in the third month, eight meteorites fell in Dong Commandery. In the summer, the sixth month, Shentu Sheng and one hundred and eighty other convicts from the iron official of Yingchuan killed their senior officials, stole weapons from the armory, and proclaimed themselves generals, traveling through nine commanderies. The Chief Clerk of the Chancellor and the Palace Assistant Censor were dispatched to pursue and capture them, treating the matter as a military campaign, and all were executed.

In the autumn, on the day of Dingsi in the eighth month, Wang Feng, the Grand Marshal and Grand General, passed away.

In the spring of the fourth year, the first month, an edict was issued: "The 'Hong Fan' outlines eight policies, with food as the foremost, which truly is the foundation for providing for households and avoiding punishments. The late emperor encouraged agriculture, reducing its taxes and rewarding those who were diligent, placing them in the same category as the filial and fraternal. Recently, the people have become increasingly lazy and negligent, with few returning to the fundamentals and many pursuing the trivial. How can this be rectified? Now, as the eastern work begins, let the officials of two thousand piculs diligently encourage farming and sericulture, traveling through the fields to offer encouragement and support. Does not the 'Book of Documents' say? 'Cultivate the fields diligently, and there will be an autumn harvest.' Let them be urged on!"

In the second month, a great amnesty was proclaimed throughout the empire. In the autumn, on the day of Renshen in the ninth month, King Yu of Dongping passed away. In the intercalary month, on the day of Renxu, Yu Yong, the Grand Master of Remonstrance, passed away.

In the spring of the first year of Hongjia, the second month, an edict was issued: "We, having received the mandate of heaven and earth, have been able to preserve the ancestral temple. However, our wisdom is obscured, our virtue cannot bring peace, and our punishments are not just. Many grievances are left unresolved, and those who come to the palace to lodge complaints are unceasing. Therefore, yin and yang are in disorder, the seasons of cold and heat are out of order, the sun and moon do not shine, and the people suffer calamities. We are deeply grieved by this. Does not the 'Book of Documents' say? 'Even though I am in charge of affairs, I cannot attain longevity; the fault lies within myself.' Now, as spring is the time for growth, we are personally sending the Grand Master of Remonstrance, Li, and others to investigate and redress the wrongful cases in the three capital regions, the three rivers, and Hongnong. Let the dukes, ministers, grandees, and regional inspectors clearly instruct the governors and chancellors to act in accordance with our will. We bestow upon the people of the empire one rank of nobility, and to the women of every hundred households, oxen and wine. Additionally, we grant silk to the widowers, widows, orphans, and the elderly. Do not collect any outstanding loans or taxes."

On the day of Renwu, the emperor traveled to the initial mausoleum and pardoned the laborers. He designated the theatrical village of Xinfeng as Changling County to serve the initial mausoleum and bestowed oxen and wine upon every hundred households. The emperor began to make incognito excursions. In the winter, a yellow dragon was seen in Zhending. In the spring of the second year, the emperor traveled to Yunyang. In the third month, during the drinking ceremony performed by the Erudites, a pheasant flew into the courtyard, ascended the steps to the hall, and crowed. Later, it gathered in various government offices and also in the Chengming Hall.

An edict was issued: "In ancient times, the selection of the worthy was based on their words and tested by their achievements, so that no official position was left unfulfilled, no commoner was left idle, education and transformation were widespread, wind and rain were timely, all grains were harvested, and the masses were content in their occupations, all enjoying peace and tranquility. We have inherited the great enterprise for more than ten years, and have repeatedly encountered disasters of floods, droughts, and epidemics. The people have suffered repeatedly from hunger and cold, and yet we hope for the rise of propriety and righteousness—is this not difficult? We have not been able to lead by example, and the way of the emperor and kings has been declining daily. Is it because the path to recruiting the worthy and selecting the talented is blocked and not open, or is it that those who are recommended are not the right people? Let those who are recommended be honest, virtuous, and capable of speaking forthrightly, in the hope of hearing earnest words and good strategies to correct our shortcomings."

In the summer, five thousand households of prominent individuals from commanderies and kingdoms with assets exceeding five million were relocated to Changling. The Chancellor, Censor, generals, marquises, princesses, and officials of two thousand piculs were granted burial lands and residences. In the sixth month, Yunke, the grandson of King Xian of Zhongshan, was established as the King of Guangde. In the summer of the third year, the fourth month, a great amnesty was proclaimed throughout the empire. Officials and commoners were allowed to purchase ranks of nobility, with each rank priced at one thousand coins. There was a severe drought.

In the autumn, on the day of Yimao in the eighth month, a fire broke out at the gate tower of the temple of Emperor Jing. In the winter, on the day of Jiayin in the eleventh month, Empress Xu was deposed. More than sixty men from Guanghan, led by Zheng Gong, attacked government offices, freed prisoners, stole weapons from the armory, and proclaimed themselves lords of the mountains.

In the spring of the fourth year, the first month, an edict was issued: "We have repeatedly instructed the officials to act with leniency and to prohibit harshness and cruelty, but to this day there has been no change. When one person is guilty, the entire clan is detained; farmers lose their livelihoods, and there are many who harbor resentment. This harms the harmony of the universe, leading to disasters of floods and droughts. There are many displaced people east of the Passes, especially in the regions of Qing, You, and Ji, and we are deeply pained by this. We have not heard of any in positions of power who are compassionate; who will assist us in our worries! We have already dispatched envoys to inspect the commanderies and kingdoms. For areas where more than forty percent of the population has been affected by disasters, and where the people's assets do not exceed thirty thousand, do not collect rent or taxes. Do not collect any outstanding loans or taxes. For displaced people who wish to enter the Passes, register them and allow them entry. The commanderies and kingdoms they go to should treat them with care and reason, striving to ensure their survival and well-being, in accordance with our will."

In the autumn, the rivers of Bohai and Qinghe overflowed, and relief was provided to those affected by the disaster. In the winter, the followers of Zheng Gong from Guanghan gradually increased, and they ravaged four counties, with their numbers reaching nearly ten thousand. Zhao Hu, the Commandant of Hedong, was appointed as the Governor of Guanghan, and he led thirty thousand troops from the commandery and Shu Commandery to attack them. Those who captured or beheaded the rebels would have their crimes pardoned. Within a month, the rebellion was quelled, and Zhao Hu was promoted to the position of Director of the Imperial Guard and was awarded one hundred catties of gold.

In the spring of the first year of Yongshi, on the day of Guichou in the first month, a fire broke out in the ice storage room of the Grand Provisioner. On the day of Wuwu, a fire broke out at the gate tower of the garden of Empress Li. In the summer, the fourth month, Zhao Lin, the father of the Lady Zhao, was enfeoffed as the Marquis of Chengyang. In the fifth month, Wang Mang, the son of the emperor's uncle Man, who held the positions of Palace Attendant, Commandant of Cavalry, and Grand Master of Splendid Happiness, was enfeoffed as the Marquis of Xindu. On the day of Bingyin in the sixth month, Lady Zhao was established as empress. A great amnesty was proclaimed throughout the empire.

In the autumn, the seventh month, an edict was issued: "We have not firmly upheld virtue, and our plans have not fully considered the people below. We mistakenly listened to the words of the Grand Architect for the Ages, Wan Nian, who said that Changling could be completed in three years. After five years of construction, the central mausoleum and the gate of the Sima Hall have not yet been worked on. The empire is exhausted, the people are weary, the borrowed soil is loose and poor, and ultimately it cannot be completed. We are deeply troubled by the difficulty and are heartbroken. It is said, 'To err and not correct it is to err indeed.' Let Changling be abandoned, and let the old mausoleum not relocate the officials and people, so that the empire may have no wavering hearts." Li, the son of King Xiao of Chengyang, was established as king.

On the day of Dingchou in the eighth month, the Grand Empress Dowager Wang passed away. In the spring of the second year, on the day of Jichou in the first month, Wang Yin, the Grand Marshal and General of Chariots and Cavalry, passed away.

On the night of the day of Guiwei in the second month, stars fell like rain. On the day of Yiyou, the last day of the month, there was a solar eclipse. An edict was issued: "Recently, a dragon was seen in Donglai, and there was a solar eclipse. Heaven has shown anomalies to manifest our faults, and we are deeply fearful. Let the dukes and ministers instruct all officials to deeply reflect on the warnings of Heaven, and if there are measures that can reduce burdens and bring convenience and peace to the people, let them be reported in detail. The relief loans to the poor shall not be collected." It also stated: "East of the Passes, there have been consecutive years of poor harvests. Officials and commoners who, out of righteousness, gather food for the poor and contribute grain to assist the county officials in relief, have already been rewarded. Those who contribute over one million shall be additionally granted the rank of Right Reviser; those who wish to become officials shall be appointed to the rank of three hundred piculs; and the officials shall be promoted two ranks." Those who contribute over three hundred thousand shall be granted the rank of Fifth Grandee, and the officials shall also be promoted two ranks; commoners shall be appointed as court gentlemen. Those who contribute over one hundred thousand shall be exempt from rent and taxes for three years. Those who contribute over ten thousand shall be exempt for one year."

In the winter, the eleventh month, the emperor traveled to Yong and performed sacrifices at the Five Altars.

In the twelfth month, an edict was issued: "Previously, the Grand Architect for the Ages, Wan Nian, knowing that Changling was low-lying and unsuitable as a resting place for eternity, petitioned to construct it, establishing a walled city, and deceitfully increasing the height with soil, imposing heavy taxes and corvée labor, and initiating sudden construction projects. The laborers suffered unjustly, and the dead were numerous, the people exhausted, and the empire depleted. The former Grand Minister of Agriculture, Hong, repeatedly petitioned that Changling could not be completed. The Palace Attendant and Commandant of the Guards, Chang, repeatedly advised that it should be stopped early and the households returned to their original places. We, considering Chang's advice and Hong's memorial, and all the discussions of the dukes and ministers, agreed with Chang's plan. He first proposed the best strategy, and Hong managed to reduce great expenses, bringing peace to the people. Hong was previously granted the title of Marquis within the Passes and one hundred catties of gold. Now, Chang is granted the title of Marquis within the Passes, with a fief of one thousand households, and Hong with five hundred households. Wan Nian, a deceitful and disloyal person, has spread poison among the masses, and resentment throughout the land has not ceased to this day. Although he has been pardoned, he should not remain in the capital. Let Wan Nian be relocated to Dunhuang Commandery." "

In that year, the Grandee Secretary Wang Jun passed away. In the spring of the third year, on the day of Jimao, the last day of the first month, there was a solar eclipse. An edict was issued: "Heavenly disasters are still severe, and we are deeply fearful. Concerned about the people's loss of livelihood, we have dispatched Grandee Secretary Jia and others to travel throughout the empire, to visit the elderly and inquire about the people's sufferings. Let them, together with the regional inspectors, recommend one person each who is honest, modest, and virtuous."

In the winter, on the day of Gengchen in the tenth month, the Empress Dowager ordered the officials to restore the sacrifices at the Great Altar of Ganquan, the Altar of the Earth at Fenyin, the Five Altars at Yong, and the Temple of Chenbao at Chencang. The details are recorded in the Treatise on Suburban Sacrifices. In the eleventh month, Fan Bing and twelve other men from Weishi plotted rebellion, killed the Governor of Chenliu, plundered officials and commoners, and called themselves generals. Li Tan and four others together fought and killed Bing and his followers, and all were enfeoffed as marquises.

In the twelfth month, Su Ling and 227 other convicts from the Shanyang Iron Office attacked and killed senior officials, stole weapons from the armory, and called themselves generals. They passed through nineteen commanderies and kingdoms, killing the Governor of Dong Commandery and the Commandant of Runan. The Chancellor's Chief Clerk and the Palace Assistant Censor were dispatched with credentials to supervise and expedite their capture. The Governor of Runan, Yan Xin, captured and beheaded Ling and his followers. Xin was promoted to Grand Minister of Agriculture and awarded one hundred catties of gold.

In the spring of the fourth year, the first month, the emperor traveled to Ganquan, performed the suburban sacrifice at the Great Altar, and divine light descended and gathered at the Purple Palace. A great amnesty was proclaimed throughout the empire. Officials and commoners of Yunyang were granted noble ranks, women were given cattle and wine per hundred households, and the widowed, orphaned, and elderly were bestowed with silk. In the third month, the emperor traveled to Hedong, performed the sacrifice to the Earth, and granted the same to officials and commoners as in Yunyang, with no land rent collected in the areas passed through. In the summer, on the day of Guiwei in the fourth month, the Linhua Hall of Changle Palace and the East Sima Gate of Weiyang Palace both suffered disasters.

On the day of Jiawu in the sixth month, the gate tower of the Ba Mausoleum garden suffered a disaster. Those from Duling who had never served were sent home. An edict was issued: "Recently, there have been earthquakes in the capital and frequent fires, and we are deeply fearful. Let the officials diligently and clearly address these calamities, and we will personally review them."

It also stated: "The sage kings established rituals and regulations to order the ranks of the noble and humble, differentiated carriages and attire to distinguish the virtuous. Although they had wealth, without the proper rank, they could not exceed the regulations, thus the people were inspired to act, valuing righteousness over profit. Nowadays, the customs of the world are extravagant and unruly, with no limit and no satisfaction. The dukes, marquises, relatives, and close ministers, who are models for the four directions, have not been heard to cultivate themselves and follow the rituals, sharing the same heart to worry for the state. Some are indulgent in luxury and idleness, striving to expand their mansions, cultivate gardens and ponds, keep many slaves and maids, wear silk and fine fabrics, set up bells and drums, prepare female musicians, and exceed the regulations in carriages, attire, weddings, and funerals. Officials and commoners admire and imitate them, and it has become a custom. Yet, to hope that the people will be frugal and that every household will be self-sufficient, is it not difficult? Does the Book of Songs not say, 'Illustrious is the Master Yin, the people all look to you.' Let the officials be instructed to gradually prohibit these practices. The blue and green attire commonly worn by the people should not be stopped. The marquises and close ministers should each reflect and reform themselves. The Director of the Imperial Clan shall investigate those who do not change."

On the day of Xinwei in the seventh month of autumn, the last day of the month, there was a solar eclipse. On the first day of the first month of the first year of Yuanyan, the day of Jihai, there was a solar eclipse. In the third month, the emperor traveled to Yong and performed sacrifices at the Five Altars. On the day of Dingyou in the fourth month of summer, there was thunder without clouds, with bright sounds and light, descending from all sides to the ground, stopping at dusk. A general amnesty was proclaimed throughout the empire.

In the seventh month of autumn, a comet appeared in the eastern well. An edict was issued: "Recently, there have been solar eclipses and falling stars, and ominous signs have appeared in the heavens, with great anomalies recurring. Those in office have remained silent, and few have offered loyal advice. Now, a comet has appeared in the eastern well, and we are deeply fearful. Let the dukes, ministers, doctors, and councilors each diligently consider, think of ways to change, and clearly respond with the classics, without any concealment; let the inner commanderies and kingdoms each recommend one upright person who can speak out and remonstrate directly, and the twenty-two northern border commanderies each recommend one brave and knowledgeable in military strategy." "

The descendant of Prime Minister Xiao, Xi, was enfeoffed as the Marquis of Zan. On the day of Xinhai in the twelfth month of winter, the Grand Marshal and General Wang Shang passed away. In that year, the Lady Zhao, the Bright Consort, harmed the imperial children in the harem. In the spring of the second year, the first month, the emperor traveled to Ganquan and performed the suburban sacrifice at the Great Altar. In the third month, the emperor traveled to Hedong and performed the sacrifice to the Earth. In the summer, the fourth month, Shou, the son of the Prince of Guangling, was established as king.

In winter, the emperor traveled to Changyang Palace, accompanied by Hu guests for a grand hunt. He stayed at Fuyang Palace and bestowed gifts upon his accompanying officials. In the spring of the third year, on the day of Bingyin in the first month, Mount Min in Shu Commandery collapsed, blocking the river for three days, and the river water dried up. In the second month, Chunyu Chang, the Palace Attendant and Commandant of the Guards, was enfeoffed as the Marquis of Dingling. In the third month, the emperor traveled to Yong and performed sacrifices at the Five Altars. In the spring of the fourth year, the first month, the emperor traveled to Ganquan and performed the suburban sacrifice at the Great Altar.

In the second month, the office of the Director of the Imperial Clan was abolished. In the third month, the emperor traveled to

Hedong and performed the sacrifice to the Earth. Sweet dew fell in the capital, and the people of Chang'an were granted cattle and wine. In the spring of the first year of Suihe, the first month, a great amnesty was proclaimed throughout the empire.

On the day of Guichou in the second month, an edict was issued: "We have inherited the great enterprise of the Grand Ancestor and have served the ancestral temple for twenty-five years. Our virtue has not been able to pacify and govern the world, and many among the people harbor resentment. Not having received the blessings of Heaven, to this day there is no heir, and the empire has no one to rely upon. Observing the warnings of ancient and recent events, the seeds of calamity and chaos all arise from this. Prince Xin of Dingtao is like a son to us, kind, benevolent, and filial, and can continue the heavenly order and the ancestral sacrifices. Let Xin be established as the Crown Prince. Enfeoff Feng Can, the uncle of the Prince of Zhongshan and a Remonstrance Official, as the Marquis of Yixiang, and increase the fief of the Principality of Zhongshan by thirty thousand households to comfort them. Bestow gold upon the feudal princes and marquises, grant noble ranks to those in the empire who are to succeed their fathers, and give silk to the elders, the filial, the fraternal, and the diligent farmers, each according to their status."

It also stated: "It is said that a true king must preserve the descendants of two kings, to maintain the continuity of the three traditions. In the past, when King Cheng Tang received the mandate, he was ranked among the three dynasties, but the sacrifices to them have been discontinued. After investigation, none is more appropriate than Kong Ji. Let Ji be enfeoffed as the Marquis of Yin Shaojia." In the third month, he was advanced to the rank of Duke, and the Marquis of Zhou Chengxiu was also made a Duke, each with a fief of one hundred li. The emperor traveled to Yong and performed sacrifices at the Five Altars.

In the summer, the fourth month, the Grand Marshal and

General of Agile Cavalry Gen was appointed as the Grand Marshal, and the office of General was abolished. The Imperial Censor was made the Grand Minister of Works and enfeoffed as a Marquis. The stipends of the Grand Marshal and the Grand Minister of Works were increased to match that of the Chancellor. In the autumn, on the day of Gengxu in the eighth month, Prince Xing of Zhongshan passed away. In the winter, the eleventh month, Jing, the grandson of Prince Xiao of Chu, was established as the Prince of Dingtao.

Chunyu Chang, Marquis of Dingling, committed great treason and was imprisoned and executed. Kong Guang, the Commandant of Justice, was sent with credentials to bestow poison upon the noble lady Xu, who drank it and died. In the twelfth month, the office of the Regional Inspector was abolished, and the position of Regional Governor was established instead, with a rank of two thousand dan. In the spring of the second year, the first month, the emperor traveled to Ganquan and performed the suburban sacrifice at the Great Altar. On the day of Renzi in the second month, Chancellor Zhai Fangjin passed away. In the third month, the emperor traveled to Hedong and performed the sacrifice to the Earth.

On the day of Bingxu, the emperor passed away in the Weiyang Palace. The Empress Dowager issued an edict to the officials to restore the southern and northern suburbs of Chang'an. On the day of Jimao in the fourth month, he was buried in Yanling.

The commentary states: The aunt of the minister served in the harem as a Lady of Handsome Fairness, and her father, brothers, and cousins attended in the imperial tent. They often told the minister that Emperor Cheng was adept at cultivating his appearance and demeanor. When he ascended the carriage, he stood upright, did not look back, did not speak hastily, and did not point personally. When he presided over the court, he was deep and silent, dignified like a god, truly embodying the majestic appearance of an emperor! He was widely read in ancient and modern times and could accept straightforward advice. The dukes and ministers were competent, and their memorials and discussions were commendable. He lived in a time of peace, with harmony between the upper and lower classes. However, he was indulgent in wine and women, the Zhao family caused chaos within, and the maternal relatives dominated the court. Speaking of it, one could only sigh. Since the beginning of the Jianshi era, the Wang family began to hold the reins of the state. Emperors Ai and Ping had short reigns, and Wang Mang eventually usurped the throne. Indeed, the source of his authority and fortune was gradual!

VOLUME 11: RECORDS OF EMPEROR AI, PART 11

Emperor Xiao Ai, the grandson of Emperor Yuan and the son of Prince Gong of Dingtao, was born to Lady Ding. At the age of three, he succeeded to the throne as a prince and grew up fond of literature and law. In the fourth year of Yuanyuan, he came to court accompanied by his tutor, chancellor, and commandant. At that time, the younger brother of Emperor Cheng, Prince Xiao of Zhongshan, also came to court, but he was accompanied only by his tutor. The emperor found this strange and asked the Prince of Dingtao about it. The prince replied, "According to the regulations, when a feudal prince comes to court, he may be accompanied by officials of the two thousand dan rank from his state. The tutor, chancellor, and commandant are all officials of the two thousand dan rank in my state, so I am accompanied by all of them. The emperor then ordered him to recite the Book of Songs, which he did fluently and with understanding. On another day, the emperor asked the Prince of Zhongshan:

"Why are you accompanied only by your tutor, according to what law?" The Prince of Zhongshan could not answer. The emperor then ordered him to recite the Book of Documents, but he faltered again. When they were served food in the emperor's presence, the Prince of Zhongshan ate greedily and then left, his belt coming undone. Emperor Cheng thus considered him incapable and admired the Prince of Dingtao, often praising his talent. At that time, the prince's grandmother, the Dowager Consort Fu, accompanied him to court and privately bribed the emperor's favorite, Lady Zhao, and the emperor's uncle, the

General of Agile Cavalry and Marquis of Quyang, Wang Gen. Seeing that the emperor had no sons, Lady Zhao and Wang Gen also sought to secure their own long-term interests and repeatedly praised the Prince of Dingtao, urging the emperor to make him his heir. Emperor Cheng also admired his own talent and, upon reaching adulthood, sent him away at the age of seventeen. The following year, he appointed Ren Hong, the Commandant of the Capital Guards, as the Grand Herald and sent him with credentials to summon the Prince of Dingtao, establishing him as the Crown Prince. The prince declined, saying, "I am fortunate to inherit my father's position as a feudal prince, but my ability is insufficient to assume the role of Crown Prince. Your Majesty, with your sagely virtue and magnanimity, reverently upholds the ancestral temple and serves the deities, and should be blessed with countless descendants. I wish to remain in the state residence, attending to your daily needs, and when a holy heir is born, I will return to my state and guard the fief." The memorial was presented, and the emperor acknowledged it. More than a month later, Jing, the grandson of Prince Xiao of Chu, was established as the Prince of Dingtao to continue the sacrifices to Prince Gong, as a way to encourage the Crown Prince to focus on his duties as the heir. This is recorded in the biographies of the maternal relatives.

In the third month of the second year of Suihe, Emperor Cheng passed away. On the day of Bingwu in the fourth month, the Crown Prince ascended the throne as emperor and paid homage at the Gaozong Temple. The Empress Dowager was honored as the Grand Empress Dowager, and the Empress as the Empress Dowager. A general amnesty was proclaimed throughout the empire. Horses were bestowed upon the members of the imperial clan who were related to the emperor, one team each. Nobles were granted ranks, and every hundred households were given cattle and wine. The elders, the filial, the fraternal, the diligent farmers, the widowed, the orphaned, and the solitary were granted silk. The Grand Empress Dowager issued an edict honoring Prince Gong of Dingtao as Emperor Gong.

On the day of Bingxu in the fifth month, Empress Fu was established. An edict was issued: "The Spring and Autumn Annals state, 'The mother is honored through her son.' Therefore, the Dowager Consort of Dingtao is honored as Empress Dowager Gong, and Lady Ding as Empress Gong. Each shall have left and right attendants, and their fiefs shall be like those of the Changxin Palace and the Central Palace." The father of Empress Fu was posthumously honored as Marquis Chongzu, and the father of Lady Ding as Marquis Baode. The uncle, Ding Ming, was enfeoffed as Marquis of Yang'an, and his son, Man, as Marquis of Pingzhou. Man's father, Zhong, was posthumously titled Marquis Huaizhou of Pingzhou, and the father of the Empress, Yan, as Marquis of Kongxiang. The brother of the Empress Dowager, Zhao Qin, the Palace Attendant and Grandee of the Palace, was enfeoffed as Marquis of Xincheng.

In the sixth month, an edict was issued: "The music of Zheng is licentious and disrupts proper music, and thus was discarded by the sage kings. Let the Music Bureau be abolished." The Marquis of Quyang, Gen, who had previously proposed the strategy for the state as the Grand Marshal, was granted an additional two thousand households. The Grand Coachman, Marquis of Anyang, Shun, who had a long history of mentoring and was rewarded with an additional five hundred households. The Chancellor, Kong Guang, and the Grand Minister of Works, Marquis of Fanxiang, He Wu, were each granted an additional one thousand households.

An edict was issued: "The Prince of Hejian, Liang, mourned the Empress Dowager for three years, setting an example for the imperial clan, and is granted an additional ten thousand households."

Another edict stated: "Regulating expenditure and adhering to standards to prevent extravagance and licentiousness are the foremost principles of governance, and the immutable way of all kings. The feudal princes, marquises, princesses, officials of the two thousand dan rank, and wealthy commoners often hoard slaves and maidservants, and their fields and residences are without limit, competing with the people for profit, causing the common people to lose their livelihoods and suffer severe hardship and insufficiency. Let there be a discussion on setting limits." The officials presented a memorial: "The feudal princes and marquises may own fields within their states, the marquises in Chang'an and the princesses may own fields in the counties and districts, and the marquises within the passes, officials, and common people may own fields, but none shall exceed thirty qing. The feudal princes may have two hundred slaves and maidservants, the marquises and princesses one hundred, and the marquises within the passes, officials, and common people thirty. Those over sixty and under ten are not included in these numbers. Merchants are not allowed to own fields or serve as officials, and violators shall be punished according to the law. Any fields and slaves exceeding the prescribed limits shall be confiscated by the county officials. The three textile offices of Qi and the various offices weaving brocade and embroidery, which are difficult to produce and harm women's work, shall all cease and not be delivered. The edict also stated: "The practice of appointing sons and the laws against slander and defamation are hereby abolished. Palace women in the lateral courts under the age of thirty shall be married off. Government slaves over the age of fifty shall be freed and made commoners. The commanderies and states are prohibited from presenting rare beasts. The salaries of officials below the three hundred dan rank shall be increased. Investigate and dismiss officials who are cruel and oppressive in a timely manner. The officials shall not bring up matters prior to the amnesty. The parents of the students of the Erudites, upon their death, shall be granted three years of mourning leave."

In autumn, the Marquis of Quyang, Wang Gen, and the Marquis of Chengdu, Wang Kuang, were both found guilty. Wang Gen was sent to his fief, and Wang Kuang was stripped of his title and made a commoner, returning to his original commandery.

An edict was issued: "I bear the heavy responsibility of the ancestral temple, trembling with fear, lest I lose the favor of Heaven. Recently, the sun and moon have lost their light, the five planets have strayed from their courses, and the commanderies and states have experienced frequent earthquakes. Earlier, the waters of Henan and Yingchuan commanderies overflowed, killing people and destroying homes. My lack of virtue has caused the people to suffer, and I am deeply fearful. I have already dispatched the Grandee of the Palace to conduct inspections and compile registers, and to provide coffins and three thousand coins for the deceased. Let it be ordered that the counties and towns affected by the floods and other commanderies and states where disasters have affected more than forty percent of the population, and where the people's wealth does not exceed one hundred thousand, shall be exempt from this year's taxes and levies. "

In the first year of Jianping, in the first month of spring, a general amnesty was proclaimed throughout the empire. The Palace Attendant and Commandant of Cavalry, Marquis of Xincheng, Zhao Qin, and the Marquis of Chengyang, Zhao Xin, were both found guilty, stripped of their titles, and made commoners, and were exiled to Liaoxi. The Grand Empress Dowager issued an edict that all the fields of the Wang family, her maternal relatives, that were not ancestral graves, were to be distributed to the poor.

In the second month, an edict was issued: "It is said that the governance of the sage kings begins with the acquisition of the worthy. Let the Grand Marshal, marquises, generals, officials of the two thousand dan rank, regional inspectors, governors, and chancellors each recommend one person who is filial, fraternal, sincere, and capable of speaking frankly and understanding governance, and who is approachable and can be close to the people."

In the third month, the feudal princes, princesses, marquises, chancellors, generals, officials of the two thousand dan rank, and the officials of the central capital were granted money, gold, and silk, each according to their rank. In winter, the Dowager Consort of Prince Xiao of Zhongshan, Yuan, and her brother, Marquis of Yixiang, Feng Can, were both found guilty and committed suicide. In the second year, in the third month of spring, the Grand Minister of Works was abolished, and the Censor-in-Chief was reinstated.

In the summer, in the fourth month, an edict was issued: "The system of the Han dynasty is to promote kinship to highlight respect. The title of Prince Gong of Dingtao should no longer be used. The Empress Dowager Gong shall be honored as Empress Dowager, residing in the Yongxin Palace; the Empress Gong shall be honored as Empress, residing in the Zhong'an Palace. A temple for Prince Gong shall be established in the capital. A general amnesty is proclaimed for all exiles." The regional inspectors were abolished, and the inspectors were reinstated.

On the day of Gengshen in the sixth month, Empress Dowager Ding passed away. The emperor said: "I have heard that husband and wife are one body. The Book of Songs says, 'In life, they dwell in separate rooms; in death, they share the same grave.' In the past, when Ji Wuzi completed his resting place, the burial of the Du family was at the west steps, and he requested to be buried together, which was granted. The custom of joint burial began with the Zhou dynasty. 'How rich and splendid is the culture! I follow the Zhou.' A filial son serves the deceased as if they were alive. Empress Dowager Ding should have a tomb built in the garden of Prince Gong. "Thus, she was buried in Dingtao. Fifty thousand people from the nearby commanderies of Chenliu and Jiyin were mobilized to dig the burial mound.

The court scholar Xia Heliang and others spoke of the prophecy of the Red Essence, saying that the Han dynasty's mandate had declined midway and should be renewed, and that the era name should be changed. An edict was issued: "The Han dynasty has risen for two hundred years, and the calendar has opened a new era. The supreme heaven has bestowed blessings on the unworthy, and the Han state has once again received the mandate. How dare I not comply! The fundamental destiny of the empire must be renewed with the world, and thus a general amnesty is proclaimed. Let the second year of Jianping be changed to the first year of Taichu Yuanjiang. Let the emperor be titled the Emperor of Chen Sheng Liu Taiping. The water clock shall be set to one hundred and twenty degrees."

In the seventh month, the area of Yongling Pavilion on the northwestern plain of Weicheng was designated as the initial tomb. The people of the commanderies and states were not to be relocated, allowing them to live in peace.

In the eighth month, an edict was issued: "Earlier, Xia Heliang and others proposed changing the era name and increasing the water clock, claiming it would bring eternal peace to the state. I mistakenly listened to their words, hoping to bring blessings to the realm, but in the end, there was no auspicious response. Their proposals were contrary to the classics and ancient practices, and unsuitable for the times. The decree issued on the day of Jiazi in the sixth month was not an amnesty and is hereby annulled. Xia Heliang and others, who misled the people with their heresy, shall be handed over to the officials for punishment." They were all executed.

The Chancellor Bo, the Censor-in-Chief Xuan, and the Marquis of Kongxiang, Yan, were found guilty. Bo committed suicide, Xuan's sentence was reduced by two degrees, and Yan had a quarter of his household removed. Details are recorded in Bo's biography. In the third year, in the first month of spring, Guanghan, the younger brother of the King of Guangde Yi, was appointed King of Guangping. On the day of Guimao, the main hall of the Empress Dowager's Gui Palace caught fire. On the day of Jiyou in the third month, the Chancellor passed away. A comet appeared at the constellation Hegu.

In the summer, in the sixth month, Min, the Marquis of Wuxiang and son of Prince Qing of Lu, was appointed king. In winter, on the day of Renzi in the eleventh month, the altars of Taiyi at Ganquan and Houtu at Fenyin were restored, and the southern and northern suburban sacrifices were abolished. Yun, the King of Dongping, his queen Ye, and Fang, the wife of the Marquis of Ancheng Gong, were all found guilty. Yun committed suicide, and Ye and Fang were executed in the market.

In the fourth year, in spring, there was a severe drought. The people of Guandong spread the message of the Queen Mother of the West, passing through the commanderies and states, and entering the capital from the west. The people also gathered to worship the Queen Mother of the West, and some took torches to the rooftops at night, beating drums and shouting to frighten each other. In the second month, Fu Shang, the Palace Attendant and cousin of the Empress Dowager, was enfeoffed as Marquis of Ruchang, and Zheng Ye, the Palace Attendant and younger brother of the Empress Dowager, was enfeoffed as Marquis of Yangxin.

In the third month, the Palace Attendant and Commandant of the Imperial Carriage, Dong Xian, the Grandee of the Palace, Xifu Gong, and the Governor of Nanyang, Sun Chong, were all enfeoffed as marquises for their reports on the King of Dongping. Details are recorded in Xian's biography. In the summer, in the fifth month, officials from the two thousand dan rank down to the six hundred dan rank and all the men of the empire were granted noble titles. In the sixth month, the Empress Dowager was honored as the Grand Empress Dowager. In autumn, in the eighth month, the north gate of Prince Gong's garden caught fire.

In winter, an edict was issued for generals and officials of the two thousand dan rank to recommend those who were well-versed in military strategy and possessed great foresight.

In the first year of Yuanshou, on the first day of the first month of spring, a solar eclipse occurred. An edict was issued: "I have been fortunate to preserve the ancestral temple, but being neither wise nor diligent, I have been anxious and toiling day and night, without rest. The yin and yang are out of harmony, and the people are in want, yet I have not seen the cause of these calamities. I have repeatedly admonished the high officials, hoping for improvement. Up to now, the officials enforcing the law have not been just, some being cruel and tyrannical, gaining fame through power, while the gentle and lenient have fallen into ruin. Thus, the harm has grown, harmony has declined daily, and the people are filled with sorrow and resentment, with no place to turn. "Now, on the first day of the first month, a solar eclipse has occurred. The fault is not far off; it lies with me alone. Let the high officials and ministers each devote their hearts and lead the officials diligently, promote the virtuous, and remove the cruel, aiming to bring peace to the people. Expose my faults without any concealment. Let the generals, marquises, and officials of the two thousand dan rank each recommend one person who is virtuous, upright, and capable of speaking frankly. A general amnesty is proclaimed."

On the day of Dingsi, the Grand Empress Dowager Fu passed away. In the third month, the Chancellor Jia was found guilty, imprisoned, and died. In autumn, in the ninth month, the Grand Marshal and General of Agile Cavalry Ding Ming was dismissed. The bronze tortoise and snake door knockers of the temple of Emperor Xiaoyuan's temple made a sound. In the second year, in the first month of spring, the Xiongnu Chanyu and the Great Kunmi of Wusun came to court. In the second month, they returned to their countries, and the Chanyu was displeased. Details are recorded in the Xiongnu biography.

In summer, on the last day of the fourth month, Ren Chen, a solar eclipse occurred. In the fifth month, the positions of the

Three Excellencies were officially divided. The Grand Marshal and General of the Guards, Dong Xian, was appointed Grand Marshal; the Chancellor, Kong Guang, was appointed Grand Minister of Education; the Censor-in-Chief, Peng Xuan, was appointed Grand Minister of Works and enfeoffed as Marquis of Changping. The positions of Sizhi, Silij, and Sikou were established, but their duties were not yet finalized. On the day of Wuwu in the sixth month, the emperor passed away in the Weiyang Palace. In autumn, on the day of Renyin in the ninth month, he was buried at the Yiling tomb.

Commentary: Emperor Ai, from his time as a feudal prince to his tenure in the crown prince's palace, was known for his literary talent and intelligence, earning a good reputation from a young age. Witnessing the decline of the imperial family's fortunes and the shift of power away from the throne during the reign of Emperor Cheng, he frequently executed high officials upon his accession, aiming to strengthen the emperor's authority and emulate the reigns of Emperors Wu and Xuan. He had a natural distaste for indulgence in music and women, occasionally enjoying archery and martial displays. However, after ascending the throne, he suffered from paralysis, which worsened in his later years. His reign was short-lived—alas!

VOLUME 12: RECORDS OF EMPEROR PING, NO. 12

Emperor Ping, a grandson of Emperor Yuan and son of Prince Xiao of Zhongshan, was born to Lady Wei. At the age of three, he succeeded to the throne as king. In the sixth month of the second year of Yuanshou, Emperor Ai passed away, and the Grand Empress Dowager issued an edict: "The Grand Marshal Dong Xian is too young and does not command the hearts of the people. Let him surrender his seal and ribbon and be dismissed." Dong Xian committed suicide the same day. Wang Mang, Marquis of Xindu, was appointed Grand Marshal and put in charge of the Secretariat. In the seventh month of autumn, General of Chariots and Cavalry Wang Shun and the Grand Herald Zuo Xian were sent with credentials to welcome the King of Zhongshan. On the day of Xinmao, Empress Dowager Zhao was demoted to Empress Xiao Cheng and retired to the North Palace, while Empress Fu of Emperor Ai retired to the Gui Palace. Marquis of Kongxiang Fu Yan, the Minister of the Imperial Household Dong Gong, and others were stripped of their official positions and titles and exiled to Hepu. On the day of Xinyou in the ninth month, the King of Zhongshan ascended the throne as emperor, paid homage at the temple of Emperor Gao, and proclaimed a general amnesty.

The emperor was nine years old, and the Grand Empress Dowager ruled in his stead, with Grand Marshal Wang Mang in control of the government. All officials reported to Mang. An edict was issued: "Amnesty decrees are intended to give the empire a fresh start, sincerely hoping that the people will reform their ways and purify themselves, preserving their lives. However, officials often report on matters that occurred before the amnesty, accumulating charges and punishing the innocent, which is hardly in line with the principles of trust and cautious punishment, nor the intent to cleanse hearts and renew oneself. As for those involved in elections, if they are experienced and renowned individuals, they are considered difficult to protect and are thus not recommended, which greatly contradicts the principle of pardoning minor faults and promoting the worthy."

"Henceforth, for those who have hidden crimes or internal faults that have not been exposed but are recommended, they shall not be investigated. Let scholars strive diligently for advancement, and do not let minor flaws hinder great talents. From now on, officials must not report matters that occurred before the amnesty. Those who do not comply with this edict shall be considered ungrateful and treated as having committed a grave offense. This shall be established as a law and proclaimed throughout the empire, so that all may clearly understand it."

In the first year of Yuanshi, in the first month of spring, the Yuechang people, through multiple translations, presented one white pheasant and two black pheasants. An edict was issued for the Three Excellencies to offer them at the ancestral temple. The ministers petitioned that the achievements and virtues of Grand Marshal Wang Mang were comparable to those of the Duke of Zhou, and he was granted the title of Duke of Anhan. Additionally, Grand Tutor Kong Guang and others were granted increased fiefdoms. Details are recorded in Mang's biography. All the people of the empire were granted one rank of nobility, and officials in positions of two hundred dan or above were fully confirmed in their ranks as if they were permanent.

The former crown prince of the late King Yun of Dongping, Kaiming, was established as king, and Chengdu, son of the late Marquis Qing of Taoxiang, was made King of Zhongshan. Thirty-six descendants of Emperor Xuan, including Xin, were enfeoffed as marquises. Twenty-five individuals, including the Grand

Coachman Wang Yun, who had previously deliberated on the posthumous title of Empress Dowager Fu of Dingtao, adhered to the classics and laws, did not flatter or follow improper orders, and were loyal ministers like General Sun Jian. The Grand Herald Xian, who had previously upheld righteous discussions without flattery, later carried the credentials to welcome the King of Zhongshan, along with the Director of the Imperial Clan Liu Bu'e, the Commandant of the Capital Ren Cen, the General of the Household Yong Kong, the Prefect of the Masters of Writing Yao Xun, and the Governor of Pei Commandery Shi Xu, all of whom had participated in the earlier planning and welcomed the emperor to the east for his enthronement, serving diligently and meticulously, were enfeoffed as Marquises of the Interior, with varying fiefdoms. Officials from the rank of two thousand dan down to assistant clerks in the counties and cities through which the emperor passed before his enthronement were granted varying ranks of nobility. It was also decreed that princes, dukes, marquises, and Marquises of the Interior who had no sons but had grandsons or sons of their brothers could have them as heirs. If the heir of a duke or marquis committed a crime punishable by hard labor or worse, a prior petition was required. Members of the imperial clan who had not exhausted their lineage but were cut off due to crime had their lineage restored. Those who were recommended as incorruptible assistant clerks were appointed to positions of four hundred dan. Officials throughout the empire of the rank of two thousand dan or above who retired due to old age were granted one-third of their former salary for the rest of their lives. Censor Grandees were dispatched to the three metropolitan regions to register officials and commoners and compensate those who had been subjected to arbitrary levies during the turmoil of the second year of Yuanshou. Tombs of the people at Yiling that did not obstruct the palace were not to be disturbed. Officials throughout the empire were not allowed to store utensils in their residences.

In the second month, the position of Xihe was established, with a rank of two thousand dan; the positions of Waishi and Lüshi were established, with ranks of six hundred dan. Education was promoted, and illicit sacrifices were prohibited, while the music of Zheng was banned. On the day of Yiwei, the divine robes of the Yiling tomb were found in their case, but by dawn on the day of Bingshen, they were on the bed outside. The tomb director reported this urgent anomaly. A grand sacrifice with a great offering was conducted.

In summer, on the first day of the fifth month, Ding Si, a solar eclipse occurred. A general amnesty was proclaimed. The Three Excellencies, generals, and officials of the rank of two thousand dan were each to recommend one honest and outspoken individual. In the sixth month, the Junior Tutor and General of the Left Feng was sent to present a seal and document to the emperor's mother, Lady Ji of Prince Xiao of Zhongshan, appointing her as Queen Dowager of Zhongshan. The emperor's uncles Wei Bao and Bao's brother Xuan were enfeoffed as Marquises of the Interior. The emperor's four younger sisters were granted the title of Jun, each with a fiefdom of two thousand households.

The descendants of the Duke of Zhou, Gongsun Xiangru, were enfeoffed as Marquis of Baolu, and the descendants of Confucius, Kong Jun, were enfeoffed as Marquis of Baocheng, to continue their sacrifices. Confucius was posthumously honored as Duke Xuan Ni of Baocheng. The Mingguang Palace and the imperial highways of the three metropolitan regions were abolished.

Female convicts throughout the empire who had been sentenced were allowed to return home, with a monthly compensation of three hundred coins. One chaste woman from each village was exempted from corvée. The positions of Sea Assistant and Fruit Assistant in the Office of the Imperial Household were established, with one each; the Ministry of Agriculture established thirteen Regional Assistants, each assigned to a province to promote agriculture and sericulture. The Grand Empress Dowager reduced her personal fiefdom of ten counties, which were placed under the Ministry of Agriculture, with their rental income separately accounted for to aid the poor. In autumn, in the ninth month, a general amnesty was granted to convicts.

The county of Kuxing in Zhongshan was designated as the personal fiefdom of the Queen Dowager of Zhongshan. In spring of the second year, the state of Huangzhi presented a rhinoceros. An edict was issued: "The emperor's two names are common in objects; henceforth, he shall be renamed in accordance with ancient customs. Let Grand Tutor Guang offer a great sacrifice and report it at the temple of Emperor Gao."

In summer, in the fourth month, Ruyi, a descendant of the great-grandson of King Xiao of Dai, was established as King of Guangzong; Gong, Marquis of Xutai and grandson of King Yi of Jiangdu, was established as King of Guangchuan; and Lun, great-grandson of King Hui of Guangchuan, was established as King of Guangde. The descendants of the late Grand Marshal and Marquis of Bolu, Huo Guang, including Yang, a great-grandson of his cousin; Qingji, a great-grandson of Marquis Xuanping Zhang Ao; Gong, a great-grandson of Marquis Jiang Zhou Bo; and Zhang, a son of a great-grandson of Marquis Wuyang Fan Kuai, were all enfeoffed as marquises and had their titles restored. One hundred and thirteen descendants of the late Marquis of Quzhou Li Shang, including Li Mingyou, were enfeoffed as Marquises of the Interior, with varying fiefdoms.

There was a severe drought and locust plague in the commanderies and kingdoms, particularly in Qingzhou, causing the people to flee and wander. Two hundred and thirty individuals, including the Duke of Anhan, the Four Regents, the Three Excellencies, ministers, officials, and commoners, donated their fields and residences to aid the impoverished. Envoys were dispatched to capture locusts, and commoners who brought locusts to officials were paid by the stone. Commoners throughout the empire with assets less than twenty thousand coins and those in disaster-stricken commanderies with assets less than one hundred thousand coins were exempted from taxes. Those suffering from epidemics were housed in empty residences and provided with medical treatment. Families with six or more deaths were granted five thousand coins for burial; those with four or more deaths, three thousand coins; and those with two or more deaths, two thousand coins. The Huchi Garden in Anding was abolished and established as Anmin County, with official buildings and markets constructed to recruit and relocate the poor, providing food along the way. Upon reaching their new locations, they were granted fields, residences, and utensils, and were lent plows, oxen, seeds, and food. Additionally, five neighborhoods were established within Chang'an city, with two hundred residences to house the poor.

In autumn, one courageous and disciplined individual knowledgeable in military strategy was recommended from each commandery and sent to the capital. On the last day of the ninth month, Wushen, a solar eclipse occurred. A general amnesty was granted to convicts. Forty-four officers from the Grand Marshal's staff were sent with credentials to inspect the border troops.

Commandant of the Capital Chen Mao was sent with drums and gongs to recruit three hundred brave officials and soldiers from Runan and Nanyang. Over two hundred bandits, including Cheng Zhong, surrendered voluntarily and were sent to their homes to resume their duties. Zhong was relocated to Yunyang and granted public fields and residences. In winter, officials of the rank of two thousand dan were to recommend one individual each year who was fair in handling legal cases.

In spring of the third year, an edict was issued for the officials to arrange the emperor's betrothal to the daughter of the Duke of Anhan, Wang Mang. Details are recorded in Mang's biography.

Another edict appointed Grandee of the Palace Liu Xin and others to compile wedding rituals. The families of the Four Regents, the Three Excellencies, ministers, erudites, courtiers, and officials were all to marry according to these rituals, with the groom personally welcoming the bride in a carriage with paired horses.

In summer, the Duke of Anhan proposed regulations for carriages and attire, as well as standards for the livelihood, funerals, weddings, slaves, fields, residences, and utensils of officials and commoners. Official granaries and educational institutions were established. In commanderies and kingdoms, they were called "xue"; in counties, districts, towns, and marquisates, they were called "xiao." Each xiao and xue was to have one Classics teacher. In villages, they were called "xiang"; in hamlets, they were called "xu." Each xu and xiang was to have one teacher of the Classic of Filial Piety.

Ren Heng of Yangling and others proclaimed themselves generals, stole weapons from the armory, attacked official buildings, and released prisoners. The Grand Minister of Works' assistants pursued and captured them, and they were all executed. The heir of the Duke of Anhan, Yu, conspired with the Wei family, the emperor's maternal relatives. Yu was imprisoned and died, and the Wei family was exterminated. In spring of the fourth year, in the first month, Emperor Gao was honored in the suburban sacrifices to match Heaven, and Emperor Wen was honored in the ancestral temple sacrifices to match the Supreme Deity. The Duke of Yin Shaogai was renamed Duke of Song, and the Duke of Zhou Chengxiu was renamed Duke of Zheng.

An edict was issued: "When husband and wife are upright, then father and son are close, and human relations are established. The previous edict ordered officials to restore chaste women and return female convicts, truly aiming to prevent wickedness and preserve chastity and trust. The elderly and those in mourning are exempt from punishment, as the sage kings decreed.

However, harsh and cruel officials often detain the relatives of lawbreakers, including women, the elderly, and the weak, creating resentment and harming morality, causing suffering among the people. Let it be clearly decreed to all officials that women who are not personally guilty of crimes, and men over eighty or under seven, whose families are not implicated in heinous crimes or named in arrest warrants, shall not be detained." Those who are to be examined shall be questioned immediately. Let this be established as a law."

On the day Dingwei in the second month, Empress Wang was established, and a general amnesty was proclaimed. Eight individuals, including the Grand Coachman Wang Yun, were sent as deputies with credentials to travel throughout the empire and observe customs. Officials from the Nine Ministers down to those of six hundred dan, and members of the imperial clan with registered lineages, were granted noble titles, ranging from Fifth Rank Grandee upwards. Commoners throughout the empire were granted one rank of nobility, and the elderly, widowers, widows, orphans, and the childless were granted silk.

In summer, the empress was presented at the temple of Emperor Gao. The Duke of Anhan was granted the title "Prime Minister." The duke's mother was honored as "Lady Gongxian." The duke's sons, An and Lin, were enfeoffed as marquises. The Duke of Anhan proposed the establishment of the Hall of Enlightenment and the Piyong. The temple of Emperor Xuan was honored as "Zhongzong," and the temple of Emperor Yuan was honored as "Gaozong," with the emperor offering sacrifices for generations. The Xihai Commandery was established, and lawbreakers from throughout the empire were relocated there.

King Li of Liang committed a crime and committed suicide. The capital was divided into the Qianhuiguang and Houchenglie commanderies. The titles and ranks of the Three Excellencies, ministers, and eighty-one chief officers, as well as the names of the twelve provinces, were changed. The boundaries of commanderies and kingdoms were redrawn, and many were abolished, established, or altered, causing widespread confusion that officials could not keep track of. In winter, a great wind blew off most of the roof tiles of the eastern gate of Chang'an city.

In spring of the fifth year, in the first month, a grand sacrifice was held at the Hall of Enlightenment. Twenty-eight kings, one hundred twenty marquises, and over nine hundred members of the imperial clan were summoned to assist in the sacrifices. After the rituals, all were granted additional households, noble titles, gold, and silk, and were promoted or appointed to official positions in varying degrees.

An edict was issued: "It is said that emperors and kings pacify the people with virtue, and next, they treat their relatives with affection. In the past, Yao harmonized the nine clans, and Shun esteemed and ordered them. I, as the emperor in my youth, oversee the governance of the state. The members of the imperial clan are all descendants of the Great Ancestor Emperor Gao and the brothers Wu Qing and Chu Yuan. From the Han's beginning to the present, there are over one hundred thousand of them. Although some are kings and marquises, none can correct each other, and some fall into crime, which is the fault of insufficient instruction. Does the tradition not say, 'When the gentleman is devoted to his relatives, the people are inspired toward benevolence'? Let the imperial clan, from the Supreme Emperor down to the present, be organized by generation and surname, and let each commandery and kingdom establish a Clan Master to correct them and provide instruction. Let officials of two thousand dan select those with virtue and righteousness to serve as Clan Masters. They shall investigate those who do not follow instructions or have grievances and lost positions, and the Clan Masters may report to the Clan Chief via postal stations for consideration. Each year in the first month, Clan Masters shall be granted ten bolts of silk." "

Xi and Liu Xin, along with three others, were appointed to

oversee the Hall of Enlightenment and the Piyong, ensuring that the Han dynasty's achievements matched those of King Wen's Spirit Tower and the Duke of Zhou's construction of Luoyang. The Grand Coachman Wang Yun and seven others were sent to propagate customs and promote virtuous transformation, uniting all states. All were enfeoffed as marquises.

Scholars throughout the empire who were knowledgeable in lost classics, ancient records, astronomy, calendrical calculations, music theory, philology, historical texts, esoteric arts, materia medica, and the Five Classics, the Analects, the Classic of Filial Piety, and the Erya were summoned. Each was provided with a single-horse carriage and sent to the capital. Several thousand arrived. In the intercalary month, a descendant of King Xiao of Liang, named Yin, was established as king.

In winter, on the day Bingwu of the twelfth month, the emperor passed away in the Weiyang Palace. A general amnesty was proclaimed. The officials deliberated: "According to ritual, a minister does not mourn a young ruler. The emperor was fourteen years old and should be encoffined with ritual and crowned posthumously." The proposal was approved. He was buried in Kangling. An edict was issued: "The emperor was benevolent and compassionate, and all grieved for him. Each time he fell ill, his breath would rise and harm his speech, so he could not leave a final edict. Let the palace ladies be released to return home and marry, as in the time of Emperor Wen." "

Commentary: During the reign of Emperor Ping, governance came from Wang Mang, who praised the good and highlighted achievements to enhance his own prestige. Judging from his writings, the barbarians beyond the borders were all submissive; auspicious signs and favorable responses were accompanied by songs of praise. However, when anomalies appeared in the heavens and the people grumbled below, even Wang Mang could not gloss over it.

Printed in Dunstable, United Kingdom